CONFESSIONS OF LADY GRACE

RACHEL ANN SMITH

PENFORD
PUBLISHING

First Edition August 2020

Developmental Edit by Gray Plume Editing

Edited by Victory Editing

Proofread by Jennie Ladd and Magnolia Author Services

Cover design by Impluvium Studios

Copyright © 2020 by Rachel Ann Smith

ISBN 978-1-951112-08-0

PROLOGUE

LONDON 1815—LORD HARRINGTON'S PRIVATE STUDY…

The rules of the game were simple. It was her opponent who posed the challenge.

Lady Grace Oldridge picked up the stack of cards from the table and split the deck in two. "What are we to play for this time?" She bent the well-worn cards at their center, then fanned and intermingled them with seemingly effortless skill. Grace continued to shuffle over and over, her gaze trained on the man seated opposite her. Matthew Stanford, Marquess of Harrington, returned her stare with one eyebrow raised, leaving Grace with no doubt what the stakes would involve—her future.

The man was relentless.

She should have ordered one of the Foreign Office agents under her command to inform Matthew of a potential threat to his best friend, the Earl of Devonton. Instead, she had entered his London townhouse in the dead of night, via a secret entrance. And after her mission was complete, rather than returning to her own bed, she had found herself blissfully tangled in his sheets. Throughout the early-morning hours, Matthew had employed various inventive methods to tempt her into marrying him. She had nearly succumbed, but in the end, Grace denied his pleas.

As the first rays of sunlight peeked through the drapes, Matthew had charmed Grace into staying to break her fast with him and then a game of brag.

Grace admired Matthew's elegant, straight nose, warm blue-gray eyes, and his full lips that had wickedly kissed her senseless. She set the deck on the table an equal distance between them. "I won't marry you until Lucy has chosen a husband."

"While it is my greatest wish to make you mine, my sister has no desire to marry."

"Very well," Grace gave in. Matthew had already captured her heart, and she had willingly given him her body, but the man wanted more. He wanted a family—and so did she, just not now. "If you win, I shall marry you as soon as the banns have been read."

Matthew's head slanted and his lips slowly curved into a lopsided grin as his eyes raked over her, sending shivers along her inner thighs. She crossed her ankles beneath her skirts and banished images of his head between her legs.

"And if you win?" Matthew asked.

Unless one was skilled at reading their opponent, brag was a game of chance. Her lips curved into a smile. Understanding a person's body language came as naturally to Grace as learning a foreign tongue. And in this case, she knew her opponent exceptionally well.

The stakes were high, but she would not relent. "My

terms remain the same. We shall be married after Lucy is happily wed."

Matthew picked up the cards and grumbled, "Lord, help me."

The first round revealed who would have luck on their side. It required absolutely no skill—the highest card won.

Matthew deftly dealt two cards facedown to each of them. She held her breath as he flipped the third card in front of her—a nine of hearts. A midrange card, no need to panic, and it was one that might work in her favor for the second and third rounds.

Revealing his next card, Matthew smiled. "Knave of spades. I win the round." Matthew collected his winnings.

They had each wagered two wooden coins. With the first round lost, Grace's heartbeat sped up in anticipation of the next round.

Grace lifted the bottom left corner of each card. Ace of clubs. Queen of hearts. Years of practice controlling her facial expressions in front of a looking glass meant Grace was able to mask her reactions with confidence, except in the presence of the man opposite her. Careful not to reveal any clue as to what cards she held, Grace scrutinized her opponent. Matthew flipped the corners of his own cards up. His jaw muscles clenched. A tell that gave her a hint that neither card was a royal. If she had read him correctly, then it was more than likely she had him beat—unless he held a pair. Statistics and mathematical calculations were his twin sister, Lucy's, strengths. Neither Grace nor Matthew would claim to share such skill. However, both were quite capable of determining the overall odds of winning based on the cards dealt. The key to winning was deducing with accuracy what cards the other person held in their hand.

Before she decided upon whether to brag or not, she

ran the pearl pendant he had gifted her back and forth along its silver chain. Matthew's gaze fell to her décolletage, and he shifted in his seat. He was easily distracted, which meant he didn't hold a pair.

She pushed one-third of her coin pile to the center of the table, a sizable wager but not too large to make Matthew believe she had him beat.

Without hesitation, Matthew said, "I shall match your bet." He flipped his cards over to reveal the king and seven of spades.

She had him beat with the ace. But Matthew had bamboozled her with his tells. She had concluded the man didn't hold a royal card in his hand. Heat flooded her cheeks. She hated being wrong. Perhaps she didn't know the man as well as she thought.

"Ready to lose?" Matthew taunted as he shoved the remaining coins in his pile to the center. The man had bet his entire pile—typical Matthew, all in.

Grace counted their scores. Matthew had twenty-seven, and she had twenty-nine. Closest to thirty-one, she'd need a two.

Matching his pile of coin, Grace said, "Let's see who the winner is, shall we?"

Chuckling, Matthew slid a card off the top of the deck.

A scratch at the door halted his movements and he called out, "One moment."

Grace raced to curl up in one of the wingback chairs facing the fire. Skirts tucked tightly under her feet and teetering on the edge of the seat, she rolled her shoulders and rested her head on her knees, making herself as small as possible.

The door creaked open.

"Sorry to bother you, Matthew, but Lucy is visiting Ms. Lennox, and Mama... Well, Mama is in her rooms."

Matthew's little brother's tentative voice tore at Grace's heart.

"What is it you need?"

"I was wondering if you might have time to take me to the park today. I made the most extraordinary kite with…"

The excitement in Edward's voice was infectious. Grace found herself smiling and then her heart burst with joy when Matthew interrupted to say, "Perhaps I could make time." But the bubble of happiness was short-lived. Matthew continued, "After I'm done with the estate ledgers." Grace's ire rose as the image of a dejected Edward floated in her mind.

"I shall wait for you in the library. But if Lucy returns before you are ready, it will be you who will miss the experiment."

Why had Edward's reply not been laced with held disappointment? Not having any siblings of her own, she found the dynamic between Matthew and his brother and sister at times confusing.

The click of the door latch falling into place spurred Grace into action. Standing before Matthew, she said, "You should take Edward to the park."

"I did not lie." Matthew pointed to the stacks of books and papers that lay scattered upon his desk. "I do have estate matters to attend to."

"I know you are not a liar. But family should come first."

Matthew ran a hand through his hair. A hint to his agitated state. "Would it please you if I took my brother to the park *and then* attended to the pile of paperwork that awaits me?"

"It would." Grace placed her hands upon his sturdy shoulders and leaned in to kiss him.

He kissed her back with a fierceness that demonstrated

his desire to marry her. "Very well. I did promise to always see to your happiness."

Matthew's openmouthed kisses heightened Grace's pulse and sent pleasure coursing through her body all the way to her toes. Crushing herself to him, she came into contact with Matthew's hard form. Every curve of her body melted into his. His groans of pleasure left no doubt as to the effect their kisses had upon the man she intended to marry—one day.

Breathlessly Grace said, "You need to leave, or I might change my mind." With a playful shove, she hurled him toward the door.

Before he crossed the threshold, Matthew said, "I shall expect you to save a waltz for me tonight." Not waiting for a response, he left, closing the door behind him.

With no social engagements or meetings arranged for the afternoon, Grace lingered a moment longer. The card table by the window caught her attention. Meandering to stand next to their unfinished game, she turned over the next card from the top of the pile—eight of diamonds. She would have had a score of thirty-seven. Unable to resist knowing if she would have won or lost, Grace flipped the next card—six of diamonds.

Grace gasped. Had they continued to play; Matthew would have won.

Was the tightness in her chest due to disappointment—or relief that their game had been interrupted? Grace turned to leave through the secret passageway, her hands trembling as she tried to ensure the concealed entrance was closed correctly.

It wasn't that she didn't love Matthew.

No, she would happily marry him if another man didn't stand between them.

There was the unresolved matter of the traitorous Lord Burke and—most importantly—the threat that his schemes would ruin certain members of Grace's family.

CHAPTER ONE

BROKEN PROMISES AND TWO YEARS LATER...

a sliver of white parchment peeked out from behind a jagged rock in the garden wall. Grace froze midstride, blinking twice. For one hundred and eighty-one days in a row, she had walked along the same path without any indication that the rock had been moved, giving up hope that Matthew would once again return to their secret spot.

She stared at the note as blood rushed from her head. Dizzy and in disbelief, she inhaled until her lungs were about to burst with the cool night air before exhaling. Time was supposed to ease pain and heartache. But as each day passed, the ache in her heart continued to grow. The reality that she must marry Tobias Bixley, the Earl of Ellingsworth, heir to the Marquess of Burke, caused the knots in her stomach to tighten.

Her pulse returned to a steady beat, yet here she stood, paralyzed.

What the blazes was wrong with her? She was the head

of the Foreign Office, for goodness' sake. Granted, she didn't hold the official title on paper; her papa, Lord Flarinton, held the position. But Grace had acted as the department leader for years—renowned for being fearless in her actions. Then why was she behaving like a lovesick debutante? Grace released a groan. Damnation! After all these blasted months, she still pinned for Matthew.

Drawing upon her reserves, she squared her shoulders and moved to stand next to the wall. A quick glance behind her, she spotted her guards. They were positioned a fair distance away, far enough to grant her privacy yet close enough should danger present itself. Her hand shook as she shimmied the rock loose. Her heartbeat thudded so loudly she glanced about once more. She reached for the note and hastily slid the stone back into place. Matthew's bold script flowed across the paper, setting her pulse racing. Curse her heart for still caring for the man.

Grace tilted the note toward the moonlight.

I resign.
Best wishes.

The words blurred before her. Her suspicions Matthew no longer cared for her were confirmed. She squeezed her eyes shut. Anger replaced the hurt.

Two measly lines!

She had sacrificed her future and her happiness to save the wretched man's life, and all he could manage to write was four blasted words. Poised to rip the missive in half, Grace froze. Now was not the time to act rashly. She balled the parchment in her fist and shoved it into her skirt pocket. She would keep the miserable note, even if the words crushed her heart and soul.

Ready to return to the sanctuary of her room, Grace

turned and came face to chest with the two footmen prepared to escort her back to the house. They must have sensed her change in mood. Grace momentarily regretted her decision to heed the Home Secretary, Lord Archbroke, and his wife, Lady Theo's, advice and order her men to provide twenty-four-hour protection. Then Theo's sweet but firm voice rang clear in Grace's mind: *Your future father-in-law intends for you to come to an untimely death as soon as you are wed to his ninny of a son.* Nonetheless, it was challenging to adjust to having bodyguards around the clock. With the official announcement of her engagement mere days away, Grace's shoulders sagged as the risk of losing control of the Foreign Office settled in her heart. Head bowed, she walked back along the garden path that led straight to the servants' entrance of her papa's townhouse.

Crossing the threshold into the kitchens, Grace waved off her men. She needed a moment alone. The jagged edge of the parchment poked through the material of her pocket and against her thigh. Matthew. Urgh. She wanted to shake the man until he provided an explanation for the shameful excuse of a note. *No.* What she really wanted was to rail and scream at Matthew for blatantly dismissing her and her orders to remain on home soil twenty-two months ago. If he had listened to her wishes and not broken his promise to always see to her happiness, she wouldn't be in this predicament—betrothed to the son of her sworn enemy.

"Where have you been?" Lord Flarinton, her papa, stood a few feet away from her.

Grace jumped. "Papa!" She eyed the man leaning against the kitchen prep table with a shiny green apple raised halfway up to his mouth. The old man's eyes were clear and focused. *Blast.*

"Gracie, I'm waiting."

Her mind scrambled for a plausible excuse to be out well past the midnight hour. "I needed a bit of fresh air."

Grace smiled as her papa bit into the tart apple Cook used for pies. He chewed with one eye closed and the other squinting. Grace stifled her giggles.

Her papa finally swallowed and asked, "Air, you say, at this hour?"

"I was... I was reviewing the seating arrangements for tomorrow's dinner party." A task she would have to undertake after reading Matthew's paltry four-word message. Her original plan had Matthew seated close to her. Now she wanted the man as far away from her as possible. No. That was a lie. Her heart still longed to have him close.

"Is that so? Has Harrington provided you with a full report?" Her papa asked her the same question daily. Sadly, her answer remained the same.

Grace shook her head. "No."

"That is unlike Harrington to ignore an order. He must have a sound reason."

Drat. Grace's papa chose the most inconvenient times to be fully alert and cognizant of events. "He sent word that he wishes to resign."

The green blur of the apple being waved about ceased. "Resign? Why would he do that? You must pay him a visit. I'm certain he has an explanation." Apple midway to his mouth, her papa stood, staring at the fruit. His eyes became unfocused, and his brow creased in confusion.

Grace eased the apple from his grasp and tossed it onto the marred kitchen table. "Come along, Papa. Up to bed."

Flustered, Lord Flarinton asked, "Gracie girl, what are we doing in the kitchen?"

"Partaking in a nice late-night chat." Grace patted his arm and smiled.

He cocked head to one side. "Is that so?" He looked

about as Grace took his hand in hers and guided him up to his chambers.

As they entered the master's bedchamber, her papa's long-standing valet jumped to his feet and placed a book on the small table next to the fire.

Grace released her papa's hand. "Lord Flarinton is ready to retire."

"Yes, my lady."

Grace backed out of the room. She released a sigh as she shut the door. Her mind should be void of distractions. She needed a clear head for tomorrow's event—it would be the first time she and her intended met.

Grace made her way down the hall to her own chamber. Her papa's words, *you must pay him a visit*, burrowed into her thoughts like a burr in her foot. Swiveling away from her door, Grace practically ran down to the foyer. She wouldn't rest until she confronted Matthew and attempted to explain the events that had led to her betrothal to another man.

Silverman was waiting at the door with her great cloak and a black wide-brimmed hat. The family butler had the peculiar ability of always being one step ahead of her. Grace smiled and said, "I don't know how you do it, but I'm forever grateful."

With a grunt, the ever-loyal servant wrapped her coat about her shoulders and slapped the hat atop her head. "The lads are out back waitin' for you, my lady."

Grace stepped through the threshold, her bodyguards immediately by her side as she proceeded down the front stairs to the awaiting coach.

A footman held open the coach door. "My lady, Lord Harrington was spotted leaving his club not long ago. If we depart immediately, we may be able to get you to the Harrington townhouse in time."

Grace halted—one foot rooted to the ground. "Lord Harrington was at his club this eve, was he?"

The footman ducked his head and shrugged.

Regretting the censure in her tone, Grace said, "My thanks for passing along the information." The coach door closed behind her. Settling onto the coach bench, she tugged on the lapels of her coat. She mumbled, "If Matthew was well enough to go about town, why the blazes did he not simply give his resignation in person?" No more waiting. She was going to obtain the answers she needed and hopefully regain some semblance of rationality.

For nearly two years, she'd lived with guilt and doubt. Guilt for not agreeing to marry Matthew when he had asked. Doubt that he would ever forgive her for agreeing to Lord Burke's demands. They had played havoc with her sanity, and altered her person in the worst of ways. Snapping at the staff, tirelessly working agents until they found their voice and complained, ignoring her friends who continued to remain empathetic and supportive. If she had the chance to change the events of the past, she would have finished the game of brag, agreed to marry him, and then sent him off to spend the afternoon with his brother.

Time travel was impossible. The reality was if she was to fight to retain control of the Foreign Office, she needed her sanity back. For that to happen, she needed to explain to Matthew the events which had led to what he probably believed to be the worst betrayal by her—an engagement to another man.

Grace had drafted numerous missives to Matthew since his return, attempting to outline the incidents. But she couldn't find the right combination of words. Lord Burke, the devil, had been the only person who held the information she needed to ensure Matthew's safe return. The bastard had set the terms and would not relent. Her fear of failure had driven her to convince her papa to sign the marriage contracts.

Tonight, she would explain everything, and in return, she'd ask Matthew for a full report as to the events that led to his capture and the happenings that occurred during his captivity. She was certain Matthew held the key to understanding her future father-in-law's motivations and dastardly plans.

Grace sighed. Her plans for the evening were riddled with flaws. Needing a distraction from the ache in her chest and the pounding in her head, she pulled back the curtain and counted the gas lamps as the coach continued to rattle along the cobbled streets. As the number increased, so too did her level of anxiety in seeing Matthew once more. There was so much at stake. She needed him to understand.

An image of the four-word missive she received earlier from Matthew floated before her mind's eye. Her blood boiled once more. Grace released her tight grip on the curtain, crossed her arms, and huffed. She had traded her future, her dream of a loving family, for his life. The least the man could do was provide a full report.

CHAPTER TWO

*E*yes shut, Matthew's nose twitched at the alluring scent of lilacs. This was no dream. Grace was definitely in his chambers. This was his ultimate nightmare —the woman he loved within reach. Hauling her into his bed was not an option. Every muscle in his body tensed, and he held in a groan. Eight bloody hours—it took less than a day for his resolution to ignore the woman to disintegrate into an afterthought. He shouldn't have left the note. He should have… No, he'd already resolved not to rehash the countless *should-haves*.

His lungs burned. Inhaling the sweet smell of the woman who inspired him to survive months of grueling captivity was pure torture. He'd endured enough of that for a lifetime. He took in a deep breath through his mouth to relieve the ache in his chest. But the harsh reality that once again playing cards, dancing, and making sweet love to Grace were no longer possibilities caused a sharp pain deep in the walls of his ribs. He expelled the breath.

Betrayed by the one woman who he had believed loved him like no other. His months away at Halestone Hall had given his body time to heal, but his heart and mind had metamorphosed into organs he no longer had control over. Apparently, he lacked control over other parts of his body in her presence. She had given him her virtue, heart, and soul before his disastrous mission on the Continent. His body remained in tune with hers. Matthew rolled slightly to his side to ensure Grace didn't see the impact her presence was having on him. If he feigned sleep, perhaps she would leave and let him wallow in peace.

Leaving him alone with the memories that deprived him of slumber and refused to die. Muffled sobs of men. Putrid odors that turned his stomach. Rope abrading his neck, ankles, and wrists. And the black rats. Lord, the giant black rats. His entire body shuddered, erasing the painful recollections he vowed he would never taint Grace with.

The susurrus of slippers against the wood floor brought his thoughts back to the present. Time to confront the woman whom his heart steadfastly refused to forget.

Through gritted teeth, Matthew said, "Why are you here?"

Soft ungloved hands lifted his arm to uncover his eyes and face. In a tone that brooked no argument, Grace asked in turn, "Why did you fail to obey orders?"

The heat of her touch threatened to warm his heart once more. He needed to put distance between them. Matthew clenched his hand tight as she laid his arm to rest above his head. As her hand left him, only months of practiced self-control prevented him from reaching out and grabbing it back, pulling Grace down over his body, naked under the linens, every muscle at the ready to experience her soft curves.

Eyes half-closed, he peered up at Grace through his eyelashes.

She loomed above him like an avenging angel. Fire

blazed in the golden flecks of her dark brown eyes. *Why was she angry?* He wasn't the one who had returned home engaged to another.

He counted to ten. "You shouldn't be here."

"What was I to do? You left me with no choice."

Grace's accusatory tone spurred his ire. Damnation, the woman had plenty of choices, and she had chosen the devil's own son, Ellingsworth. A wastrel and a simpleton if Matthew's sources were to be believed. Lingering bitterness remained on the tip of his tongue. He didn't move, didn't blink, simply asked, "What is it you want from me?"

Her eyes widened for a brief moment before her lips thinned into a straight line.

He glared at her.

She glared back.

Frowning, she finally broke the silence. "Why did you not provide a full report as requested?"

The woman was here for her report and no other reason. No surprise—Crown matters before all else; after all, he too had shared the sentiment, before his imprisonment. Curse his delusional mind for hoping she might be seeking more from him. She more than likely saw him as merely another informant. The stab of pain in his chest nearly had him acting savagely, and he fought the urge to tell her to go to hell. He was no longer the gentleman Grace had known, yet he would prefer she not see the angry brute he had become. He moved his arm back to shield his face and eyes.

The soft patter of her toe-tapping meant Grace would not be leaving until she received what she came for—a full accounting of events he dearly wished to never speak of again. Relenting, Matthew rose to a sitting position and shifted his back against the headboard. He let the bed linens drop to his waist, revealing his scarred and battered bare chest.

Grace gasped. Precisely the reaction he had expected. He hadn't anticipated her knuckles turning white as she clasped her hands tighter. As if she was holding back from touching him. As if she cared that his skin was marred from burns and whippings, or that his ribs remained clearly visible. His liquid diet of brandy and whiskey fueled his appetite for revenge, not his body. The possibility that Grace might still care had him hungry for the woman who stood by the side of his bed.

Matthew continued to stare. Grace's eyes slowly returned to his. While her gaze had softened, her body remained rigid. She had never been self-contained with him when they were alone, only in the presence of others.

When she didn't offer him a smile and continued to frown, Matthew folded his arms across his chest. After inhaling deeply, he began his report. "Madame Foreign Secretary. I beg your pardon for…" He paused to scratch his chin that had a day's worth of stubble. His list of transgressions was long, and he was willing to admit to only a few.

He removed his hand from his face and raised his index finger into the air. "Ah, yes. First, not obeying your direct orders to report immediately upon my return from the Continent." His middle finger joined his index finger. "Second, ignoring your summons while I was recovering at my country estate." He released his ring finger to join the others, which he waved in front of his chest. "And lastly, neglecting your requests to appear at headquarters as soon as I returned to London."

Grace's gaze roamed his face and lower, over the outline of his body shielded by the bedclothes. Her features revealed nothing of her thoughts. "I was informed you were well enough to visit your club this eve. Begs the question as to why you were remiss in your duties."

His hand quivered, the shaking uncontrollable. He tucked the offending appendage into the crook of his elbow before Grace could detect that anything was amiss. "Still spying on me. I imagined you would be too busy planning for your wedding. What will your fiancé think of your activities?"

Grace dipped her chin to her chest. "I've been told he's not one to form much of an opinion on anything but perhaps which horse to favor at the races. He's reported to favor hells and brothels. I'm certain he won't be bothered with what I choose to do with my days… or nights." She turned away from him to face the door.

What the devil was wrong with him? His words were unkind. How childish of him to lash out at her. He knew better. That was not how to treat someone you love, even if they no longer returned your regard and were betrothed to another. He should apologize. Console her at the very least. He sat up, ready to jump from the bed. The bed linens grazed against his bare skin. Naked—he wouldn't be able to leave the bed. His heart screamed at him to beg for her forgiveness. Forgive him for his wretched behavior both this eve and the night he went in search of his best friend's kidnapper—Lord Addington.

None of that mattered now. Grace was engaged to Ellingsworth, and he was a man on a personal mission—one that did not involve the Crown or any of its government offices.

Grace walked to the door without a sound. His lips firmly sealed and a breath trapped in his lungs, he waited for her to leave.

With her hand on the door handle, Grace swiveled to

face him. "I will expect a FULL written report on my desk in the morning, Lord Harrington. No more excuses."

The click of the latch falling into place echoed through the room.

Grace was gone.

He threw back the covers and reached for his night-shirt. Slipping the garment over his head and punching his arms through the sleeves, he began to pace. The lingering lilac scent had him waving his arms about like a lunatic. Was he trying to rid the room of the smell or catch and hold onto it?

He froze, closing his eyes tight. The image of Grace's gaze, devoid of emotion as she spoke of her intended, seized his heart. Opening his eyes, his gaze fell upon the empty bed. Images of Grace naked wrapped up in his bed linens came rushing back, causing his body to ache for the woman. With no possibility of sleep, Matthew turned and marched to the window. The view of the street front gave no sign of Grace or her coach. The woman had made haste, wasting no time leaving.

Leaving him.

It was for the best. The farther removed from her he remained, the better. It would ensure her safety and happiness.

Matthew stepped away from the window to pace. Perhaps, if he repeated the adage, *she is better without me* enough times, his heart would listen, and he could be happy for her. That day had yet to come. His heart remained faithful though she was to marry Ellingsworth within the month. His right hand shook at his side. A reminder he needed to focus on other matters—the demise of his sworn enemy, Lord Burke.

Turning and changing directions, Matthew's mind followed suit. He focused on devising a list of the tasks he would need to see to tomorrow. As a court-appointed advisor, Lord Burke possessed access to information and resources that would be hard to match. Still, Matthew was determined Burke would pay for his misdeeds once and for all. But what of his son—was Lord Ellingsworth as frivolous and devoid of mental shrewdness as informants had led Matthew and Grace to believe?

CHAPTER THREE

*G*race squinted into the small looking glass that hung above the porcelain washbasin. Dark circular stains around red puffy eyes stared back at her. With a groan, she splashed cold water on her face. Her maid had insisted she sleep with slices of potato upon her eyes, to reinvigorate her pale, tired features. She patted her face dry with a piece of square linen and peered at her image. Brown rings beneath her eyes remained, making her appear as if she hadn't slept in months, which was not far from the truth. It was Matthew's doing.

For months she had waited to hear from him. But the man in Matthew's chambers last night was not the same man who had promised to love her with his every breath, the man to whom she had most willingly—ardently!— given her virtue. Yes, his emaciated state and the white lines slashed across his bare chest had shocked her, making her heart ache, but it wasn't those physical changes that had caused her restless night. Grace whipped her shawl about her shoulders with quick, decisive movements that revealed her ire as she stewed over Matthew's rude, condescending behavior. No, that man last night was a dark, lost soul, filled with anger and hatred—and it was all her fault.

Platters clattering, and the hurried footsteps of servants brought Grace out of her reverie. Now was not the time to dwell on the changes to the man her heart pined for. She had prayed for a reprieve or an event that might delay the inevitable. Her prayers remained unanswered. The reality was, in a matter of a few hours, she would meet her fiancé and would have to come to accept a future that placed her at the mercy of an evil father-in-law and a bumbling husband.

She rolled back her sagging shoulders and lifted her chin. Her tightly tied corset ensured her spine was already straight, preventing her from appearing like a weeping willow. Worrying over Matthew and her agents' safety for the past two years and constantly questioning her decisions had made Grace weary. She gave herself a good shake and paced the length of her bedroom.

Focus was required. Clasping her hands behind her back and adjusting her posture once more for good measure, she recited the list she had crafted days ago.

Listen intently.

Avoid entering into conversations with Lord Burke.

Keep close to Papa.

Feign interest in her fiancé.

Ignore the man who still possessed her heart.

It would be imperative she executed her list without issue. When she drafted the list, nothing had appeared to be overwhelmingly difficult. Yet her pulse faltered every time she came to the last item. Avoiding Matthew would have been a test of her will, but evading the man she confronted last night seemed an easier task.

She froze as a dark figure appeared in the doorway. Grace glanced up to see her papa entering her chambers.

She scanned his features—who was the man approaching her? The brilliant man who held the title of the head of the Foreign Office or her papa with an aging disease?

Her papa's eyes were bright and held a sharpness to them. "Gracie."

"Yes, Papa."

"I'm confused."

The confession tore at her heart. She stepped forward to embrace the man who was her hero.

"There. There." He patted and rubbed her back. "I was just informed the servants are preparing for a formal dinner. Guests are expected later this eve to celebrate your betrothal to Lord Burke's heir." Her papa leaned back to peer down at her. "How can that be? You love Harrington."

Her papa often repeated statements during moments of clarity as if reinforcing memories and facts for himself. She, however, did not need a reminder of her feelings for Matthew.

She took a step back, releasing her papa. "I'm to marry Tobias Bixley, the Earl of Ellingsworth, son of the Marquess of Burke. We discussed this when you signed the agreements."

She hadn't lied. They had discussed the matter at length during one of her papa's lucid moments. It was a deal they had made with the devil—Lord Burke. The man wielded too much power, having held the position of private counsel to the king for the past decade and now the Prince Regent.

Her papa frowned. "I would not have agreed to such a ridiculous union!"

Grace quickly tried to explain before he became too agitated. "Months and months ago Lord Burke sought you out... us out. He knows of your condition. To guarantee his silence and gain information regarding Harrington's location upon the Continent, you offered my hand to his son."

"Girl, my memory may fail me at times, but I'm not that heartless. I would never have agreed to you marrying that imbecile. Pfft… Ellingsworth."

She wanted to buckle, bury herself in the comfort of her papa's strong arms, and confess that he hadn't. It had been she who had agreed to Burke's demands, with the caveat that the betrothal announcement to be postponed until the start of the upcoming season.

Her papa's lips were pressed tight into a straight line, signaling his displeasure, the look she feared most as a child. It pained her to disappoint her papa, but she had no choice. In order to preserve control of the Foreign Office and ensure the safe return of Matthew and others held in captivity with him, she had agreed to marry Lord Ellingsworth, and her papa had signed the marriage settlement.

In previous moments of lucidity, Grace had shared her concerns in marrying Burke's son. Lord Ellingsworth ran with an entirely different set. She could only recall one instance of having been near the man, and that was many years ago. Her fiancé was admiring the Elgin Marbles, surrounded by his cronies, acting the fool he was reported to be. Lord Ellingsworth had made the most indecent gestures, causing his mates to giggle like a pack of hyenas. She was fully aware that it would take every ounce of fortitude she possessed to convince the ton she was happily engaged to a man who was purported to have air for brains.

Her papa continued to stare at Grace as if he was waiting for her to provide some reasonable explanation. She needed a diversion. There was no time today to rehash the matter. Nothing came to mind. Grace wrapped her arms around her waist. What was she to do? Lucy had confirmed that Matthew would be in attendance per orders from Archbroke. Her head ached. She would soon come face-to-face with Lord Ellingsworth. A wave of nausea rolled through her.

Grace asked, "Will you escort me down?"

He took one of her hands in his and gently rubbed his thumb over the back of her hand like he had when she was a little girl and upset. "Gracie girl, you know my wish was for you to marry Harrington." Her papa released her hand and huffed, "I should have drawn up the contracts prior to him venturing off. A partner is what you require— someone to assist you with Foreign Office affairs. Harrington wouldn't have abused the status, and I could retire. All the agents respect him and would have supported his appointment."

Grace was fully aware of her papa's wishes and hopes.

Her papa's dreams of Matthew and her running the Foreign Office in partnership would have been realized if Matthew had not dashed off on the dangerous mission of hunting down the foolish Lord Addington, who aided Lord Burke in his devilish schemes. But Matthew had made his choice. Without so much as a by-your-leave, he left for the Continent, got himself captured, and had been held until Grace managed to arrange for his rescue. What irked her the most was that the blasted man had returned to England and completely ignored her.

"I won't ask again." Her papa cringed at his last words but continued, "Explain the events that have resulted in you being betrothed to the scallywag Ellingsworth."

Grace sighed. "There is no time, Papa. There is much to do before Lord Burke, his family, and the other guests arrive."

27

"No more excuses, Gracie girl. I will have this out with you now."

Her papa was in fine form today. She should be grateful he was of sound mind for this auspicious occasion, yet it rankled her that he pressed her for details of the events she sorely wished had never occurred. "Very well. I... we received word that Harrington, Addington, and Hereford, along with a Home Office agent named Mr. Jones, were being held captive in Salamanca, Spain. Lord Burke came to us and informed us he had critical information that would assist us in obtaining their release. He also indicated he was aware of my role at the Foreign Office and that it would be his duty to advise the Crown to appoint a new head of the department."

With a frown, her papa declared, "He has no authority over who is appointed."

"Lord Burke may not have direct authority, but he is a formidable man with many resources. He has the potential to make things difficult for us. I... we needed Lord Burke's assistance. The price for Harrington's safety and your condition to remain a secret is one I am willing to pay."

Her papa stroked his chin and began to pace. "Burke wants his son in place to take control of the office, thus gaining additional resources to aid in his private affairs."

She smiled broadly at her papa. This was the man she admired and who had taught her everything she knew.

She took advantage of his lucid state. "What do you suppose those affairs comprise?"

"Power and coin. Burke has always been a greedy bastard, unlike his papa before him."

Grace fell into step alongside her papa. She had noted that when he exercised, the periods of lucidity were lengthier and successive.

Her papa continued. "By putting his son in place, he

would have access to foreign trade deals, information on diplomatic arrangements and agents readily available to do his bidding. Hmmm… There is more to his plan." His blue eyes caught her gaze. "Gracie, remind me of the timeline of events, please."

This was her chance. Her papa was in fine form this afternoon. While he had made the request before multiple times during the past six months, each time she had refined her response, kept succinct, not knowing when he might lose his concentration. All in the hopes he would assist her in devising an alternate plan to avoid life with Lord Ellingsworth.

"Two seasons past, we issued orders for Devonton to return from the Continent. Midway through the season, we received word of a plan to abduct Devonton. Against orders, Harrington and Devonton attended the Redburn House party, from which Devonton was kidnapped. Lucy deciphered intercepted missives indicating Addington was involved in the matter."

"Addington? But he is one of our agents."

She too had initially been confused by Addington's betrayal. "Lord Burke had threatened to ruin Addington's sister, Lady Cecilia, who was set to make her debut the following season."

Her papa paused to look at her directly. Grace needed to steer the conversation back on course. "In any case, Lucy ventured to the Continent to fetch Devonton, which resulted in her becoming Lady Devonton."

"Ah, as it should be. A love match, no less." He resumed pacing, but with shorter strides to match hers this time.

Grace sighed, "Yes, well, not all marriages can be a love match. Back to the timeline, Papa. Harrington left in search of Addington against our orders. I sent Lord Hereford to assist. Archbroke, the meddling fool, sent Mr. Jones, one of his own messengers, from the Home Office to the Continent."

Her papa came to stand next to her. "Lord Archbroke broke protocol? That's unlike the man."

Grace said, "Yes. Well, he did."

"What happened next?" Her papa hooked his arm about hers and began to walk once more.

"After Lucy's wedding, Aunt Emily and I went to the Continent in search of Harrington. However, we discovered that they were being held as prisoners in a Spanish insurgent camp. Heeding Aunt Emily's advice, we returned to London. I made further inquiries, which led to Lord Burke presenting us with the deal that landed me in this predicament."

"Who then rescued Harrington and the lot?"

"Archbroke sent Waterford."

He tapped her arm. "And who did you send?"

Grace smiled as she recalled the night she stole Lady Cecilia away from Lord Archbroke to assist her in carrying out the complicated rescue plan. "Lady Cecilia. I might have also seen to it that certain information fell into the hands of the newly minted Lord Hadfield."

"Smart girl, Gracie."

His belief and trust in her were unfailing while her own confidence in her abilities had waned. Grace continued, "With the information Lord Burke provided, Lady Cecilia, Waterford, and Hadfield successfully tracked down Harrington and the others and freed the lot. Harrington and Hereford returned home. Addington and Lady Cecilia fled to Canada. Neither wanted to face Lord Burke."

"And what of Mr. Jones?"

Curious. Papa hadn't shown any emotional reaction to the others. Grace eyed her papa for clues as she answered.

"I believe Archbroke ordered him to follow Harrington to Halestone Hall."

His shoulders relaxed, and a smile Grace hadn't seen in months appeared. "Wonderful. Now, what of Waterford and Hadfield?"

She missed the wise man before her, the mastermind who recalled details and never let a loose end go unanswered.

"They did not return with the others. According to the intelligence I received, Hadfield wished to remain and tour the Continent. It was rumored Hadfield was avoiding his new cousin by marriage—Archbroke."

Turning to pace in the opposite direction, her papa asked, "Have you seen Matthew since his return? How does he fare?"

Grace's heart sank. Her papa had already forgotten his advice to seek Matthew out. She chose her next words with care. "He has yet to obey our orders."

Matthew had again failed to provide her with the information she requested. There had been no written report awaiting her this morning. Initially, she was disappointed, but then the idea he might come in person to present the information had her giddy with anticipation. She had even delayed leaving the gazebo for a full extra hour in the hopes he would comply, but neither man nor report had appeared.

Her papa said, "I would expect Harrington will accompany Lucy and Devonton to this evening's event."

"Yes, Lucy informed me that both she and Matthew are well enough to attend."

"What ails Lucy?"

"Nothing. However, she is still recovering from the birth of her sons, Pierce and Rowland. They are but six months old. Devonton shared his displeasure at having Lucy return to town so soon after her lying-in."

"Nothing slows that girl down. Twin boys, huh." Papa stopped by the window and keenly watched some activity outside. "If anyone is up to the challenge, that would be our Lucy."

On her tiptoes, Grace peeked over his shoulder but saw nothing out of the ordinary.

He turned away from whatever it was. "Gracie, one last query, and then I shall take you down to see that all is ready for the evening. Have you ascertained what Lord Ellingsworth knows of the whole matter?"

"No, Papa. But I did receive a message from him this morn asking to meet in private before dinner commences. I assume it is so he can formally propose. You and Lord Burke have already signed the marriage contract."

"I have?" Concern and confusion clouded his eyes, but he shook it off. "Not to worry, Gracie. All will be well. I'll see to it."

But she had heard that exact promise numerous times throughout the years. While her papa meant well, she understood he might not recall his pledge as early as tomorrow morn or in a day or two at the outset. Grace moved to place her hand on his winged arm but found herself caught up in an affectionate hug.

Before he released her, he instructed, "Make sure Cook prepares the same light fare for my breakfast tomorrow, and you take me for a nice long walk out in the gardens like we did this morn, Gracie. Don't forget."

"Yes, Papa, I'll remember."

CHAPTER FOUR

*C*haos. Utter Chaos.

Matthew's head pounded with the increasing volume of the voices surrounding him. Seated at his desk, fingertips steepled beneath his chin, he took another deep breath. Briefly, he closed his eyes to make the gathered group disappear. What he really wanted to do was cover his ears and order the meddling lot to get the bloody hell out of his study. Leave his townhouse. Leave him alone.

Blake and Archbroke occupied one side of the room, facing their wives, while Matthew's mama stood, quiet but present, beside him.

He slid a pleading look to Blake. His best friend always read his mind, and he was counting on the skill right now.

Blake shuffled to Lucy's side, and Matthew released a sigh of relief as he read Blake's lips. *Sweetheart, perhaps the ladies would like to adjourn to the drawing room. Allow the men a moment to partake in a drink… or two.*

His sister's gaze darted past him before landing on their mother. The crease between Lucy's eyebrows deepened as she said, "Mama, Theo, let's adjourn for tea. I need some sustenance before we continue discussing matters."

Matthew observed Blake's reassuring hand on Lucy's lower back as he escorted her and the other ladies to the door. The touch was merely one of the ways Matthew's brother-in-law displayed his love. Praise the saints, Lucy had married the only man alive who had the skill and patience to handle her.

Matthew waited for the ladies to leave the room, but before the door even clicked closed, Archbroke faced Blake. "What the devil? We were finally getting somewhere in the discussion…"

Blake glared down at the man. "How many times must I remind you? You may be the head of the Home Office and Lucy's superior, but you are *not*—"

"Will the two of you shut up!" Matthew said before the discussion deteriorated. "I need a bloody drink!"

Both men stared at him as if he had grown horns and a third eye. Matthew wasn't the devil or a monster, but he was no longer the carefree, indolent marquess who sought to restore the peace. Damnation. If they weren't going to pour him a drink, he'd do it himself. Matthew pushed back his chair and quickly stood—and just as quickly grabbed for the back of his chair.

Stars appeared before his eyes, a reminder of his months of captivity. Beating after beating had left him with constant headaches and sudden dizziness. He opened his eyes to a double image of Blake inches away and a glass of brandy being urged into his shaking hand. He didn't care about the concerned looks he was receiving. He didn't want or need pity. He put the glass to his mouth and poured the fiery liquid down his throat.

At least, that is what he had intended, but the glass slammed down on the desk. His judgment of distances was impacted during these irritating episodes. While their frequency had lessened over the past few months, they still bedeviled him.

"Steady on there." Blake refilled the glass and pushed it closer.

Alcohol no longer dulled the ache in Matthew's head, but he accepted the drink anyway, and Blake came back into full focus. He was more than a best friend and brother-in-law. Blake was Matthew's hero. Against all the odds, the man had survived and escaped enemy captivity numerous times during the war. Blake was considered the Foreign Office's most valuable agent. He never once uttered a complaint when his tour abroad was extended.

Matthew had advised Grace to summon Blake home many times, for his sister's sake, but the acting Foreign Secretary had argued that Lucy was resilient and would manage without the assistance of a man. It was true Lucy had managed. But having seen the unparalleled love and understanding the pair shared, after experiencing captivity himself, guilt ate at Matthew's soul for having failed to persuade Grace to order Blake's return home sooner.

Matthew hadn't understood Blake's annoyance when he first returned at how frivolous and selfish the majority of the ton behaved. Matthew did now. He had been guilty of taking the lavish meals, the conveniences of bed, bath, and clean clothes for granted. Lucy had told him of the scars evident on Blake's body. But her husband never shared the horrific conditions he must have endured during his time on the Continent with anyone.

Blake showed no signs of the distress that Matthew was now experiencing after being held prisoner. Matthew hadn't been alone like Blake. Held captive with three others, they were now like brothers, sharing a deep bond that would never be broken.

Matthew glanced down at the glass in his hand. It was empty, like him.

The crimson material of Archbroke's waistcoat caught his attention as the man paced in front of him.

Matthew barked, "Speak up, Archbroke. What the devil are you rambling on about now?"

The Home Secretary came to stand mere inches away. "I remain your superior. I do not take orders from my subordinates."

They stared at each for a full two minutes. Matthew respected Archbroke. The man was a genius and a fabulous leader, but Matthew had plans for his time, and they didn't involve the Home Office. Matthew was the first to release his gaze and lower it to the floor.

Archbroke released a barely audible sigh before saying, "Devonton, since you shooed your wife away, you will have to answer my questions. Did Lucy receive any further news from Lady Grace?"

"No." Blake's lips curved into a devilish smile. Unlike Matthew, Blake dared to question the Home Secretary. "Has Mr. Jones provided a report? I assume he was able to immerse himself into Ellingsworth's set."

Archbroke's shoulders slumped. "To his dismay, yes."

Matthew didn't want to hear Grace's betrothed's name uttered in his house. Every single muscle in his body tensed, and he carefully placed the empty glass on the sideboard before it shattered in his hand.

How was he to endure an entire evening in Grace's presence along with her fiancé?

An image of Grace floated in his memory. Candlelight glinting off her bright eyes as he twirled her about the dance floor. Her laughter filling his heart with happiness. Leaning down, he tucked a wayward tendril behind her ear, but instead of seeing his own reflection in the depths of her eyes, Ellingsworth's idiotic grin stared back.

Matthew's heart seized. His only solace was that Burke would pay for upending his life.

Blake joined him at the sideboard and poured two healthy fingers of brandy for each of them. His best friend took a long sip and swallowed. "Archbroke, if we are to puzzle out why Lord Flarinton and Lady Grace would agree to the outrageous match, you must share the intelligence in your possession. Don't make me subject Theo to an inquisition."

"Threaten to burden my wife again," Archbroke returned, "and I'll pound you into the ground. She is in no condition to worry about these matters."

How had Matthew's overbearing superior convinced sweet Theo, a woman Matthew had known since childhood, to marry him? Even more perplexing was the fact that she appeared to be in love with Archbroke. Matthew's lungs deflated as feelings of love permeated his mind. He never had reason to question Grace's feelings for him. Even when he received the news of Grace's betrothal, he had initially believed it a mistake, a farce of some sort. But when Lucy informed him Lord Flarinton had indeed signed the marriage agreements, Matthew resigned himself to the fact that the woman had gone and betrothed herself to another.

He shook his head. "What is with the empty threats, Archbroke? You are no match for Devonton." He raked his gaze over his superior standing in front of him. Archbroke's waistcoat was no longer tight around the belly, and the material about his shoulders was pulled taut. Where was the man who spent hours, days even, behind a desk, mindlessly consuming beefsteaks that were placed before him?

Archbroke stood with his hands on his hips. "Is that a fact? Devonton, what do you say to a round at Gentlemen Jackson's tomorrow?"

Blake's eyes lit with interest.

The instinct to smooth the situation over with a glib statement flittered through Matthew's mind. Choking back the comment, he asked, "What did Jones find out about Ellingsworth?" A bitter taste remained in his mouth as Grace's fiancé's name rolled off his tongue. He needed another drink.

Moving his hands from his hips to clasp them behind his back, Archbroke said, "I'll repeat Jones's observations verbatim. *Lord Ellingsworth is of a similar temperament to that of Lord Devonton. He should not be judged by those who surround him.* I will add that Jones was required to report back merely after spending a day and a half with Ellingsworth's set."

"What!" Blake ran his hand through his hair. "From all accounts, Ellingsworth has nothing but air for brains and spends his days at the worst gaming hells, whorehouses, and opium dens. And here I assumed after journeying with Jones, he would know me better." Blake was clearly disappointed.

Matthew replayed Jones's words again before saying, "I too spent time with Jones, and he is extremely astute, an excellent judge of character. I'd say Jones was conveying his suspicions that there is more to Ellingsworth than what might appear." Had he inadvertently defended the man he swore to hate?

Blake said, "We still have to ascertain what information Burke used to blackmail Flarinton."

Archbroke said, "It can't be the obvious. Flarinton's aging disease has plagued him to varying degrees for years." Tapping a finger against his lean waist, he continued, "Burke probably advised Prinny it was of no matter since it was in his favor."

Archbroke was right. Neither the king nor the Prince Regent were interested in state affairs. Prinny was only interested in his building projects and lavish parties.

Archbroke mumbled, "Admittedly, while it took me a few months to adjust to working with her, Lady Grace did admirably for the duration of the war."

Who was this man? Archbroke never praised Grace for her capabilities.

"What are you gawking at, Harrington?"

Matthew turned to Blake, "He's an impostor!"

Blake chuckled, "He is not an impostor. The man before you is the result of Theo knocking sense into him."

"Theo?"

Blake was right. The man's whole demeanor softened as he uttered his wife's name. Matthew was surrounded by men in love, the punishment he deserved for abandoning Grace.

Archbroke continued, "Perhaps obvious to others, but Flarinton and Grace might be under a different impression. We need someone they trust to discuss this with them both at a… well, at the right time."

Blake and Archbroke looked at Matthew pointedly.

"Me? You want *me* to be alone in the same room as her!"

"No, in the same room as Lady Grace *and* her papa," Archbroke replied.

"I won't do it." He would rather resign than be trapped in a room with the woman who had betrayed him.

Crown before all else. Damnation. He was no novice agent. He'd simply have to treat this like any other assignment. Doubts about his ability to ignore the lingering emotions that refused to be banished from his heart and mind resurfaced.

Standing to his full height and adopting a tone that brooked no argument, Archbroke said, "Lord Harrington, your assignment is—"

Matthew raised his hand. "No need to be overdramatic." It was inevitable that he would see Grace at social events. Better to figure out the best way to deal with her now before she was married and enceinte with another man's child. Matthew conceded, "I'll try to speak to her in private this evening."

"Splendid." Archbroke slapped his gloves across his thigh and headed for the door with a spring in his step Matthew had never seen before.

Frowning, he said, "I don't care for that man. I want the old Archbroke back. At least he was predictable. This new version..." The image of his superior a year ago was vastly different from the man who strode from his study. "Has Archbroke lost a stone or two?"

"Yes. These days you can find him fencing at Angelo's at least twice a week and at Jackson's at least once a week. Add that to activities he enjoys with Theo."

"Devonton!"

"Get your brain out of the gutter, Harrington. I wasn't referring to bed sport, although from her condition, that may have something to do with his altered physical condition. I expect you will find his counterpart, Lady Grace, has also greatly changed since you last saw her. I want to warn you..."

Warn? Did Matthew want to hear it? He unsteadily poured himself another drink and swallowed it in one gulp before turning his full attention back to Blake.

"Yes? Warn me..."

"My superior did not appreciate you ignoring a direct order."

"She ordered me to stay put and let Hereford do my duty. I was the one who was ordered to protect you. I would never let another clean up or fix my mess. It was unreasonable for her to issue such an order."

"She wanted to protect you. She was in love with you."

"Yes. Was. As in no longer is. Grace now belongs to Ellingsworth."

"She believed you acted rashly and abandoned her."

"Of all the people we are acquainted with, she should have understood."

"Grace understood, all right. You chose duty rather than her."

No, Blake had it all wrong. He had a job to do. Grace should have supported his decision. It had been the right and honorable thing to do to hunt down his best friend's kidnapper, even if it meant leaving her.

CHAPTER FIVE

Spying Silverman's dour features at the door, Grace vacated her favorite velvet upholstered chair in her papa's private study. Her movements caused Lord Flarinton to cease his pacing and face her. Grace slipped her tired feet back into her slippers and said, "I believe Lord Ellingsworth has arrived. It is time I met my intended."

"I shall accompany you."

"My thanks for your support. However, it would be best if you and Mama entertained and greeted the other guests as they arrive." She preceded her papa to the door.

Silverman said, "Lord Ellingsworth is awaiting you in the green drawing room. I shall escort Lord Flarinton to the garden room."

With a nod, she turned to her left and made her way down the corridor. Nervous at leaving her papa alone for more than a few minutes, Grace lengthened her stride. Glad she wasn't to meet her fiancé for the first time at the altar, she was simultaneously annoyed with the entire situation. She came to an abrupt halt.

Matthew was there—with his ear pressed to the draw-ing-room door. He raised his hand in a warning not to approach.

Oh no. This was her house, and she'd do as she pleased. Sidestepping the board that creaked, she headed straight for the door while Matthew anticipated her move and shifted quickly to block her way.

For a moment, Grace stood mesmerized by his blue-gray eyes. Her body longed for him to haul her into his arms, and her mind wished he'd reassure her all was right between them. She gave herself a good mental shake.

In a harsh whisper, she demanded, "What are you about?"

In typical Matthew fashion, he replied with a question of his own. "Can you explain why Ellingsworth would be meeting with Theo and her husband?"

The slight upturn of Matthew's mouth and the curiosity in his eyes told her one thing. He was still pursuing his investigations into the existence of what most considered an old wives' tale. Three families, who have for generations sworn to serve the Crown, referred to as the Protectors of the Royal Family, PORFs. She suspected that his absurd obsession in identifying the three family names was part of the reason why Matthew ignored her pleas to remain in England.

Jaw clenched, Grace answered, "I haven't the slightest clue."

Matthew's narrowed gaze bore into hers. She'd witnessed the look many a time as he interrogated enemy spies, but she'd never been on the receiving end. The man's stare was relentless as if he had the ability to look into her soul and determine if she were telling the truth. She was on the brink of confessing her love for him when a flash of guilt appeared in his eyes.

Matthew looked away. "I need to speak with Archbroke."

His words crushed the last ounce of hope Grace possessed. Of course, he wasn't sneaking about searching for her. She was no longer of any interest to him.

Holding back the hurt and tears, Grace moved to step around him. His hand reached out to brush against her shoulder. She whirled around to face him. "I need to meet with my intended."

His hand dropped from her. "I apologize. I should not have touched you."

Grace closed her eyes as she willed the pain of his words away. She shouldn't want him to touch her. She shouldn't want him at all. "That is the problem, my lord. I'm about to meet my fiancé for the first time, and all I can think about is you."

"First time?"

Her sorrow briefly forgotten as Matthew's features transformed from a disgruntled bear to a gaping fish. Registering it was the first time she'd ever managed to catch Matthew off guard only had the sadness seeping back into her as she confessed, "The contracts and agreements were all arranged by his papa, Lord Burke."

The door to the drawing room swung open, and Theo popped her head out. "Would the two of you care to join us, or are you going to loiter about in the hall all evening?"

Matthew finally regained his voice. "Where is your husband? I wish to speak to him."

Archbroke appeared next to his wife in the doorway. "Lady Grace, I must say you look lovely this eve. With your permission, Harrington and I shall adjourn to the library."

At Matthew's incredulous look, Grace said through barely parted lips, "Theo has had a most profound effect upon the man." She moved forward to stand in front of Theo and Archbroke, leaving Matthew behind. "The library is yours to use." Grace found herself engulfed in a hug from Theo. Pulling back, she looked into Theo's brilliant green eyes. "You are looking well." Theo had a glow that could only be attributed to one condition—she was with child.

A blush appeared on Theo's cheeks. "Yes. Thank goodness I have not suffered as Lucy did."

Over Theo's shoulder, Grace's gaze fell upon the outline of a gentleman standing by the window. A pang of jealousy hit her. Both of her closest and most trusted friends were happily married to men who adored them. They were also embarking upon the next stage of life as wife and mother, while here she was about to meet Lord Ellingsworth, a purported dullard, with whom she was to spend the rest of her living days. Stifling a groan, Grace stepped farther into the drawing room.

The fabric of her betrothed's coat wrinkled across his back as his shoulders straightened. Only a few feet away, Grace noted the man's dark brown hair was trimmed shorter than the current fashion sported by Mr. Brummell and his set. Grace called upon all her years of training to mask any signs of surprise. Lord Ellingsworth's skin was not pale from lack of sunlight, nor did it sport a yellow tinge that would have indicated years of debauchery and swill. No. The man standing before her was hale and showed no signs of having air for brains. His light blue eyes sparkled with clarity. There was no indication the man was befuddled in the least.

Grace squared her shoulders and dipped into a curtsey. "Lord Ellingsworth."

"We are to be married. Please address me as Tobias."

Placing her hand into his upturned palm, she raised to

stand. "Tobias. It is a pleasure to meet you." The warmth of his touch calmed her nerves.

"Ah, but the pleasure is all mine." They were not alone, and Tobias withdrew his hand.

His tone was clear and precise. It wasn't laced with mockery or malice like his papa's. Frowning, Grace found it challenging to reconcile the man standing before her and the man described by her informants.

Theo broke the silence. "Archbroke, let us join the other guests. It's time we leave and allow Lord Ellingsworth to get to know Lady Grace better."

Archbroke moved to obey his wife's command but came up short as Matthew blocked his progress. Grace lifted her foot to go to Matthew, but she froze as Tobias placed a hand at the small of her back.

Matthew glared at Theo. "You are going to leave Grace alone with…"

Theo slapped Matthew on the arm. "What is the matter with you? They are betrothed!"

Matthew shifted, avoiding Theo's attempt to turn him about. He'd once looked at Grace with naked desire, but now his eyes, deep, dark wells of anger, reflected nothing. "We should return to the garden room. Lord Flarinton needs our support."

He still cared for her papa, but not for her. Grace turned away from Matthew, squeezing her eyes tight against the deluge of tears threatening to overflow. Tobias's hand rested upon her shoulder.

From behind her, Matthew emitted a feral growl followed by shuffled footsteps. Grace glanced up at Tobias. "Are they gone?"

He nodded. The concern in his eyes was overwhelming. A tear escaped, rolling down her face.

Tobias gently swiped the tear away. "He will come around in time."

Grace settled herself upon the couch. "You're wrong. You don't know him." *No one does anymore, not even me.*

"Harrington was right. We shouldn't be alone, but first, we have a few matters to discuss and reach agreement upon."

Tobias moved to stand by the window once more. With his attention drawn away from her, Grace stared at her betrothed. Physically Tobias was a younger version of his papa. He had the same refined nose with a slight upturn and lips that were now pulled taut into a straight line. They shared the same eye color, but while there was a wily edginess to Lord Burke's eyes, his son's gaze was stout and guileless. While Grace had instantly disliked Lord Burke upon introduction, her instincts told her to trust Tobias. But what if the impulse was wrong?

Tobias placed his hands behind his back, but his focus remained on the activities outside the window. "The man who sired me will be arriving soon, and I need to share a few pertinent details with you."

She waited for him to continue. When he glanced over his shoulder at her, she had regained her composure and now sat on the edge, intently listening.

Tobias lifted a hand to pull the drapes to one side. "I will go along with this sham of an engagement for a period. But let me be clear—we will not be married. I have no interest in whatever arrangements Lord Burke has made."

Too exhausted to stand, Grace muttered, "Wait. What do—"

He turned to face her and raised a hand in midair. "Let me explain, and then I'll gladly answer any questions you may have. Agreed?"

Grace stared at Tobias. Was this a trick of some sort? She didn't know the man well, but he used a hand gesture before he spoke rather than after. Liars tended to use hand movements after starting a conversation to distract their audience from their words. And his gaze never flickered away like when one was telling a fib or set out to deceive. *No*, the man steadily met her gaze. She gave him a curt nod.

Tobias returned his attention back to the street front. "I've known for years of my sire's underhanded dealings, and I want no part of his schemes."

"Is that why you associate yourself with…" Grace stopped mid-sentence as Tobias's fierce scowl fell upon her. "Sorry—I agreed to no questions until after you are finished. Proceed."

His scowl disappeared, replaced by a look of resolution. "This betrothal has come at the most inconvenient time. I was to set sail in three weeks. I have investors and business partners awaiting my arrival in New York."

Before she could stop herself, Grace blurted, "You were to tour America?"

"I see you can't help but make inquiries." Instead of a scowling, Tobias smiled and said, "No, not a grand tour. To leave and never return. I believe Lord Burke was advised of my plans and set his own in play. But the man is getting old. And I swear I will set matters straight before I take my leave. All I ask is that you agree to follow my lead. In order for my plan to succeed, I will need you to act the besotted fiancé."

Grace rolled to her feet, no longer able to sit for the conversation. "Why should I trust you? Gossips have pegged you a dimwit with few morals, if any." She walked to stand next to Tobias by the window. She needed to be able to see his facial expressions to detect the small nuances that would indicate he was behaving dishonorably.

Tilting his head in her direction, he answered, "You have acted as Foreign Secretary since the ripe old age of eighteen, which means you now have five years of experience to rely upon. For those privy to such information, you are known for your quick, decisive actions and unwavering ability to judge character within moments. Am I a dimwit?"

How was he aware of such details? None of her reports indicated he would have committed such information to memory. She narrowed her gaze upon her betrothed. None of his facial muscles were taut. His lips were curved easily into a smile, not an overexaggerated, feigned smile that would typically accompany a lie. Tobias's gaze was steady, with no rapid blinking, and his eyes sparkled clear with intelligence. He exhibited none of the traits of a liar nor a man lacking astuteness. No. The man before her was no idiot but a master of disguise.

"You're a wolf in sheep's clothing. I do not trust such beasts. Nor do I trust your papa."

"Wise of you not too. You have but two choices. Marry me, leaving London and your family forever, or play along and have what your heart desires and the rule of the Foreign Office." With a snap, Tobias released the curtain he had peeled back. "Well, what is it to be?"

Grace arranged her features into a pleasant mask of peace and happiness.

Similarly, Tobias's features transformed from sharp intellect to that of a simpleton. "Perfect. You could have managed a successful stage career on Drury Lane, my dear."

"And you, my lord, could have been master of the boards."

Placing a hand on his winged arm, they marched to the door as if heading into battle. Just shy of the door threshold, Tobias halted and, in all seriousness, said, "It is imperative everyone, including Harrington, believes we are to wed. Ours is to be a tale of love at first sight. Do you understand?"

Her shoulders slumped forward. "I do."

"I'm sorry for the pain you must temporarily endure. But if Harrington is half the man he is reported to be, and all accounts of how much he is in love with you are accurate, all will be as it should be in the end." Tobias's voice was filled with regret and sincerity.

Perhaps he spoke the truth and wanted no part in Lord Burke's activities. However, it was one thing to avoid becoming involved in his sire's misdeeds and an entirely different matter to scheme against the devil. Tobias was a conundrum.

CHAPTER SIX

*M*atthew glanced over his shoulder as he escaped into Flarinton's gardens, certain that no one would notice his absence for a short spell. How had he ever endured such trivial discussions like those of the weather? Captivity stripped a person bare. The cloak of society he once believed warm and inviting was now smothering and suffocating. All evening his attention had veered in Grace's direction. There had been a time when she would instinctively return his looks, and they would commiserate in each other's misery. But not tonight. Not once had Grace's pretty molten chocolate eyes sought him out.

Avoiding the pebbled path that led to her private retreat, a gazebo well hidden within Flarinton's gardens, Matthew weaved his way until he reached the lawn. His knees had threatened to buckle many a time during the past hour. Matthew collapsed to the ground. Forcing himself to sit upright, he slowly brought his knees up and rested his arms over them. He leaned back and ran his hands along the tops of his thighs and massaged the knots in his muscles. It wasn't the physical demands of the evening that had him seeking out solitude. Matthew could have muddled through on willpower alone if that were the issue. No, it was the emotional toll of the event that had him creeping out into the night. Without the deep-seated connection he once believed to exist between himself and Grace, he was lost among the crowd he once thrived in.

To hell with following the rules. He removed his stockings and shoes and rolled to his feet. The blades of the grass tickled the soles of his feet, reminding him—he was alive and free. With his shoes and hose held tightly in his hands behind his back, he walked the perimeter of Lord Flarinton's lawn. He glanced at the wall of windows to the garden room. Even from this distance, he could make out Grace's slight form standing next to Ellingsworth's. Matthew paused to study her. Grace's body was slightly turned toward Ellingsworth, but her weight fell all to one side, away from her betrothed. She was nodding excessively, another indication of feigned interest. All throughout the engagement dinner, Matthew had observed Grace, hoping to see her rub her right wrist—Grace's telltale sign of nervousness and uncertainty. But the meal had ended, and not once had she even come close to exhibiting anything that might have been interrupted as distaste for her betrothed.

The woman was a master of languages, especially in what people showed with their movements and not their words. She was always fully aware of her own actions and the effect they had on those about her. Her overexaggerated movements had Matthew desperately trying to deduce what Grace was trying to communicate. Fingers pressed to his temples; his head pounded as he shifted through the night's events. He grumbled, "Damnation," as nothing of note came to mind. Matthew wasn't ready to rejoin the others and place himself within twelve feet of Lord Burke. The devil had preened about the room, cleverly avoiding all contact with Matthew, as if he didn't exist. The cut direct had Matthew itching to do the man bodily harm, but Grace's engagement dinner was not the location Matthew desired to deal with the coward who hid behind his title and position at court.

A woman's raspy cough from the other side of the hedge caught Matthew's attention. He turned, intending to leave.

"Sweetheart, the soot and smoke—it's terrible for your lungs." Blake's deep baritone voice had Matthew halting his departure.

"Don't *sweetheart* me! I'll not return to Shalford Castle." His sister coughed again. It had a terrible whooping quality to it. "Matthew needs us."

Damnation. Lucy should know he would never put her safety or health at risk. Matthew was about to announce his presence when Blake said, "I'm asking you to take heed of the doctor's advice. The London air is horrendous for you and the twins. While I do not care for the idea of being away from you, I shall remain in town."

What? Blake hated being apart from his wife. The pair were inseparable. Matthew would simply adjust his plans.

Lucy responded, "Lord Burke will not be easy to defeat."

Matthew wanted to reach through the prickly bush that separated him from his brother-in-law and wring Blake's neck. He had expressly told Blake not to share his plans for Burke's demise with anyone.

Interrupting his murderous thoughts, Lucy asked, "What if you need me?"

"I am always in need of you." Blake's husky answer was accompanied by the rustling of silk.

Matthew swiveled toward the house. About to leave and give the couple privacy, he halted at Lucy's deep sigh.

"I won't leave Matthew. He…" Lucy's voice cracked. "The man who returned on the Quarter Moon is not my twin. Matthew would never let hate and vengeance rule him."

"Sweetheart, your brother was held in captivity for an extended period, and in less-than-ideal conditions. It is only natural for him to want to take revenge against the man who left him to rot. Burke held the information for months before he shared it with Grace. Burke could have easily prevented Matthew's suffering. Instead, the devil had remained silent. Don't worry. Archbroke, and I will ensure your brother comes to no harm."

Matthew could picture his twin's reaction to Blake's reassurances. He didn't need to see her. Lucy would have her hands firmly planted on her hips; head cocked to one side. She said, "Hmm. You will need to find out what Theo and Archbroke have planned. There is more to this entire matter than what we have been told. I have an awful feeling." A terrible fit of short breaths followed by coughs had Lucy wheezing the last few words. "I'm never wrong about these things."

Lucy's intuition was uncanny. Blake vocalized Matthew's thoughts. "I am fully aware that your instincts are rarely wrong. But love, I must insist you take the children and return to Shalford Castle."

The sound of lips kissing had Matthew striding toward the party. Blake's gravely tone traveled the night air. "Trust me. I will take care of matters here, and I will send word as soon as the matter is dealt with."

Matthew slowed his pace. Lucy hadn't precisely agreed to leave town, which gave him pause. His twin could be extremely difficult and stubborn when she believed she was needed. He should turn around and demand Lucy give him her word to return to the country. Whirling about, he came face-to-face with a startled Grace. How long had she been trailing him? The blasted constant ringing in his ears prevented him from hearing others approach. His shoes dropped to the ground with a soft thud. A year or so ago, Grace would have laughed and teased him at the sight of his bare feet. Now his gaze met her befuddled eyes.

Grace lowered her gaze inch by inch until it rested upon his feet. The tip of her shoe peeked out from under her dress and slid across the grass to tap his little toe. "I see you have acquired a new habit."

One of many he'd formed since his return from Continent. "Yes. The prickle against my soles reminds me I'm not dead."

Grace pulled back her foot. Head bent, she said, "Oh, Matthew. I'm sorry…"

He tilted her chin up, knowing the words she needed to hear. "Don't apologize. You did not fail. You did nothing wrong. It was I who made an unwise decision, and I paid the price."

The small curve of her lips was hardly a grin, but a genuine reaction—in stark contrast to all the smiles she had given Ellingsworth. He had simply spoken the truth. It wasn't her fault he had left London on a wild-goose chase and was captured by Spanish insurgents. No, he had fallen directly into Burke's scheme.

He let his hand fall to his side.

Grace said, "I wish…"

What did she wish for? Why had she left the safety of the house—was it possible she still cared, had noticed his absence?

Her skin pebbled, and she tugged on her shawl as a

cool breeze swept over them, reminding Matthew they were alone in the dark.

"It's not wise for you to be out here. I'm certain Ellingsworth would not appreciate the possibility of his betrothed being seen with another man."

Grace stiffened at the mention of her betrothed. "I informed Tobias that I was coming out here to look for Lucy."

"Tobias, is it?" Matthew searched her features, looking for a tell.

Straight-faced, Grace answered, "My betrothed is not at all what I expected. He's rather… charming."

Her words speared his heart. For years, the ton had considered Matthew as one of their darlings—amiable, titled, handsome, and eligible. He was no longer that man. Charisma was not going to ensure Burke's demise. No. Matthew needed to remain coldhearted and ruthless. If he could survive a year in horrid conditions as a prisoner, he could endure a season of heartbreak.

He bent to pick up his shoes and let them dangle from his fingers behind his back. He jutted out his chin and said, "I believe you will find my sister and her husband are farther along the path." Standing within reach of Grace, the devil in him couldn't resist touching her. He leaned forward and lightly brushed his cheek up against hers and whispered, "Be careful in the dark." As he walked away toward the terrace doors, he heard the catch in her breath. Grace was not immune to him. The problem was she was no longer his to touch.

CHAPTER SEVEN

*M*atthew dropped his shoes to the ground and settled back on the grass. He wiggled his free toes before stuffing them into his stockings and shoes. He had anticipated his return to London would be difficult. Deliberately delaying his plans to allow himself time to heal. Five months and twenty-six days had apparently not been long enough. Emotions Matthew thought banished and sworn never to feel again returned in full force. After only being in Grace's company twice, they were strangely stronger than ever before. Time had not lessened his love for her. Damnation, the woman was betrothed to another. How many times must he remind himself of the fact? Why could he not dismiss the useless desire to have Grace back in his arms?

As he rolled to his feet, candlelight glinting off the windows captured his attention—time to return to the party and come out of hiding. He ran a hand down his coat sleeve and tugged at his cuffs as he mentally prepared to be once again boxed in with the other guests.

Standing behind a potted plant, he peered through the

glass. *Ellingsworth is an absolute buffoon.* Matthew's jaw clenched as the man's grating laugh floated across the room out onto the terrace. Good gracious—that is what Grace considered charming?

Ellingsworth stared at Lady Mary, now Countess Waterford, as she spoke, wearing a frown of pure confusion. His eyes darted to her décolletage and then to Waterford, as if to see if her husband had caught his errant gaze. What a dolt! Waterford would pound him to the ground. Instead of rage, Waterford wore an obsequious expression. The buzzing in Matthew's brain triggered a slew of theorems to swirl about in his mind.

A rainbow of colors reflected off the glass and recaptured Matthew's attention. Mr. Jones, who had endured months of imprisonment with Matthew, stood in the corner dressed as a guest this eve instead of his usual footman's disguise. The man angled an empty glass Matthew's way, signaling that he had been spotted.

With his mind awhirl, Matthew stepped back from view, observing the interesting byplay between Ellingsworth and Waterford. Eyes shut tight, Matthew tried to recall the complex line diagram that he and Grace had compiled during the past several years. It outlined the interconnections between those Matthew believed were PORFs and those who displayed the symbol of their support. The Burke family name had continuously emerged in Matthew's investigations, which meant that Lord Burke was not only a danger to Matthew but also to the Crown. The air from his lungs left him as grief hit him square in the chest—he and Grace were no longer a team investigating matters. And specifically not the one that originally brought them together in the first place.

Seeking a glimpse of Grace, Matthew peeked around the bush. His gaze was caught by the sight of Mr. Jones staring intently at his sister. Lucy had always been a beauty, but marriage and parenthood had added an extra glow despite the dark circles under her eyes. Matthew had long considered Blake like a brother even before he married Lucy. He had missed their wedding, but he'd heard from multiple sources it was a rare occurrence for the pair to be separated.

Grace had always favored Blake. His unique skills to recall information and faces, along with his ability for illustration, was unmatched. An order from Grace was the only logical explanation for him to agree to be separated from Lucy. Didn't Grace realize with twins Lucy would need her husband's help? Blake would never disobey an order. The tightness in his chest eased a tad. He would send both Mama and Edward, his younger brother, to accompany Lucy to Shalford Castle. They could help Lucy and stay out of harm's way. The perfect plan.

A light vanilla scent wafted on the breeze. Theo was nearby. Childhood memories of him chasing Theo and Lucy down the corridors of Halestone Hall flashed before him. One corner of his lips turned upward into a grin as he recalled threatening to pull their pigtails if they tattled. Matthew turned away from the glass windows and was confronted by sparkling, emerald-colored eyes.

Theo narrowed her gaze and said, "You look rather pleased with yourself. What mischief are you planning?"

As a boy, it had been Theo, not Lucy, who had thwarted all his childish pranks. The woman standing before him now was no longer the skinny little girl he grew up with. No, the lady staring back at him was in every way Archbroke's match.

The smirk upon Theo's face gave him pause about his plans. Both Archbroke and Grace possessed the inherent ability to convince others they were acting of their own accord when, in fact, the individual's reactions were carefully devised by either the Home or Foreign Secretaries.

Perhaps Theo would provide the answer. Matthew replied, "My, my, Theo. How did you learn to sneak up upon a person without a sound?"

Theo shrugged. "One of the perks of marrying Archbroke."

"Really, I wasn't aware stealth was one of your husband's stronger suits."

"It's not. However, Archbroke's hearing is impeccable and hence the ultimate challenge."

Matthew let out a chuckle. "I'm not sure what Baldwin would have thought of you marrying Archbroke."

Theo's eyebrow's furrowed. "My brother would have been proud to call Archbroke brother-in-law. Just as you are to call Devonton so."

The prickling sensation along the back of his neck returned. Theo's modulated tone meant she was trying to hide something. Archbroke was one of the families Matthew had pegged as PORFs. It was the third family's identity that alluded to him. If his theory was correct, Theo had become a PORF upon her marriage to Archbroke.

Matthew's eyes flickered back toward the party. Archbroke flanked Lord Flarinton as if he was guarding the man.

Matthew asked, "Why is that?"

"I believe you already know the answer." Theo shivered. "I've not come out into the cold to discuss Archbroke."

Matthew glanced down at Theo's still flat stomach. "You should not risk your health, given your condition."

"My condition." She ran a hand along her midsection. "Can you tell?"

"No. Archbroke, let the information slip."

Theo snorted. "Slip? Hardly. The man never divulges information until he wants to." Matthew followed Theo's gaze as she looked over her shoulder through the glass at her husband. Archbroke had taken a step forward but then promptly returned to his discussion with Grace's papa. Interesting that Theo could command the Home Secretary, one of the most influential men in all of England, with a mere look.

He raised an eyebrow at Theo as she turned to face him once more. "Impressive."

"Archbroke will be next to me within the count of twenty. I've not much time. I need your help."

The twinkle in Theo's eyes remained. She was up to no good. "Help? With what, exactly?"

Either Theo counted quickly, or her estimation was severely overoptimistic, for Archbroke was nearly upon them.

Grabbing his wrist, Theo pleaded. "Promise. Promise, you will assist me."

She shifted her hand and tightened her grip. Surely Theo wasn't about to inflict the childish punishment they had once given each other when they were younger. Although Theo probably hadn't had cause to employ her unique technique to cause rub burns, he still clearly remembered how effective it was. His wrists burned despite Theo not having moved; they were still raw from being bound for months.

Archbroke came to a stop beside Theo. He glared at the physical touch. "Love, why are you about to inflict pain upon Harrington?"

Theo released his wrist, but her gaze never left Matthew's face.

He considered the woman like a sister, and of course,

he would do anything she asked. Which she rarely did. Matthew released a sigh of resignation. "I'll be around tomorrow to finish this discussion."

Theo's smile beamed with triumph. Possessively Archbroke placed his hand on Theo's lower back. "What discussion?"

"Oh, nothing. We were just reminiscing and discussing childhood pranks. But I asked Matthew to visit tomorrow. I haven't seen him since..." Theo's eyes watered. "Well, since Baldwin died."

At his wife's upset, Archbroke's pompous demeanor fell away and he swiped the lone tear that had escaped, rolling down her cheek. Archbroke murmured in a tone Matthew had never heard before, "Of course, Harrington should come to visit." His superior then turned to address him directly. "We would be delighted to have you visit for a drink."

Theo inched a step closer and whispered in her husband's ear. With a slight roll of the eyes, Archbroke said, "You are welcome to visit our home regardless if I'm present or not." The couple shared a look that simultaneously conveyed both a challenge and immense love for one another. How astonishing that both sentiments could be expressed within a singular stare. The dynamics between the pair were intriguing. There was a strong undercurrent of respect, freedom, and love that flowed between them. Matthew sucked in a breath. Theo and Archbroke's connection mirrored the one he once had with Grace. They possessed the type of relationship he had hoped to return to upon his release from captivity.

Archbroke winged his arm. "It's time we all return to the party."

Matthew blindly followed the pair who were still

nonverbally communicating. Why would Theo seek out his help when she had Archbroke clearly in hand?

Grace's tinkling laughter brought his attention back to the couple who were the cause of the celebration. Ellingsworth looked down at the woman whose mere smile sent Matthew's pulse racing. He couldn't blame the man for looking like a besotted fool. After all, Ellingsworth was lucky to be marrying such an astonishing woman.

Matthew had to look away. Grace's smiles were causing a cascade of emotions he dared not acknowledge. He needed to escape. He pushed his way through the crowd of guests to the foyer.

Lord Flarinton stepped in front of him, blocking his path. "Where do you think you're going?"

"Lord Flarinton. I have another matter to attend to."

"Don't lie to me, boy."

Ah. He was dealing with the astute mastermind of foreign affairs. The man he had considered like a papa since the death of his own. The man whom he wanted to model his own life after. But Lord Flarinton would never endorse the plans he had for Burke. Even if the man could recall all of Burke's devious schemes. It had taken Matthew, Grace, and Lord Flarinton years to eliminate Burke's smuggling rings and shut down his gambling halls that went without policing and drove many a man to his own death, leaving genteel families destitute. The only scheme left to disband was Burke's most lucrative—the selling of English artifacts.

Flarinton's gaze hardened. "You will stay and support Gracie, even if it kills you. That is an order."

"Yes, my lord." Matthew wouldn't dream of denying the man.

Without Flarinton, Matthew would have failed as the primary liaison between the Home and Foreign offices, a role he had held up until his absence. Upon his return, Matthew was surprised that the position hadn't been filled by either his sister or another agent, but by Theo. And from all accounts, the woman had done an outstanding job of ensuring the two departments worked together in harmony.

Matthew led Flarinton back to the party. As they reentered the room, Lady Flarinton's strained features relaxed, the worry over her absent husband replaced by relief. Placing his clenched fists behind him, Matthew stood near the entrance and watched Flarinton return to his wife's side. Ellingsworth stood slightly to Grace's right. The man's jovial smile was firmly in place until his gaze fell upon Matthew.

Matthew's mind screamed. *Turn. Leave.*

The experience of another man standing mere inches away from Grace, exhibiting all the traits of a man infatuated with his betrothed, was far worse than what he had endured upon the Continent.

CHAPTER EIGHT

A lock of hair at the back of Grace's neck brushed
against the sensitive spot Matthew loved to nibble.
Pressing her eyes closed for a moment, she let the fantasy
of having his lips upon her play out. She missed the thrill
of his kisses on her neck, along her jaw, down the slope of
her breast, and, most of all, between her thighs. Her hands
balled at her side. No matter how much she ached for him,
he remained out of reach. If her mind would refrain from
linking every event, conversation, or smell with the man,
her heart might have a chance to heal. Without Matthew
in her life, a gaping hole in the vital organ had formed. A
slight rise in her body temperature meant he had returned
from his jaunt into the gardens. Grace held her breath and
opened her eyes. Matthew stood frozen at the threshold.

What was he doing? Matthew never stood still.

His ability to breeze into a room and enter a discussion
with any group regardless of whatever event they were
attending was the one skill Matthew possessed that Grace
had envied the most. Yet he remained rooted to the spot,
his eyebrows scrunched, eyes narrowed, and lips drawn into

a tight line. He appeared as if he was preparing himself to enter a battle, not a room full of friends and family.

"It's time your papa and I retired." Her mama's sweet voice startled Grace. "You know what occurs when he becomes overtired."

Her mama placed a light touch upon her husband's arm and left with a swish of skirts. Her papa smiled at guests as he and her mama bid them a good eve. Matthew shifted to allow her parents to pass. After a brief exchange with her mama, his scowl disappeared, and a hesitant smile appeared. Not at all surprising, her mama, like Matthew, had an innate ability to set everyone at ease. Unfortunately, it was not a trait Grace had inherited.

She could feel Ellingsworth's eyes boring down on her, but she couldn't tear her gaze away from Matthew, who bowed as her parents left. He promptly made his way across the room, ignoring the other guests, to where Blake and Lucy stood talking with the Home Office messenger, Mr. Jones.

Tobias shifted to stand before her, blocking her view of the group. "I'd wager that Matthew was ordered to remain despite his wishes to leave the festivities."

She raised her gaze to his and, through lips that were plastered in a smile, asked, "Who would issue such an order?"

"Your papa." Ellingsworth's weight shifted slightly forward, breaching the socially accepted distance between them. To onlookers it might appear an intimate gesture by her fiancé, but she knew better. The man was attempting to loom above her in an endeavor to dominate her and the space between them.

Standing her ground, Grace replied, "Why would he?"

"Because your papa agreed it was best if everyone

believed we are to be wed. He has even offered to assist."
Tobias stuck his elbow out and said, "Don't look so
shocked. He was of sound mind when we discussed the
matter. Now, let's take a turn about the room. I'm sure a
riddle or two will liven up the evening."

Grace dutifully placed her hand on the crook of his
arm as she slid a glance over at Matthew. The material of
his coat was stretched taut across his back. Faced away
from her, she studied his reflection in the windows. His
scowl had returned. Their eyes met in the glass, and she
sent him a plea to see through the facade to the truth.
Matthew blinked, and the slight tilt of his head breathed
hope into Grace that he might, just might, have understood her message.

Tobias's arm muscle twitched beneath her hand. He
leaned down to whisper in her ear. "It is imperative *everyone*
believes you intend to marry me willingly. Including
Harrington."

She rolled her shoulders slightly forward and then back
before she nodded. Grace could only hope Matthew had
noted the brief movement, their private signal that she
wished to meet him at the gazebo to discuss an important
matter.

Tobias maneuvered them through the room toward
Lord Burke. Every fiber in her body bristled at being in
close proximity to the devil. The man was responsible for
Matthew and the others' captivity. Grace glanced at Tobias
as he slowed his pace. He appeared relaxed and jovial, but
Grace could feel the anger radiating from his tense body
with every step they took.

He murmured, "Burke may be my sire, but he holds
none of my respect. The man only cares for one person,
himself. We will need to convince him we remain his

pawns, willing to be easily manipulated and abide by his wishes. Am I clear?"

The edge to Tobias's words left no doubt in Grace's mind that the man had no qualms in deceiving his own papa. "Crystal."

Tobias let out a loud chuckle. "My dear, you are ever so clever."

Grace straightened her shoulders as she came to stand before Lord Burke. A tingling sensation ran along her spine. She was certain Matthew's gaze was fully trained on them. She ignored the temptation to turn around.

"Ah. What a lovely couple." Lord Burke's large hand landed on Tobias's shoulder briefly. Tobias dipped his shoulder forward and acted as if the weight of it was too mighty for him.

Her betrothed was no weakling. The muscles in his forearm were drawn taut beneath her fingers. Grace suspected Tobias simply did not care for his papa's touch.

Lord Burke smoothly placed his fallen hand behind his back. "Lady Grace, the hour grows late, and only the young remain. I shall bid you good eve." The old man leaned forward. "I've arranged for the banns to be read the weekend following the Fairmont ball."

That meant she had three weeks of hell to endure.

Tobias smiled and responded, "Splendid."

He patted her hand as her fingers dug into his arm. Her molars were about to crack from the force with which she gritted them together as she stood within five feet from the man she utterly despised.

With a grin that left Grace itching to slap the man, Lord Burke stepped around them and left.

Grace frowned. "Did your papa not expect us to move to let him pass?"

"He believes I don't possess enough sense to know

better." Tobias tapped her hand with his forefinger. "You will have to do better next time. I'd like to survive the next few weeks without incurring bodily harm."

"I beg your pardon?"

He flexed his arm. "You have an impressive grip."

Grace drew back and clasped her hands firmly in front of her. What must the others believe with her holding on to Tobias like that all this time? She searched the room for Matthew. He stood with his back to her, facing Lucy and Blake, who glared at her. There was no mistaking the meaning behind their narrowed gazes. They were furious with her.

The patter of slippers from behind had Grace whipping about to face Theo. The woman gave her a bright smile. At least one of her friends remained happy.

Theo turned to face Tobias. "My, my, Ellingsworth, you didn't perish after all." Her normally sweet tone was a tad sardonic. With a challenging twinkle in her eye, she continued, "You survived a whole three minutes in the presence of the man who sired you. Well done."

Tobias turned so only Theo had a clear view of his features. "Can I count on your support?"

Theo's brow furrowed, but she gave Grace a reassuring smile. What was Tobias asking of her? Grace shifted to gain a better view of the pair, hoping their nonverbal cues would give her a clue as to what was being discussed.

Tobias sighed. "Lady Theo, you are the only one remaining. Do I have your promise?"

Eyes wide, Theo swiveled to face her husband, "You gave him your word?"

Archbroke nodded. "As has Hadfield with—"

"I'll not give you my word." Theo didn't wait for her husband to finish his sentence. She spun around back to Tobias. "Not until I've had sufficient time to consider."

Grace took a small step away from Tobias as she spied the invisible daggers Theo was throwing at him. The tension among the trio was palpable.

Tobias glared at Archbroke, "Your wife has until tomorrow."

"I'm standing right under your nose. You can speak to me directly." Theo puffed out her chest. "While I vowed to obey my husband, he would *never* order this of me."

Grace glanced at Archbroke and Theo, who both immediately shuttered their expressions. A prickling sensation ran down Grace's spine. What if Matthew's theory was correct, and Tobias, Theo, and Archbroke were PORFs? Couldn't be. PORFs were not real. Although the amount of evidence she and Matthew had accumulated was substantial, none of it was conclusive.

Nose raised in the air, Theo continued, "You'd be wise to heed my advice—do not act in haste. Love can blind one to the obvious."

Grace's mind scrambled to assemble all the pieces of the conversation together. Theo had mentioned love. Was Tobias in love with someone? He had made it clear earlier that their engagement was to be a sham—that he had no intention of marrying her and had even made mention that all would be as it should be, alluding to the possibility that she would gain what her heart most desired—Matthew. A spark of hope had Grace's pulse racing. Buoyed by the possibilities, she returned her attention to her fiancé.

The corner of Tobias's mouth turned up once again to form the idiotic smile that he had donned most of the night. "Lady Archbroke, haven't you heard? I'm not known for being wise. I am, however, stubborn, and my plan will be carried out with or without your assistance." He raised a single eyebrow. "I hope your cousin will talk

CONFESSIONS OF LADY GRACE

some sense into you since it's obvious your husband has failed."

A man cleared his throat behind Grace, and she peered over her shoulder to see Theo's cousin. Lord Hadfield was an enigma and hadn't held the title for long. Grace would be eternally grateful for the man's help in gaining Matthew's release.

Hadfield had the audacity to wink at her before turning his attention to Tobias. "Ellingsworth. Were we not clear earlier? Both Archbroke's and my own promise were conditioned upon Theo's agreement."

How intriguing that these lords would place such power in the hands of a woman. Especially Archbroke. Her counterpart at the Home Office had been extremely resistant to her acting and making decisions on her papa's behalf. Matthew was the one who had eased the relations and acted as liaison. Grace internally sighed. That was the Lord Archbroke of old, the one before marriage. The couple reinforced her theory, born from her parents' relationship, that behind every great man stood a woman of great strength.

Archbroke gave Theo a meek smile. "You didn't give me a chance to finish my sentence, my love." He wrapped an arm about his wife's waist as he spoke to Ellingsworth. "If Theo doesn't agree, it will be because she has sound reasoning. Both Hadfield and I defer to her judgment in this instance."

From behind, Hadfield said, "I think it wise we discuss these matters at another time."

Tobias glanced at Grace. "She is my betrothed and will be my wife if the three of you deny me."

Wife! Grace nearly sputtered the word out loud but caught herself in time.

"Tobias." Theo placed a hand on Ellingsworth's arm

71

briefly before returning it to the crook of her husband's arm. "I understand your plight, but there are many individuals who your scheme impacts, and there is much to consider."

There was a strong undercurrent of familiarity among the others that she had not detected before. Matthew's voice whispered in her head—*PORFs*. She prayed Matthew would heed her earlier request to meet her at the gazebo. They had much to discuss.

Tobias's stance relaxed, and a genuine smile appeared upon his face. Theo had once again managed to use her persuasive skills to dispel the issue at hand. During the past year, Grace had repeatedly seen Theo win over two opposing parties and assist them in coming to an agreement, but tonight this discussion felt far weightier.

There was a swift shift of energy among the group as Lord Hadfield announced, "It's time we all retire for the night."

As if the king himself had made the declaration, Archbroke and Theo proceeded to say their farewells and Tobias led Grace about the room, ushering the other guests to the door.

Grace watched as Theo left her husband and cousin to whisper something into Lucy's ear. Lucy and Theo had been close friends since childhood. They shared a bond that was extremely strong—a connection forged and strengthened by shared experiences over time. Grace hadn't known Lucy as long as Theo, but she thought of Lucy as her best friend.

Lucy glanced at Grace and then turned back to Theo. Blast. Matthew had always been the one able to read lips from a distance. She could merely interpret facial expressions. Lucy hadn't liked Theo's request—not at all. Her lips were pursed, and her nose crinkled. Theo threw her arms around Lucy as she nodded with sad eyes. Archbroke and Theo promptly left, leaving Tobias and Grace alone with the group she most feared to face—Lucy, Blake, and Matthew.

Lucy grabbed Grace's hands and squeezed. "We"— Lucy's hand waved to include the gentleman—"wish you all the best, and I shall return for your wedding."

"Where are you going?" Grace asked.

Blake answered, "It's best if Lucy and the boys return to Shalford Castle for the next few weeks. I shall see to it that she returns after the banns have been read."

Grace had hoped Lucy would remain in town for support. Without Matthew and her best friend, she wasn't sure how she was going to survive the endless social route. Tobias placed a hand on the small of her back, a subtle reminder of her promise—to make everyone believe their faux engagement was real.

With a weak smile and in a fake chipper voice, Grace said, "I understand. I shall see you at Saint George's church then in three weeks."

At the mention of the church, Matthew's posture stiffened a minuscule amount. Grace doubted anyone but she had noticed. Swiveling on his heel, he turned and left without a single word. Grace prayed, *Please Lord, help Matthew find his way back… back to the gazebo.*

CHAPTER NINE

*M*orning rays of sunlight hit the tips of Grace's pink slippers as they peeked out from beneath her skirts. She lengthened her stride, eager to reach the whitewashed garden house that came into view. The gazebo. Her sanctuary. Climbing rose bushes wound up along the posts and covered most of the trellis that Matthew had ordered be installed on seven of the eight sides. He had claimed it was merely to shield the interior from wind and rain, but it had also served to provide them privacy during their numerous clandestine meetings. Grace smiled as she spied buds that would bloom into peach-colored roses in a month or so. Spring was her favorite season of the year. It signaled new beginnings.

Grace sneaked a quick glance at her papa, who appeared to be deep in thought as he walked alongside her.

Frowning, he asked, "What games are you playing with Ellingsworth?" Her papa's clear eyes were trained on her as he continued, "Last eve you were behaving as if you enjoyed the company of that buffoon. His jokes…"

Grace's smile broadened. "Did you not like the one about oranges and bananas? I considered it a rather clever parody of Shakespeare's Macbeth."

"Shakespeare?" His eyebrows crinkled. "Are you referring to the scene when a porter is awoken out of a drunken stupor by a man knocking at Lord and Lady Macbeth's door?"

"Exactly." A surge of happiness filled Grace's heart. Since Matthew's departure, she hadn't anyone to have playful intellectual debates with.

Rubbing his chin, her papa said, "Hmm… If it was, in fact, such a satire, then perhaps he is not such a dunce."

"I believe he might have the intelligence to outwit our dear friend Archbroke." Grace admittedly was impressed by Tobias's playacting abilities from the prior evening. What caught her off guard was his ability to appear totally inept. He asked questions or made statements that, if taken literally, would infer the man certainly had air for brains. But when Grace took the time to listen to his speech, she found he was far from ridiculous. In fact, he was exceedingly intelligent.

Her papa chuckled. "Archbroke. Doubtful. The man is an absolute genius."

"I've taken to viewing Tobias like an abacus."

"How so?"

Grace ceased walking to explain. "Upon first glance, one might consider the instrument simple when, in fact, once you learn how it operates, there is nothing simple about it."

Tobias was indeed a conundrum. While her betrothed was a puzzle, she sorely missed Matthew's direct honesty and openness. From their first meeting, Matthew understood her inherent need for the truth. Matthew had the unique ability of being able to share facts with her, no matter how harsh they might be, disabusing her natural instinct to mistrust others. In running the Foreign Office, Grace often dealt with men of Tobias's ilk, never knowing exactly what they meant or what their true intentions might be. With Matthew, she never doubted his intentions.

Grace glanced up. Her papa was at least six feet ahead. The snap of a twig nearby had her frantically searching the grounds for Matthew. Her pulse raced with the anticipation of seeing him. When she spotted him behind a tree that was out of speaking distance, she rose both palms. She wiggled her fingers quickly, the signal for him to wait before she clasped them behind her back and scurried to catch up to her papa.

When she came abreast with him, he said, "Gracie, I received new information early this morn regarding Burke's plans. Convince Archbroke to send Mr. Jones to monitor the docks and gain employment aboard the Quarter Moon. It is not scheduled to set sail for a few weeks yet."

She must have misheard—Mr. Jones was a Home Office agent. "Papa, who did you say you wanted to be appointed to this assignment."

With a sudden lack of certainty, he replied, "Mr. Jones. Did I—"

"Very well." Eager to restore her papa's confidence, she said, "I'll meet with Archbroke as soon as it can be arranged." However, in order for her to convince Archbroke to do anything, she would need a motive. "What is Mr. Jones's objective?"

"Burke is in dire need of funds. I believe he arranged for a private auction of the last remaining heirlooms he has in his possession. The items are being stashed down at the docks. We need to find them and the crown jewels before it is too late."

Grace nodded. "Very well, I'll share your wishes with him. Although you know how wily the man can be when we request the services of one of his men."

Her papa crouched down by the edge of the path to touch a delicate snowdrop bloom—the first early sign of spring. When he stood, he looked about, and his eyes widened at the sight of her. He smiled and said, "Gracie, is it spring already?"

Her heart sank as she answered, quoting him, "Time for new beginnings." Grace was convinced her papa's bouts of clarity would increase in frequency and length if she could manage to persuade Cook to refrain from preparing meals heavily laden with salt and fat.

Grace placed her hand on her papa's arm. "We should head back inside."

Patting her hand, her papa said, "It is a bit brisk out here. Your hands are cold as ice."

It wasn't the chill in the air that caused her blood to leave her extremities; it was the thought of her future that had them devoid of feeling. Ushering her papa back to the house, a trickle of awareness ran down her spine as they neared the garden wall. Grace glanced about. Matthew popped his head up and pointed back toward the gazebo. Grace smiled and nodded. All her worries that Matthew would continue to ignore her vanished. While she wanted nothing more than to spend the day with Matthew in the gazebo, she could not neglect her meeting with Archbroke. Burke's schemes needed to be put to an end.

Silverman waited for them by the terrace doors. "Lady Grace, you have a visitor. He is in the morning room."

She inwardly groaned at further delaying her meeting with Matthew. Who the devil was calling at such an early hour?

MATTHEW WAITED until Flarinton and Grace had reached the terrace before making his way to the gazebo. He stared at the wooden structure Flarinton had built for Grace to play in as a child. As she grew, it had become her private retreat—a refuge when she needed time and space from others.

Initially, they had met there to discuss Crown matters, but when she confessed it was her oasis from real life, he refused to discuss Foreign Office matters in the space. His mind was filled with memories from the hours upon hours they had spent together in the haven. He could almost hear Grace's laughter floating in the wind, unlike the fake laughter he'd heard her emit during her engagement dinner.

This wasn't his first early-morning visit to Flarinton's gardens since his return to London. He lacked the willpower to stay away, but he had managed to remain undetected. Arriving before dawn, he waited for Grace to arrive. Flarinton accompanying her this morn was a shock, but details of their discussions were even more so, for it provided him with the last piece of information he needed. The location of the last of the stolen antiques.

Alongside the shuffle of Grace's slippers, boots crunched on the pebbled path that led to the gazebo. As Matthew peered around the tree, Ellingsworth came into sight.

Grace had dared to bring him to their space. Matthew's hands balled into fists, and stars appeared before his eyes. How could she? Had he truly been replaced?

He flattened a hand against the tree trunk. It didn't make sense for her to invite Ellingsworth when she was aware Matthew was waiting. Unless this was her way of telling him she no longer cared for him, that Ellingsworth was her choice. His fingers dug into the bark. His heart ached—it was just one more organ bruised and hurt. He would recover. Time would heal him.

He pressed up against the rough bark as the couple passed him.

Ellingsworth asked, "Where are you taking me?"

The man's words echoed Matthew's exact thoughts. Grace was always thinking strategically and never acted without purpose.

"To the gazebo. It is the only place I can be certain we can talk freely."

"There are always eyes and ears about."

With their voices trailing off, he would have to move closer to the gazebo. Closer than he normally would dare to go. He needed to know for certain what Grace was about. He crept along the tree line. He should leave and not intrude, but he couldn't force his feet in the opposite direction. Dashing to stand next to the trellis, hidden from sight, he took a deep breath and peered through the small gap in the wood.

Grace stood facing her fiancé. "My papa believes there are valuable items hidden upon the docks."

Ellingsworth clasped his hands behind his back. "Is that so? And how did he come about this information without your knowledge?"

It was a question Matthew himself had pondered earlier.

Her fiancé paced in a small circle and continued, "Burke is the master of manipulation. I cannot tell you how many times he has boasted that life is merely a game of chess. Like Archbroke, my sire does not make information available unless he wants it known. He plies people with favors, coin, and threats into doing his bidding. Burke will lead you on a merry chase if you let him."

"And you?"

Ellingsworth stopped in front of Grace, leaned in, and pushed a loose tendril of hair behind her ear. Matthew used to execute the exact same motion. He inhaled deeply as he waited for Grace's response.

When she remained still, he slowly released the air from his burning lungs. His mind was a mass of conflicting thoughts, but his blackened heart fluttered with hope.

"I'm not one for games." The answer brought about further madding questions for Matthew. What were Ellingsworth's motives for agreeing to the engagement?

What did the man have planned?

What resources did he have at his disposal?

The scorn in his voice when he spoke of Burke left no doubt Ellingsworth had no real affection for his sire.

Matthew blinked as the blighter dared to lean in and brush his lips against Grace's cheek.

Grace turned her face away and said, "Neither am I." She stepped back, placing another foot of distance between them, before continuing. "You informed me yesterday you have no intentions of marrying me and requested a boon, which I fulfilled more than adequately last eve. It occurred to me this morn I failed to ask. If we are not to wed and I am to be jilted, what assurances do I have that you will indeed see that Burke receives his come-uppance?"

What? Ellingsworth was going to jilt Grace, and she had agreed? The woman had lost her mind; she hated being the center of attention.

Matthew's body tensed as Ellingsworth stepped forward and leaned over Grace. An attempt to intimidate her. God help him, Matthew wanted to pummel Ellingsworth for daring to embroil Grace in a scandal.

But she did not cower. Instead, Grace placed her hands on her hips and said, "My lord?"

"I give you my word, which I rarely provide, that Burke will meet his maker sooner rather than later."

"What! You intend to have him killed?" Grace expressed Matthew's own shock at Ellingsworth's calm declaration he intended to have his sire depart this earth.

"Indeed, I do." Ellingsworth sat on the cushioned bench.

What would motivate a man to take such an action without remorse? Hatred and revenge were Matthew's first thoughts, but neither motives rang true for Ellingsworth.

Ellingsworth appeared relaxed, but his gaze searched the trellis walls until his eyes landed on the section Matthew hid behind. As if Ellingsworth was talking to him and not Grace, he said, "It's imperative no one knows of our plans not to wed. We have to ensure Burke never hears a whisper that our betrothal may be at risk or a sham." Ellingsworth must know Matthew would never endanger Grace.

Reasoning the man's words were a warning for Matthew to keep his distance, Matthew's fists clenched. Ellingsworth was right. If anyone caught sight of him here, visiting Grace in secret, it would place her in peril. Pretending she no longer mattered to him while he resided hundreds of miles apart had been excruciating torture. How was he to ignore her now that she was within a few miles of him at all times?

With her back to Matthew, Grace answered, "Very well. I shall go along with your scheme. If that is all you came here to discuss, I have other pressing matters I must deal with today."

"I think it best we review the social engagements we will attend as a couple." Ellingsworth patted the section of the bench next to him.

Grace moved a few pillows aside, building a small barrier between Ellingsworth and herself. She reached between the wood of the bench and cushion retrieving a leather-bound book. Matthew recalled she used to keep detailed records outlining every social and political event hosted. What was her journal doing out here and not in her papa's study?

Grace placed the volume in her lap and opened it. The couple's social calendar was of no interest to Matthew. He needed to return home and reconsider his plans—Ellingsworth's involvement complicated matters. Tiptoeing from the gardens, he sat upon the low stone wall and pulled on his stockings and boots. He'd return later this eve to speak with Grace.

If Ellingsworth had no intention of marrying Grace, then there was still a chance she could be his. A seed of hope nestled deep into his heart.

CHAPTER TEN

*M*atthew stood in front of Hadfield's townhouse. Merely six blocks from Grace's gazebo, the brisk walk failed to clear Matthew's muddled mind. He stepped back to look at the structure in front of him—clean clear windows with a new coat of paint along the trim. The transformation from a neglected rarely used townhouse to its current refurbished state was remarkable.

Matthew quickly mounted the steps that led to the freshly painted front door. His eye was drawn to the brass door knocker. The symbol he and Grace had pieced together during the past few years was staring right back at him—a horse with a falcon perched on its back, circled by laurel leaves. It wasn't the official Hadfield family crest. No. It was the mark he believed only three families could claim, that of a PORF. What the devil!

The front door swung open to reveal the old butler, Morris. "Lady Archbroke is awaiting your arrival, my lord."

Matthew nodded as he stepped forward to enter. His eyes darted back to the symbol one last time as Morris closed the door. If Grace and he had correctly assembled the design, it meant Hadfield was a PORF, which meant Theo would have been a PORF even before marrying Archbroke. Damnation—the last family in the trinity he sought had been right in front of him all this time. The burst of excitement the revelation caused was dampened by the fact he couldn't immediately seek out Grace and share the information with her. Grace had signaled her wish to meet with him. This new information provided him a valid reason to meet rather than admit his wish to simply be alone with her once again.

Morris ushered him into an empty drawing room. Matthew paused to gaze about the room, elegant but rather utilitarian in fashion, the walls and furniture covered in muted fabrics and not one decorative pillow in sight.

Decorative pillows. The Oldridge drawing room was full of them—there was a time when he and Grace would lie upon them, scattered about the floor, discussing everything and anything for hours.

Theo breezed into the room, breaking his train of thought. She strode directly to the fireplace and placed her hands before her to soak up the warmth. "I expected you much earlier. It's nearly time for luncheon. Have trouble sleeping?"

"My apologies for keeping you waiting. Why are we meeting here, at your cousin's residence?" He joined her by the fire.

"Archbroke and I were summoned here early this morn. Rather than return home, I decided to stay and visit with Aunt Henrietta while I waited for you."

Theo's military-like posture indicated the woman was in no mood to socialize. He too was eager to be done with matters here. His mind was on the woman who had stolen another night's sleep from him.

Matthew said, "Then you are ready to explain exactly what it is you need my assistance with, and why you simply do not ask for your husband's aid."

"You need to return the crown jewels that my cousin left in your possession to Archbroke." Theo turned to face him, but her gaze lowered to his hands, which were shaking slightly at his side.

"Why is it so cold in here? Did Hadfield not fix the drafty windows?" Trying to avoid Theo's prying eyes, he pressed his palms together and rubbed them in front of the fire.

"Don't attempt to distract me." Theo turned back to the fire and balanced on one foot while she raised the other to warm it near the grate before it slipped back under her skirts. Back on two feet, she continued, "My cousin is not pleased with you. He believes he gave you clear instructions to return the jewels as soon as you returned to England. You have been home for more than six months, and not once did you attempt to reach out to Archbroke to return the treasure."

He folded his arms across his chest. This was his opportunity to see what information, if any, Theo would divest about the PORFs. "Who is Hadfield to give orders? Your cousin is a peer, not my superior."

Theo's steady gaze remained on the fire. Oh, how he wished Grace was here to assess Theo's reactions. He was good at interpreting nonverbal cues, but Grace was far more skilled than he.

"Don't be obtuse. You know exactly what the right course of action is—return the jewels to Archbroke." Theo tilted her head and met his gaze.

He didn't need Grace by his side to tell him the woman's features were strained with concern.

Theo continued, "As long as I've known you, you have

always done what is right. And I also can tell when you are up to no good. Revenge will not give you peace." She released a sigh.

His jaw clenched, and he focused on the flames before him. "It's not peace I seek."

"Then what?" Theo's skirts shifted. "What type of revenge do you mean to extract from Burke? Why wait for the season to begin before executing your plan? You allowed Burke additional time to aggregate his resources. You have placed Grace in grave danger."

Every question and statement Theo threw at him arrowed into his gut. He had no clue how to address her litany of questions. Matthew wanted Burke to suffer as he had, experience the devastation he had caused others to experience. Ultimately, Matthew wanted the man dead. He had no intention of placing those he loved in danger. But Theo was right—he had placed Grace in danger the moment he decided to leave for the Continent.

A mixture of guilt and anger spurred his reply, "She didn't appear to be in any danger last night with Ellingsworth by her side."

"You are a fool. Grace was blackmailed into the betrothal. Who do you think obtained the necessary information for your rescue?" Theo tugged at his arm until he turned to face her.

"Archbroke, of course." A terrible knot formed in his stomach as her features set in disbelief told him he was wrong.

Theo's eyes raked over him as if she wasn't sure who he was. She blinked and shook her head. "Granted, my husband is a genius, but it wasn't he who left the security of home and went searching for you on the Continent." After a long sigh, Theo continued, "Grace discovered Burke was the one behind Devonton's kidnapping and the missing crown jewels. She realized the potential danger. She, along with her aunt, left right after Lucy's wedding in the hopes of finding you first. When Grace learned Burke meant to be rid of you once and for all, she took matters into her own hands."

What was Theo saying—that Grace had ventured across the channel in search of him? That she had negotiated her hand in marriage for his safe return?

Matthew's head ached. Why had the woman done such a thing? Grace's musical voice filtered through his mind —*Because I love you*. The same sweet words she had uttered the night she had given her innocence to him. The phrase that had given him the strength to endure the beatings and survive his captivity.

Matthew flinched as Theo placed a hand on his arm. Her tone softened as she continued, "Burke discovered it was you who shut down every one of his underhanded money-making schemes. There were whispers he was orchestrating your demise. Plans were hastened when you made your way to France."

Impossible. The events Theo described would have placed many at risk. "Grace left Flarinton and went in search of me?"

Theo emitted a growl. "Yes. Have you not been listening to me? Grace returned home distraught after discovering you were being held captive, and that only Burke held the answers." She angled her head to fully capture his gaze. "Her actions came as no surprise to any of us. Why are you in shock?"

Leaving Theo to stand alone by the dying fire, Matthew paced about the room. "You are telling me that Grace left the Foreign Office devoid of a leader. Made the treacherous journey across the channel. Traveled the Continent. Agreed to deals with the devil. Madness—utter madness." He came to a stop and faced Theo, who had her arms crossed and was briskly rubbing her bare skin. "Why did no one stop her?"

"No one stopped Lucy when she went to Devonton's rescue." Theo took a seat upon the settee and arranged her skirts as if they were merely talking of the weather or of some other trivial matter. But when she returned her gaze to his, her eyes were sad and serious. "If it had been Archbroke in your place, no one would have been able to prevent me from taking the same actions. I need to know, if you have no plans to hand over the crown jewels to my husband, what do you intend to do with them?"

When he remained silent, Theo said, "Sit."

She pointed to the wingback chair directly opposite her. He hated having his back to a door, but sunk into the chair, relieved to be off his feet for a moment.

"How can I assist you if you will not share your plans with me?" Theo asked.

"I didn't ask for your assistance, nor will I."

Through narrowed eyes, Theo said, "You need help. You have no idea of what and whom you are up against."

The air hung heavy between them. "Burke is a lord, as am I. While he may hold the privy position of Crown counsel, I too am well respected at court."

Theo stiffened. "You and Burke are not the same. Burke…"

Matthew finished her sentence, "Burke is not the only one with a network of supporters."

"And what do you know of Burke and his network?"

Theo's ambiguous tone was one she rarely used with him but one that put him on high alert.

Matthew answered, "While I'm not a genius like your husband, I am fully capable of devising a stratagem that will succeed."

"Then share this brilliant plan of yours."

"Are you mad? I will not involve a woman who is enceinte."

"I might be breeding, but that doesn't prevent my brain from working." Theo leaned forward and whispered, "What if I were able to arrange matters so that no one would attempt to remove the jewels from your possession?"

"How could you possibly convince Archbroke to leave off?"

Theo wagged her eyebrows at him. Surely Theo wasn't hinting at using seduction to persuade her husband. Grace had never used her wiles to ply information or seek a boon from him. No, she had other methods to gain those from him. Matthew cleared his throat and said, "Like I said before, I do not need your assistance."

The patter of Theo's toe tapping beneath her skirts indicated she was thinking. "Very well. I'll speak to Landon and have him deal with Archbroke." She stared at Matthew and said, "If the most logical players were kept unaware of your plans, Burke might too be caught off guard. Tell me, what is your plan?"

"Not until after Archbroke provides the information I've requested."

Theo's head tilted to the side. "What are you carrying on about?"

He leaned forward, placing his elbows on his knees. "My investigations into Burke's artifact scheme brought to light information concerning what I had once regarded a mere children's fable. But there are signs all over Britain, if one looks closely enough, that would indicate the existence of a secret network of families who swear to protect the royal family—three families who have been honor-bound for generations to protect the Crown."

Since his return, Archbroke had skillfully evaded

Matthew's inquires. It remained a point of frustration with his superior and admittedly had been part of the reason which had led Matthew to his rash decision to leave for the Continent. To leave Grace.

Theo lowered her gaze and shifted back, resting against the arm of the settee. Interesting—she was not so chatty now. Theo shivered. Was she cold, or had the mention of the PORFs caused her unease?

Matthew walked over to check that the windows were sealed. "Do you believe in the tale of the PORFs, the honorable families sworn to serve in secrecy?" He found one window cracked open and slammed it closed.

Theo jumped. Agitated, she asked, "What has this to do with the crown jewels you have in your possession?"

Instead of returning to sit in the winged chair, Matthew sat next to Theo on the settee and turned to face her. Oddly, she refused to make eye contact.

Matthew said, "I discovered that long ago—I'm speaking of generations ago, not a few years—the power among the three families was not divided equally as it is today." He'd been told it was a child's fairy tale so many times it was only fitting he began his findings with, "Once upon a time, there were three loyal families who were devoted to the protection of the Crown. One day the king decided to have a coin fashioned out of gold. He summoned the three lords, who were called PORFs. The king declared the holder of the coin would wield full control over all PORFs and the network sworn to serve them. The king threw the coin in the air, and the three men scrambled to take possession. And for decades, the three families fought among themselves for possession of the coin. Countless lives were lost in the fight for power until one day three sons, one from each family, made a pact and swore that if any of them were to come into possession of the coin, he would hide it from all and never reveal its existence or disclose where it was hidden."

He enjoyed telling the facts he and Grace had accumulated over the years which he had woven into a story during the countless nights of boredom while in captivity.

"Matthew, we are too old for fairy tales. Get to the point."

With a sigh, he continued, "Our king believes in such fairy tales. I believe he discovered the coin among the crown jewels, and—not in a fit of madness, but in a moment of clarity—he ordered them to be buried on the Continent."

"Who told you such an outlandish story?"

"No one. I've been investigating the existence of PORFs from a young age. Ever since Baldwin dared me to prove it to him." He intentionally left out Grace's involvement.

"Why would my brother issue such a dare?"

"We were but maybe eleven or twelve, that's what boys do at that age. But once I began looking for evidence, I found clues that were actually in plain sight if you knew what to look for. I hypothesize, Burke too, found out about the existence of the coin among the crown jewels and sought out your brother's assistance to find them."

"Baldwin never mentioned any of this to me when he was alive."

"Of course, not. Your brother would not want to endanger you in any way. But I suspect he had an inkling that Burke was up to no good." He didn't want to tell Theo his theory that Burke was behind Baldwin's death, but when Theo looked directly at him, he didn't have to say the words.

Her cheeks shone a bright red color. She was of an

91

even temperament, slow to anger, but once angered, she did not forgive or forget.

Theo said, "You suspect Burke was after the coin, and when Baldwin found it, Burke had him killed."

"Yes."

"And you suspect Burke to be a PORF?"

"Yes."

Theo gave no indication or clue to confirm Archbroke was indeed a PORF.

She rose from the settee. "If you do not succeed in burying Burke, I will."

He grabbed Theo's hand as he stood. "You can't involve yourself; it is too dangerous."

"Then, we shall have to work together."

Damnation—he would have to share his plans with Theo after all.

CHAPTER ELEVEN

*G*race approached Gunter's tea shop, her footmen on her heels. Over her shoulder, she ordered, "Take Tilman around to the back and order ices for yourselves. My meeting with Archbroke shan't be overly long."

Archbroke had a particular fondness for lemon ices and routinely visited the establishment in the afternoons. Grace counted on the man's preference to stick to the daily routine. Taking the parchment with Gunter's tea shop selections for the day from a server, Grace searched the crowd. No sign of Archbroke. *Yet.*

Head bent; Grace reviewed the list. Lemon. She shook her head. Eww. The tart flavor was offered every day without fail. No doubt it was due to the fact it was Archbroke's favorite.

Tapping the edge of the paper with her forefinger, her eyes were drawn to the corner where the letter G was incorporated into an intricate design that Matthew would be most interested in. Granted, she had assisted Matthew in his search for the identity of the mysterious PORFs and their elaborate underground network, but it didn't mean she believed in their existence. She stared at the seal. Years ago, Matthew had formed the theory that both Burke and Archbroke were PORFs, but he hadn't managed to determine to his satisfaction who the third family was. If Archbroke was a PORF, why had he assigned Matthew, a Home Office agent, to meticulously take down each and every one of Burke's schemes instead of someone within the secret network? Her breath caught in her chest for a moment. If Burke was a PORF, that meant Tobias was one too.

A shadow fell over the parchment. "I recommend lemon." Archbroke chuckled as Grace startled at the sound of his voice.

Annoyingly, the man was as stealthy as Matthew, yet Archbroke rarely employed the talent. She lowered the parchment in her hand to find Archbroke grinning down at her. "I prefer the peppermint. However, it's not being offered today."

Archbroke snatched the list from her hands and signaled for a server. As soon as the harried server was within hearing, Archbroke said, "One lemon and one peppermint."

With a nod, the server rushed away to see to their order.

"How is that poor footman to retrieve a flavor that is not available?"

"Not to worry. He'll find a way. Trust me."

Grace leaned closer. "I do." She glanced about. No one was within hearing. "Papa wishes Jones to be reassigned to the docks."

"I'll take it under advisement."

It wasn't a confirmation he'd see to it, nor was it a decline. Which meant unless there was a sound reason not to Archbroke would have Jones carry out the assignment. Now that she had seen to matters, she was eager to leave. Matthew could return at any moment, and she wanted to be waiting for him at the gazebo. Grace had sensed the moment Matthew had decided to leave her alone with Tobias. She needed to speak with him in person, but if she wasn't present when he arrived, at best, he'd leave a note in the wall.

Archbroke tugged on his waistcoat, "You can't leave before your ice arrives. I'm sure the lad is going to extremes to ensure the order is to your liking."

Blast the Home Secretary—he was nearly as good as her at reading body language.

His movement drew Grace's attention to his attire. His dandy threads of high-tip collars and extravagant amounts of lace about the cuffs were long gone. While Theo had seen to it that he now wore outfits that were conservative in cut, the color of his waistcoats remained questionable. Archbroke was often seen in the awful shade he called gamboge. She never understood why Archbroke favored the abhorrent shade of orange. When he wore such a color before he married, the man reminded her of the round citrus fruit.

While they waited for their order, Grace decided to share the riddle Tobias shared with her last eve. "Archbroke, humor me and play along. Knock. Knock."

"Beg pardon?" His gaze sharpened and scanned the few patrons close by.

No one paid them any heed. Grace pressed on and said, "You say 'who's there.'"

It was the first time she'd managed to catch Archbroke totally off guard. She smiled and began again, "Knock. Knock."

"Who's there?"

Grace answered, "Banana."

Archbroke arched an eyebrow and merely stared at her.

"You say, 'Banana, who'"

At Archbroke's contorted features Grace swallow the burst of laughter that threatened to escape. She tried again. "Knock. Knock."

Archbroke replied, "Banana, who?"

Grace released a sigh. "Not banana who! First, you respond who's there. If being married dulls a person's wit, I shall have to tell Ellingsworth the marriage is off."

"Marriage has nothing to do with this silly game."

Grace, nonplussed by Archbroke's comment, said, "It isn't game. It's a joke. Let's try again, shall we? Knock. Knock."

"Who's there?"

"Banana."

"Banana who?"

Ah, finally, the man had caught on.

Grace continued, "Knock. Knock."

"Who's there?

"Orange."

Archbroke frowned but asked, "Orange who?"

"Orange you glad I didn't say banana?"

A chuckle escaped Archbroke's lips. "I'll have to regale that one to my niece. She will enjoy the play on words."

The young server reappeared, cheeks flushed and wearing a barely visible satisfied grin. Grace's mouth briefly gaped in surprise as she accepted a bowl of green-colored ice.

She said, "It is rather interesting how things come about."

"Who told you such a clever riddle?" Archbroke asked.

As he spooned a mound of lemon ice into his mouth,

Grace answered, "Ellingsworth." She released the most unladylike snort-chuckle combination at the sight of Archbroke's cheeks sucked in, mouth puckered, and raised eyebrows. Regaining her composure, she said, "Actually, the two of you have a lot in common."

"Is that a fact?"

"Ah… Hmm." Grace let the peppermint flavor soak into her tongue. It reminded her of Matthew's first kiss. Did Matthew still carry peppermint treats in his pocket? She needed to hurry and finish her ice and return home. Blinking her eyes open, she expanded upon her answer, "Yes, you both utilize the ton's gossips to hide your true nature. You are no dandy, and Ellingsworth is by no means a dullard." In her haste to leave, Grace swallowed a rather large spoon full of ice. She gave her head a slight shake and found Archbroke staring down at her. Spoon held halfway to her mouth, she continued, "And then there is the matter of your family—"

Archbroke's cutting stare cut off the rest of Grace's sentence. In a tone that sent chills through Grace, he said, "Enough. This is not the location to discuss such matters."

Assessing Archbroke's hard ice-blue eyes, Grace realized the man had never genuinely attempted to intimidate Grace until now. His extreme reaction solidified Matthew's suspicions. Information from a reliable source indicated a power shift had occurred among the PORFs. She was told the upheaval could resort in deadly consequences for PORFs. If Archbroke was really a PORF, then he and Theo could be in danger.

Returning the spoonful of uneaten ice to her bowl, Grace steeled herself and said, "My sources have reported an increased amount of interest and chatter regarding a certain children's story since your cousin by marriage returned from the Continent."

"I've heard the same. Merely an old wives' tale told to children." Archbroke's gaze continued to search their surroundings.

Archbroke wiped a napkin across his lips, avoided eye contact, and shifted his weight away from her—all signs he was definitely lying. Perhaps a different tact was needed.

"Shame that Theo and you did not venture abroad after your wedding."

Straightening, Archbroke said, "Theo would not have missed the birth of our godchildren. But now that the twins have arrived, perhaps I might yet still be able to convince her to go on an adventure."

Grace pulled back as Archbroke shifted closer, peering from his empty bowl to hers. "I would highly recommend it."

Archbroke eyed her bowl once again. "For any specific reason?"

She waited for his gaze to return to her. "The conditions are safe now upon the Continent. Why not take advantage?"

"Are you trying to get rid of me?"

Grace licked the spoon and placed the bowl on the railing that Archbroke was so casually leaning against. "Why would I want that?"

Archbroke crossed his arms in front of his chest. "I don't know. You tell me."

"I was merely suggesting a short trip now that I've ensured it is safe."

"I'll admit Britain has benefited from all your hard work. But in consideration of Theo's condition, I believe we shall remain on home soil."

Fustian! The man had an answer for everything. Their conversation went around in circles. Archbroke manipulated their discussion like Tobias had used riddles the night prior, appearing befuddled when, in fact, it was his audience who was left confused. It proved her point. They were similar.

Rose-pink silk caught Grace's attention. Theo's signature color appeared as if from thin air. "Lady Grace, I hope my dear husband has been fine company while you awaited my arrival?"

Grace hadn't been waiting for Theo—what was she about? Going along with her friend's scheme, Grace replied, "He has indeed."

Archbroke scanned the area before stepping forward to confront his wife. "Where is your maid, or any of the three footmen I've employed to accompany you?"

Ah. Archbroke knew of the dangers and had increased protection for Theo. Wise man. Their meeting only provided more items for her to discuss with Matthew. A giddiness brought a smile to her face. Not only was she eager to see Matthew, but the opportunity to once again work as a team had her pulse racing.

Energy and tension filled the air between the pair. Theo gave Archbroke a peck on the cheek. "Stop your worrying. I've sent all of them round to enjoy some ices. I can assure you they carried out your orders not to let me out of their sight until I was safely within two feet of you."

Archbroke seemed mollified. "And you, my dear, do you wish for an ice?"

"Not today. I've got a message for you, dear husband, from Matthew. He hopes you will join him for supper this evening at White's."

"I'd prefer to spend the evening with you."

"Oh, I won't be home tonight. I'll be accompanying Grace to Hereford's dinner party since her dear aunt, Lady Emily Allensworth has come down with a cold."

Grace's aunt, her chaperone for all social engagements,

was never ill. Deciding it best to play along with Theo's scheme, she remained silent. Theo hooked her arm in Grace's. "Ready to depart? I'll have Jack bring round the carriage."

Blast. She had discussed attending Hereford's dinner earlier with Tobias, but in her eagerness to see Matthew, she had forgotten about the bloody event. No, not forgotten. Merely wishful thinking she wouldn't have to attend. Why in the world had Matthew requested to meet with Archbroke this eve? Everyone was aware that the Home Secretary had a propensity to hold lengthy meetings. He was also known to have sequestered agents until dawn on more than one occasion. It could be hours before either of them would be able to finally return to the gazebo. Grace released a deep breath. Duties first and then Matthew. She prayed she wasn't wrong, and that Matthew still cared for her.

CHAPTER TWELVE

*M*atthew sat slumped in his preferred chair, facing the fire in his study. His head pounded after hours of poring through reports, journals, and notes that both he and Grace had made over the years. Matthew lost count of how many attempts he'd made at re-creating the interconnected schematic of the various individuals and their association with one another —an agonizing reminder that he needed Grace.

She had a brilliant, agile, and tactical mind that worked in parallel with his. She would plot and draw out tables and charts while he would isolate key data points and patterns. Matthew's knuckles cracked as he crumpled the parchment in his hand, his last attempt at updating the convoluted diagram, and threw it into the fire. The small burst of flames fizzled out just as his hope of regaining Grace's attention once more had as the afternoon wore on.

The shuffle of boots upon the plush carpet had him straightening. Blake must have returned. But it wasn't Blake who appeared. It was Archbroke, who promptly said, "I detest having to track down my agents."

Matthew rubbed his temples in a circular motion with the pads of his forefingers. "How many times must I repeat myself? I no longer wish to be an agent of the Home Office." He had sent missive after missive informing Archbroke of his decision. Yet, each time they returned with one word boldly scribed across the parchment —DECLINED.

"You will remain an agent of the Crown until either one of us is taken from this world. Do I make myself clear?"

"Perfectly." Archbroke had not shared specifics as to why he insisted Matthew remain a part of the organization, but Matthew suspected the man wanted to keep tabs on him and his investigations related to the PORFs. He hated to admit it, but Archbroke's refusal to accept his resignation provided Matthew with a sense of being needed.

Sliding into the chair that Blake usually occupied to his right, Archbroke stretched his long legs in front of him and crossed them at the ankles as if he intended to stay awhile. "Now, Theo would not have had me hunt you down unless there was a purpose—out with it."

Theo. The woman had transformed from the sweet, mischievous girl of his childhood into a merciless strategist right before his eyes. She had prodded, poking holes in Matthew's plan to take down Burke until they were both satisfied it would ultimately reveal Burke for the devil he was. Why had she not simply shared the scheme with her husband? Why send Archbroke here?

Before delving into the details, Matthew needed a drink. Placing his quaking hands, palms down, on the arms of the chair, he pushed himself up to stand. Stars appeared. He wavered slightly before he took a steadying step forward. Certain Archbroke had noticed, he stomped over to the sideboard and grabbed the decanter of French brandy. Narrowing his eyes on the two empty glasses, he poured a large portion into each glass. This morn he had declared he'd get through the entire day without seeking relief from the pain and misery by drowning himself in spirits. His determination had doubled upon finding out Grace's betrothal was a sham, but as the day wore on frustration at his inability to hold his quill steady, his failure to muddle through the information and document his new findings only reinforced the conclusion he had reached during his time at Halestone Hall. Grace was better off without him. She didn't need to care for another man who was damaged and incapable of caring for himself in her life.

Without hesitation, he raised a glass to his mouth and consumed the liquor in one swallow before quickly refilling it. A flash of bright orange in his peripheral vision caught his attention. Archbroke had removed his jacket and was now unbuttoning his atrocious gamboge waistcoat. With an inward groan, Matthew resolved to spending the rest of the evening in Archbroke's company. Eyeing his glass, he sighed and picked up the two tumblers and returned to his seat.

Handing Archbroke his drink, Matthew said, "The location of the remaining stolen artifacts is common knowledge. Burke has ensured others are aware. It may be a trap."

"Might be, but I care little about those particular items." Archbroke raised his glass in the air before taking a healthy gulp. "I preferred it when you were working *with* the Foreign Secretary rather than alongside her. It would save me from enduring multiple meetings regarding the same matter."

Archbroke was not the only one who had a preference

for how things were before, but Matthew ignored the comment. "If you allow Burke to succeed in selling the artifacts, he will…"

Silencing Matthew with a hand in the air, Archbroke countered, "I'll be reassigning Jones to the docks in the morn as a precaution. But even if Burke does manage to sell the goods, Hereford has replaced Burke's ally within the court."

So Grace had already met with Archbroke. The woman was efficient as ever. The news of Hereford's appointment came to Matthew as a surprise. Hereford was an agent of the Foreign Office, not under Archbroke's rule. Neither Grace nor Lord Flarinton wielded enough influence within the court to see to his appointment. A critical link or piece of information was missing. Matthew leaned forward, resting his elbows on his knees, and rolled his empty glass between his palms. "Tell me why Hereford."

Archbroke narrowed his gaze. "Do you not remember? You were the one who recommended him for the position."

Oh, he remembered the discussion. Clearly. It had occurred two years ago at Grace's insistence that Matthew be the one to convince Archbroke that Burke's collaborator be removed from the court. At the time, Matthew had argued Hereford, the most honorable of men, was mature enough to balance the conflicting nature of matters dealt with at court and more than capable of simultaneously dealing with multiple objectives. He also recalled his recommendations had fallen upon deaf ears. Archbroke had simply disregarded the issue, stating a man of Hereford's years, at the time, only two and thirty, would never be respected at court.

Matthew should have worded his question differently. Archbroke was a master of evasion. Who had power and influence over court appointments? Matthew closed his eyes, and the image of the PORF design appeared. He must be hallucinating, or the effects of too much drink were beginning to affect his mental well-being. If only he'd had an opportunity this morn to meet with Grace. She would have detangled his thoughts.

Returning the conversation to simpler matters, Matthew asked, "Do you not care that the items will be sold?"

After he emptied his glass, Archbroke answered, "Not particularly, since my sources believe they are French artifacts, not British. The most pressing dilemma I currently face is you."

An unreasonable chill raced down Matthew's spine. "Me?" He endeavored to feign innocence. He probably failed. Perhaps his investigations into the PORFs and his attaching the Archbroke name to the triad of families had reached the Home Secretary's ears.

"Indeed. You *and* Grace."

"What are you babbling on about?"

Archbroke handed Matthew his empty glass. "Grace— the woman whom you have pined over for years. The lady you had hoped to marry before you went and got yourself captured."

Slowly rolling to his feet, intending to refill their empty glasses, Matthew paused before the fire. Ellingsworth's earlier warnings that no one was to suspect that his engagement to Grace was a farce came back in a flash. He continued to the sideboard. Both glasses hit the wood surface with a crash. "Grace has agreed to marry another. You saw yourself last eve she appears quite happy with the arrangement." It grated on his nerves to have to reiterate the lie, but he'd do or say whatever necessary to keep her safe.

"What is the matter with you?" Archbroke asked. "Them brutes must have damaged your brain and your eyesight. That is not at all what I surmise."

His body tensed and momentarily froze at the mention of the beatings he had received. Forcing his arm to move, Matthew grabbed the neck of the decanter with one trembling hand and splashed the dark amber liquid into their tumblers. Steadying his breathing, he choked out the words that had his stomach recoiling. "Grace is no longer my concern. Ellingsworth, as Mr. Jones assessed, is quite capable and despite the rumors is rather shrewd." The words left a bitter taste in his mouth. Seizing his glass, he quickly downed the contents and refilled it before returning to his seat.

Archbroke eyed the glass presented to him before accepting it with a nod. "Ellingsworth is much like his papa. No one really knows the real man behind the facade. Both are unpredictable, and I have serious concerns regarding Grace's safety."

"As she is your counterpart and is currently on home soil, you should be concerned."

The Home Secretary's response was to level Matthew with a glacial glare. The growl of Archbroke's stomach was probably no louder than a cat's purr, but to Matthew, it was a roar. Unwanted memories came flooding back. Days upon days he had lain curled on his side, clutching his stomach. The ache of having food and water withheld was one he never wanted to experience again, nor the taste of putrid scraps they had been fed. But a starving man filled with rage will eat anything to ensure he brought justice against those who had dared to threaten him and his loved ones.

The click of the door latch broke through Matthew's thoughts.

Blake's gravelly baritone voice filled the silent room. "Archbroke, why are you here? Shouldn't you be at Hereford's celebration dinner?"

"My wife is in attendance. No need to suffer through another tedious dinner party."

The grumble of Archbroke's stomach was louder this time. Matthew clutched the armrest. He wanted to be rid of Archbroke and find out if Blake had managed to obtain the resources they needed for the next stage of his plan. But the Home Secretary sat calmly, eyeing them both. Clearly, the man wasn't going anywhere. Blake disappeared from sight. The clink of glass and splash of liquid had Matthew wishing for another drink.

Blake reappeared and said, "Perhaps we should adjourn to White's for a delicious beefsteak."

Simultaneously both Archbroke and Matthew hauled themselves to their feet and replied, "Grand idea."

As the three of them made their way out, Archbroke turned to address both Matthew and Blake. "Whatever the pair of you are up to, do not tell me. I'm certain I'll not want to be involved. However, should you need my assistance, please ask."

Matthew stared at Archbroke. Why would his superior of over a decade make such an absurd statement? Archbroke was always the first to insist he be informed of any activity that was even rumored to occur on home soil. As Home Secretary, Archbroke had always made it his business to know the exact comings and goings of his agents. Matthew searched the man's features for a clue. The small upturn at the corner of his lips was a new facial tell that Archbroke must have adopted since marriage. Theo. His wife was a master chess player and could predict her opponent's move three turns before you even thought of it yourself. Theo must have succeeded where Matthew had failed in convincing Archbroke to see to Hereford's appointment.

A sharp stabbing pain at his temples momentarily blurred his vision and thoughts. Matthew shook his head. No, not Theo. Someone else, but who? He would have to lay off the liquor tonight. He needed his wits about him in order to visit Grace. The irritating ringing in his ear silenced as his heart skipped a few beats at the thought of seeing her.

CHAPTER THIRTEEN

*S*eated at Hereford's dinner table, Grace ran a finger along the edge of the handle of her knife. It was of the finest quality, sharp and precise.

Lord Burke, seated across from her, boasted, "Don't they make a fine couple?"

She contemplated the potential risks and benefits of hurling the blade into the heart of her fiancé's sire. The pink tip of Tobias's tongue appeared at the corner of his mouth, distracting her. She reluctantly shifted her narrowed gaze from Lord Burke to his son. Tobias's ridiculous smile was gone, and the man was indeed sticking his tongue out at her. It reminded her of when the girls from her childhood would stick their tongues out at her when she would quote a passage from one of the many etiquette books her mama had made her read. Grace was a rule follower. Life was much simpler that way. But the rules of the game were changing. The players were changing. Matthew was not in attendance, and Tobias, who was usually never seen at such events, occupied the seat next to her.

Her betrothed said, "You'll hang at Newgate if you kill him in front of witnesses." The man's idiotic smile returned.

Grace prayed; *Lord, grant me the patience to endure this evening of torture.* Every muscle in her neck and back ached. The tension of having Tobias a stranger so close two evenings in a row took a toll on her body, the same body that longed for Matthew's reassuring touches at these arduous events. Matthew would skillfully set her at ease with a slight brush against the back of her hand as he reached for a glass or utensil or by merely shifting his booted foot next to hers. Thoughts of Matthew helped her focus on relaxing her grip on the knife.

Grace glanced at Theo, who sat next to her on her left, and laid the weapon on the table before turning her attention back to Tobias. "I'm not certain anyone present would report me. Would you?"

He tilted his head to capture her gaze. "I would..." Tobias paused as he lifted his knife and deftly sliced through a piece of chicken upon his plate. His eyes remained on her the entire time. "I'd prefer that you gave me the honor of taking care of the matter."

Of course, he would. He'd already said as much that morning. But Grace placed little trust in those she was not well acquainted with. Reaching for her glass of watered-down wine, Grace said, "You have many who are competing for the pleasure."

"That is why I will act first." He stabbed the piece of meat with his fork. "With your assistance."

Grace stared at her betrothed. He hadn't made a request, nor were his words phrased as a statement. It was an order. She did not take direction from strangers. Grace only took orders from her papa. She released a sigh. That was not true; there was one other person she used to take instruction from willingly—Matthew.

Tobias popped the forkful of food into his mouth and chewed loudly. Making a show of swallowing, he asked, "Wishing I was another?"

God, she hated his disguise. While Tobias acted the fool, his words were cutting. Her fiancé had an uncanny ability to read her thoughts, or perhaps she was failing rather miserably at masking them.

As he leaned back into his chair, he muttered, "The irises of your eyes dilate, and you tilt your head slightly to the right every time you think of him." His astute observations had Grace shifting food about her plate.

"Jealous?"

Tobias chuckled. "I'll admit, a little." His admission was the last thing Grace expected him to say. Why would he be jealous?

Confident he wouldn't care for her next thought, she speared a piece of fish, the least likely item before her to make her choke upon his reply. "If you wish for me to aid you, I will require the particulars of your plan." She glanced over her shoulder as she chewed.

With a toothy smile, he said, "I've already informed you of my scheme."

Telling her to pretend to be madly in love with him until the royal surgeon declared Burke dead and that he intended to be aboard the Quarter Moon well on his way to America by the time word had spread of his sire's death was hardly enough information.

Narrowing her eyes, Grace said, "Vaguely—I need the details."

Tobias leaned forward and shuffled his seat a tad closer to her. "I've already told you. For the safety of everyone, it's best you are unaware of the finer points."

She wanted to frown and growl at the man who now sat inappropriately close. Instead, Grace plastered a smile on her face. Glancing about the table, it appeared their farce was working. No one paid them any attention. Not willing to give up, she said, "Very well. Tell me what is in America that beckons you, and I won't press further."

Tobias's glass of wine precariously tilted as he reached for it. It would have spilled if he hadn't deftly caught it without the notice of others. But Grace had witnessed his swift reflexes. It was the first time his clumsy actions had not been intentional.

Recalling Theo's reference to love, Grace pressed on and said, "Or perhaps I should ask, who." His spine stiffened. "What is this beauty's name who has caught your attention?"

Raising his glass to his lips, Tobias answered, "Come now, Grace, beauty is in the eye of the beholder. It is why you do not find me handsome. The reason why your pulse remains steady when we are close, yet your skin prickles, and your heart aches to be close to him as soon as Matthew enters the same room as you. Appearances alone have nothing to do with whether you are attracted to a person." As if to punctuate his statement, he licked the corner of his lips, capturing an errant trickle of wine. Had Matthew performed the same motions, her cheeks would be flooded with heat, but Grace's face remained aloof, and frustration roared through her at the thought, *Tobias is sticking his tongue out at me again.* Her fiancé was right. He did not evoke the sensual fantasies Matthew could.

"You must love her." Grace wasn't certain, but she suspected he hid a smile behind his napkin as he dabbed his mouth.

Looking down as he replaced his napkin to his lap, he said, "She is to me as Harrington is to you. The one person who makes the rest of the world disappear as soon as they appear."

How poetic and not at all idiotic. The man was clearly in love with another. Yet here he sat next to Grace, playing the role of a besotted fool, exhibiting none of the strains she was experiencing.

Tobias raised his eyes to meet hers. They were filled with sadness. "I feel empty without her." His gaze shifted away from Grace. "But she, like Archbroke and your dear friend Theo beside you—who, by the way, is throwing daggers at me at this very moment—places duty before her own desires."

Grace swiveled to see Theo was indeed glaring at Tobias. Turning back, Grace declared, "You know nothing of Theo or Archbroke."

Tobias's indolent smirk returned. "I believe you are the one mistaken. It is you who is unaware of the true bond they share. And unfortunate as it may be, a connection that I too share alongside them."

The man was always talking in riddles. He leaned forward and nodded at Theo.

In a harsh whisper, Theo said, "You know better than to refer to such matters."

Letting out a loud laugh, Tobias brought the entire dinner party's attention upon himself. "My dear, Lady Theo, you two are the most astonishingly intelligent women of my acquaintance. I know not what you speak of, but no matter, you are both highly entertaining." His gaze landed squarely on Grace's décolletage.

Hereford, their host, was the first to recover from the shock. "Lord Ellingsworth, perhaps you will join the other gentlemen and me in my study for a drink."

"Hereford, I don't suppose you managed to smuggle

any whiskey or cigars from the Continent upon your return?"

Tobias rose, and the rest of the gentlemen followed suit. Grace's gaze fell upon Hereford. She was responsible for sending him there to ensure Matthew returned safely. It was her orders that resulted in Hereford being held captive and tortured for many months. Grace cringed as Hereford's eyes darkened.

How rude and uncaring of Tobias to purposefully bring up the matter. Tobias eyed his papa. Lord Burke shifted uncomfortably. The comment wasn't intended to offend Hereford. It was to send a message of sorts to Lord Burke. A warning. It was the first indication that Tobias had the mettle to see to Lord Burke's demise.

Theo's sweet voice interrupted Grace's reflections. "Your betrothed is rather crafty, but do not let him underestimate you. You are a brilliant strategist and let no one convince you otherwise." Theo squeezed Grace's hand that lay fisted upon the table.

Grace glanced about the room. The tension between Tobias and Lord Burke escalated. All the gentlemen remained standing, ready to leave. Hereford shifted his weight uncomfortably. It was Lord Hadfield who broke the strained silence. "Gentlemen, let's adjourn."

How peculiar that it was Lord Hadfield who assumed the lead in Archbroke's absence.

Theo leaned closer and whispered, "Now, tell me of your plans."

Grace hadn't sorted through the myriad of ideas that she had formulated throughout the day. She shook her head and replied, "I've not yet decided on the best course of action."

Theo nodded and stood to move to the seat next to Mary. Grace should follow, but she remained in her chair, stealing a moment for herself. Theo was an excellent mediator, but Grace wanted a partner. She needed Matthew.

SQUEEZING HER EYES TIGHT, Grace moaned as the pounding in her head resumed. She'd returned home from Hereford's dinner party intending to wait for Matthew at the gazebo, but the intense shooting pain in her brain had her seeking out her bed. She rolled her head forward, then from side to side, attempting to alleviate the tension in her neck and the knots in her shoulders.

Doubts and concerns regarding her scheme and Tobias's motives plagued her. She threw the coverlet back and wrapped her favorite thick wool tartan about her. Fresh air and the comfort of the gazebo might ease her mind.

She tiptoed her way down the hall but hesitated as voices wafted up from below. Pushing against the side panel, the click of the lock sliding open revealed the secret passageway her papa had installed. Grace slipped into the narrow space and sidestepped a few feet before it opened up wide enough for her to walk comfortably. She made her way through the dark, hand pressed against the familiar fake wood walls. Her mama's laughter halted Grace in her tracks. Peeking through the spy hole into the family drawing room, she saw her mama cradled in her papa's lap.

With love-filled eyes, her papa looked down at his wife. "You are the love of my heart."

Her mama chuckled. "That may be the case now—but love, it was not always that way. If Gracie marries Ellingsworth, I only hope he too comes to love her as you grew to love me."

"I was a fool. I apologize, my dear. I should never have treated you so."

Her mama placed her hand upon his cheek. "Hush, that is all in the past. Alex has settled nicely among us and is back safe and sound."

Grace placed a hand over her mouth—silencing the gasp that threatened to escape. Who was Alex?

"Yes, I'm exceedingly proud of my son."

His son! She had a half-brother.

"My dear, he had a rough year held in captivity with Harrington. You should visit soon."

Fustian. There was no one named Alex imprisoned with Matthew. Lord Addington's given name was Benedict, and Lord Hereford's was Sebastian. The only other person rescued was Archbroke's Home Office messenger, Mr. Jones. Grace pressed her aching head against the faux door. Mr. Jones was her brother.

Her papa's sleepy voice floated through the wall. "You are correct. I should like to visit with him. Would you arrange for Alex to come at an opportune time, my love?"

Why had her parents kept the existence of Alex a secret from her? Her papa should have integrated her brother into the Foreign Office's network, not allowed him to be under the supervision of Archbroke. Did Alex know she was his sister and had refused to work under a woman?

Her mama's soft voice brought Grace's head back up to peek at the loving couple. "For you love, anything."

Her mama placed a kiss on her husband's forehead. Grace had believed her parents to be one of the few couples who had married for love when, in fact, they had not been in love. The truth of her father impregnating another sent Grace's mind into a thousand different directions.

She had always wanted a sibling. If Alex was her brother, she would claim him as such. But first, she needed more information. Summoning Alex was not an option, for he did not report to her, and she was loath to seek out Archbroke's assistance in this matter.

There was only one man she trusted to help her muddle through everything—Matthew.

If Archbroke had already assigned Alex to monitor the docks, her brother could be in grave danger. Abandoning the idea to retreat to her gazebo, Grace swiftly made her way to the study. Seated at her papa's well-worn wooden desk with her quill poised midair, Grace mentally composed several reiterations of the message she needed Matthew to respond to. Ultimately, Grace settled upon:

M,
Friends in peril. I'll be waiting.
G.

With a drop of wax, she sealed the missive. Silverman, the crafty butler, appeared flanked by two footmen.

Silverman said, "I shall see to it that it is delivered. But I must insist you not leave the house unaccompanied again."

She handed him her missive. Silverman's eyebrows shot up as he read to whom it was addressed. How uncharacteristic of the old man to reveal any reaction.

Grace said, "I'm perfectly safe here."

"I'll have young Jamison posted here until Lord Harrington arrives." Silverman didn't wait for a response. He simply left as quietly and swiftly as he had arrived.

CHAPTER FOURTEEN

*P*eeking from behind the hundred-year-old oak tree, Matthew spied Grace sitting with a tartan about her shoulders. His heart stopped. The deep crease between her furrowed eyebrows, her downcast gaze, and her stiff posture all meant one thing—her thoughts were dire. Matthew pulled out Grace's note from the pocket of his greatcoat.

It was no love letter, yet his heart soared at her uniquely lovely script. Grace wasn't one for dramatics— when he read that their friends were in danger, he had immediately set off to meet her. It had nothing to do with his desire to speak with her or to be close enough to smell the scent of lilacs once more. Satisfied he convinced himself of the lie, he tucked the correspondence back into his pocket. Matthew stepped out from behind the massive tree trunk and nodded to the young footman standing guard.

Relieved of his duty, the footman trotted down the path, breathing into his hands. How long had Grace been waiting in the gazebo? It was an extremely cool night. The wool wrap would hardly suffice to keep her warm. What-ever preoccupied her mind, had her oblivious to the cold and her surroundings. He used to seize these rare moments when he could catch the woman unaware with a kiss to the sliver of skin on the back of her neck just below her hair-line. Grace would sigh and lean back, allowing him to wrap her up in his warmth. She had claimed the only place she ever wanted to be day and night was in his arms. Reluctant to reveal himself, he stood staring, wondering how to broach the subject of her betrothal, to thank her for going to such lengths to see to his safe return home, and to tell her he still loved her.

Grace stiffened, her tartan falling from her shoulders to her waist as she swiveled to meet his gaze. "How long have you been standing there?"

She was a few feet away from him. "I came as soon as I received your note." He hated the prospect of discussing Crown matters here. This was her retreat. Previously, their oasis—a place for forbidden kisses. "Should we adjourn inside?"

Tugging the tartan back to her shoulders, Grace turned away from him and shook her head. "I've become accus-tomed to working out matters here." She sank to the bench and arranged her skirts.

"Since when and why?"

Grace let out a defeated sigh. "Two years."

Damnation. In essence, since he left.

He took three quick strides and crouched beside her. A single candle illuminated the interior of the gazebo. Not much had changed. Silk cushions were still strewn about the floor and along the benches guarded against the elements by the very roses he had gifted her. Grace's skin flushed, tempting him to nuzzle and breathe her in. Inhaling sharply, he took in the dark smudges under her eyes. Evidence of how profoundly he had hurt this woman. "I'm sorry for leaving you."

Grace closed her eyes. A tear escaped and trickled down her cheek. Matthew cupped her face and brushed the solitary droplet away. "Can you forgive me for placing you in this terrible predicament?"

To his relief, she nodded.

Matthew continued, "You are the reason I remain alive today."

Grace pressed her cheek against his palm, but her eyes remained closed. He guided her head down to his until their foreheads touched. A breath away from a kiss, he reigned in his desires and said, "When we were initially freed, my first thought was to make you my marchioness as soon as I set foot upon English soil." He took a deep breath in. He had to finish confessing to his mistakes. "When Lady Cecilia passed along your note informing me you were betrothed to Ellingsworth, I felt betrayed. I fled to Halestone Hall, not only to recover from my injuries but also in the hopes that my love for you would subside. I ignored your missives and left you alone during a time when you needed me most. I don't know how to make things right…"

Grace pulled away, and he let his hand fall to his knee. The loss of contact plunged his thoughts back to the darkest day of his life. With his heart crushed at the news that she was betrothed to his sworn enemy's son, he had vowed to destroy Burke—the man who had robbed him of freedom and love.

Her eyes filled with unshed tears, she asked, "Do you still love me?" Grace never let anyone but him see this side of her. Among agents, she was known and referred to as the iron lady. Grace was tough as nails, and many believed her emotionless. But he knew better.

She didn't need another injured soul to care for. He wasn't fully healed and may never return to his former self, the man she had fallen in love with. Regardless, the truth slipped from his mouth in a whisper, "Always."

Her cool hands reached out. Before she could touch his cheeks, he engulfed them in his as he rose to take a seat next to her upon the bench. Avoiding her gaze, he focused on warming her hands. "Tell me who is in trouble."

"Mr. Jones. My brother—Alex."

His hands stilled. When had she discovered Alex was her brother? Perhaps Theo was wrong, and Grace had sacrificed herself for Alex and not him. "Alex is well protected. He'll not be harmed." He placed her hands gently back upon her lap and stood. Turning away from her, he stuffed his hands in his coat. His fingers grazed against her note. Grace valued family above all else. It was no wonder she had summoned him as soon as she believed Alex in danger.

"How long have you known Alex was related to me?" Grace's voice was steady and even, no trace of the upset he'd seen in her eyes before.

"In Spain, when we all thought we might not survive the ordeal, Alex confessed that he wished he'd thanked your mother for her kindness and generosity in seeing to his care after his own mama died." It was one of many admissions shared, and Matthew would take the rest of them to the grave.

"I don't understand why my parents withheld his existence from me. They knew how desperately I wished for a sibling." Her voice cracked. Matthew swirled around. Grace stood and lifted her beautiful tear-streaked face and met his gaze. Out of pure habit, he reached for her, and like a million times before, she wrapped her arms about his neck and crushed her body to his.

With strength he didn't know he still possessed, Matthew lifted her and carried her to the corner where bolsters and pillows were strewn about. Lowering to one knee, he tried to place her upon the cushioned floor, but she refused to release him. With little energy left, he fell onto his bottom and scooted back to rest against the wooden bench. Soft sobs escaped Grace as he sat cradling her. He wanted to hold her like this forever, be there for her in these times of distress.

Grace hiccupped. "Why did they not trust me with this information?" She wiped the tartan across her eyes and nose but kept her face down, nested in the crook of his neck.

He didn't have an answer. All he wanted was to soothe her hurt. Matthew lightly ran his palm up and down her arm. She fit so naturally against him. He wanted to pull her tighter to him and absorb all her pain.

"I believed my parents' match to have been one born out of love. Tonight, I overheard them talking of Alex, only to find out that they did not even like each other in the beginning and that my papa… How could he have not loved and respected Mama… and his vows to her?"

Her reaction was similar to his own when Alex had confessed who his papa was. Disappointment was one of many emotions Matthew experienced as he realized Flarinton, the man on whom Matthew had wished to model his own behavior, had broken his vow to love and honor his wife. He imagined Grace experienced the same.

Grace stiffened in his arms. "You said he was well protected—by whom?"

His hand stilled. "Your betrothed." Ellingsworth's warning raced through his mind. Grace shouldn't be in his arms, but he wasn't ready to relinquish his hold on her.

"Tobias? Why would…"

Drawing her chin up, he said, "Archbroke sequestered Blake and me into a private room at White's for supper—he was in a rather chatty mood." Matthew grinned. Married to Theo, Archbroke's priorities had undoubtedly changed. "Alex and Ellingsworth have much in common. Both seek to escape the societal bonds linked to their lineage." Grace's brow furrowed. He wasn't being succinct as he struggled to diplomatically explain, "Neither of the men were birthed by a titled women. It was one of the reasons Archbroke assigned your brother to become better acquainted with your fiancé. It also explains why Ellingsworth has no love for his sire."

Grace's eyes widened as his words registered. "While you were gone, I've come to the conclusion you are absolutely correct."

That was a first. Grace rarely confessed to any matter, let alone to another being right. "About what?" Matthew asked.

With a sigh, she leaned her head back against his chest. "The existence of PORFs, their supporting network. I've amassed enough evidence that supports your theory that both Burke and Archbroke are indeed PORFs." She slid her hand up to rest between his heart and her cheek.

Did she feel his increased heartbeat? Would she recognize how much her words had meant to him? Grace had not abandoned their secret project, which meant she'd never lost hope in him.

Clearing his throat of emotion, Matthew asked, "What of the third family?"

"You mean Hadfield."

"When did you piece all of this together?"

"The other night at my engagement party. But today, while I was at Gunter's tea shop, is when I came to the conclusion that your theories were not merely old wives' tales.''

He flinched back an inch as she reached up to touch his face. Matthew relaxed his fingers that were digging into her waist. The reminder of her betrothal dinner had Matthew shifting her off his lap. "You're engaged to Ellingsworth." He had no right to be holding her.

After wriggling back into his lap, she settled herself firmly and waited until he met her gaze. "Tobias is in love with another. He told me himself last night. He has plans to be reunited with his true love in America."

Fantasies of having Grace back in his arms was what drove Matthew to continue to breathe and awaken during his darkest days. Having her upon his lap, as she was now, snuggled against him, was heaven. For months he had believed he'd never be able to hold her, touch or kiss her. Grace placed her lips upon his, and he released the groan that threatened his sanity. She traced her tongue along the seam of his mouth.

He kept his lips sealed but ached to let her in. Ellingsworth had admitted their engagement was a sham. If the man planned to jilt Grace, she could be his. She would never act dishonorably. He would figure it all out— later. As soon as his lips parted, her sweet tongue darted into his mouth. The taste of honey flooded his senses as he kissed her back until they broke for a breath.

Continuing to place light kisses along his jaw, Grace mumbled, "I've missed you."

He too had yearned for her touch. Months of attempting to banish her from his heart and soul were wiped away with her kisses. "We shouldn't." But even as he uttered the words, his hand sneaked under the tartan and cupped her breast.

"Tobias keeps insisting that all will be as it should be,

and I shall obtain what my heart truly desires. My heart has always desired you. If what he says is true, and I believe him, must we wait?"

Two months shy of two years, they had been apart— twenty-two months of longing for the woman, warm and willing in his arms. He didn't have the willpower to insist they postpone their kisses and intimate touches. Grace tugged on his coat buttons. Moments later, she had skillfully managed to snake her hands under his shirt. He had not donned a jacket or waistcoat in his haste to meet her. He was particularly glad he had forgone the extra layers, for the feel of her hands upon him once more was like a soothing balm.

His muscles twitched under her palm. The woman knew his favorite spots to taunt and tease. She ran a finger over his nipple, and a jolt of pleasure shot right to his loins. Memories of her tongue gliding over his flesh and swirling about his nipple had him shifting.

On a ragged breath, he said, "Honey."

Grace ran her tongue along his lower lip, and the rest of his speech faltered. Her lips fused to his, granting him the soul-searing kiss he had dreamed about night after night. His brain fogged over. All he wanted was to have her soft skin under his palms. He tugged at the neckline of her nightgown and eased his hand over her bosom. Rolling her pert nipple between his fingers, Grace released a raspy moan. She always rewarded him with verbal cues of what she did and did not find pleasure in. Grace wiggled, and his hands were dislodged from her chest and slid to her waist. She removed her hands from under his shirt and placed them on each shoulder. Leaning in to kiss him, she kept her lips on his as she shifted and hiked up her skirts to allow her to straddle him. His hands immediately skimmed lower to seek out her lush thighs. He rubbed her skin chilled by the cool air as she rocked against him. With the material of her gown out of the way, he ran his thumb over her slit.

"Touch me. Please don't stop." Grace let out a contented sigh and rocked harder. "It's been too many months. Matthew, I need you…"

He didn't want to be reminded of his time away from her. Pushing away the dark thoughts that threatened to intrude, Matthew devoured her mouth. His thumb slid easily back and forth. She was wet and ready. Plunging two fingers into her core, a wave of energy rolled through him. Just as he remembered, her channel was tight and slick. It was frighteningly familiar and mirrored his dreams of having her in his arms, her inner muscles clenching about him. Except it wasn't his fingers that her core tightened around, it was his manhood that currently strained against his damn breeches.

Nibbling on her neck, he pounded his fingers deep, his palm slapping against her.

"Oh. Matthew, please…" Grace's pleas hastened his movements until he could feel her muscles spasm.

She ground against his palm in a circular motion. He was close to finding his own release as she rubbed over him. Grace's head fell back, and hard shudders rocked her body.

Resting her forehead upon his, she smiled. "Oh, how I've longed to be right here—with you."

The crunch of gravel under boots filtered through Matthew's foggy brain. Lifting Grace's limp body from him, he stood and sat her upon the bench. He grabbed the discarded tartan and wrapped it tightly about her. There was nothing he could do about her torn nightgown but hide its condition. He turned away from the entrance and hastily tucked his lawn shirt into his breeches. Fumbling with his coat buttons, he turned at the rap of knuckles against the wood post.

Ellingsworth stepped out from the shadows. "Harrington."

"Lord Ellingsworth." Matthew came face-to-face with Grace's furious betrothed.

"You can dispense with the formalities, Harrington. I'm here to discuss a few matters with my intended, including the details of our wedding." Ellingsworth's cold stare remained on Matthew.

Grace spoke before he could. "But you told me you are in love with another."

Ellingsworth didn't blink at the mention of his love. He simply replied, "What does love have to do with our nuptials? You gave your word, and there is nothing more to it."

There was a message in Ellingsworth's gaze that Matthew's guilty mind couldn't decipher. He turned to Grace, lifted his left shoulder, and let it fall casually in a half shrug. A signal to ignore his words and trust that he would explain later. "Ellingsworth is right. You gave him your word." As he passed Grace's intended, he added, "Give her the respect she is due."

Ellingsworth nodded and turned his attention to Grace.

As Matthew walked behind the gazebo, he heard, "You were supposed to convince him to go along with this farce, not…" The man ceased speaking and waited. Waited for Matthew to leave. Ellingsworth's speech would not be received well, for it was delivered in a decidedly conceited tone that Grace would not care for, not in the least.

He trudged through the garden and noted the young footman had returned along with Ellingsworth. Matthew's shoulder relaxed. Glad he had not left Grace alone with

Ellingsworth, he replayed her betrothed's parting words as he made his way home.

What the bloody hell was the man up to? When was the sham to end? Matthew froze as the answer to his own question, hit him—the church.

With a bounce in his step that had been missing for many months, Matthew returned to his townhouse eager to share the half-concocted scheme to marry Grace with Blake. If the stars would align, he'd manage to time the ceremony with the departure of the Quarter Moon, upon which Ellingsworth would be aboard. But in order for his plan to succeed, he'd need to call in a few favors.

CHAPTER FIFTEEN

*G*race glared at her fiancé. The gall of the man to barge into her retreat and attempt to lecture her. She pulled the soft tartan tighter about her shoulders. Her skin tingled, still sensitive from Matthew's skillful attentions. Blast Tobias and his bloody timing. Reining in her ire, Grace said, "I'd prefer you not speak to me in that tone."

Tobias raked his ice-blue eyes over her face and lowered his gaze to the vee of the tartan. "Watching you come undone with your legs spread wide, Harrington's fingers inside you, was the most pleasurable experience I've had in over a year."

Shocked, Grace asked, "You saw us?"

"I would have been a fool to interrupt. Your features in the height of pleasure can only be described as exquisite. Eyelashes fluttering upon rosy red cheeks and… your oh-so-plump lips parted and shaped to form an *O*." He shifted his weight and, without hesitation, adjusted his manhood right in front of her. "No one should be denied those heights of pleasure and gratification. Oh no, my dear. That would have left you in a rather foul mood."

Though she was normally slow to anger, Tobias's loathsome statements had Grace's ire blazing. Foul mood indeed. Men and their bloody belief that obtaining climax was the sole purpose of having intimate relations. Bah. It might be the pinnacle of the experience, but certainly not the most pleasurable.

Grace arched her brow sardonically. "I suppose you like to watch."

Tobias chuckled. He finally raised his gaze to meet hers. "Since I do not partake, yes. Albeit not as satisfying, observing does assist in relieving some of the tension."

Grace's pent-up frustrations had hardly been reduced by her interlude with Matthew. In fact, it had fortified and intensified her desires for him.

Refocusing on the man standing before her with a wolfish grin, she asked, "Are you stating the gossip about your debauchery is *all* lies?" She didn't bother to mollify her tone.

"Hmm. I'm not familiar with the nattering that filters through the drawing rooms of my so-called peers. But I can honestly state I've not had the pleasure of a woman's lips"—his gaze narrowed on her mouth—"nor body in fourteen months, sixteen days, and"—he pulled out his pocket watch—"eight hours."

"Impossible!" He was reported to be a frequent patron of Madame Sinclair's establishment.

Tobias leaned back slightly to look out the entrance. "I'd ask Harrington to testify that such self-restraint was possible. However, it appears he has indeed left. If I were a betting man, I'd wager Harrington would be able to quote the exact period of his abstinence down to the minute prior to this evening."

To the minute would have been a feat. Grace was fully aware it had been twenty-three months, three days, and six hours since Matthew had last made love to her, but she could not attest to the minutes.

She shook her head, clearing it of doubts and images that made her ill. "Why are you really here?"

"I already told you—to discuss our wedding." He meandered over to peek through the trellis and then returned to sit next to her at a socially acceptable distance.

It appeared Tobias intended to keep his word and give her the proper respect that was due to her. Never mind that her nightgown was in shatters and her hair was a tangled mess, falling about her shoulders and down her back.

Legs stretched out before him, crossed at the ankles, Tobias said, "Three weeks hence, I shall be aboard the Quarter Moon and headed west for America."

She shouldn't care what was on the other side of the pond that held his interest, but her curiosity got the best of her. "How do you even know if this woman you claim to love remains unwed?" If it had been over a year, there was a possibility this mystery woman might have already married and birthed a child.

"You are not the only one with connections in foreign lands. Friends of Eliza have been providing updates. They do not know the cause, but Eliza has postponed the announcement of her betrothal thrice now. My hypothesis is she is waiting for me to figure out how to escape from the clutches of the devil who sired me."

"Hmmm… How well do you know these *friends* of Elizabeth?"

He pivoted to glare at Grace. "Her name is Eliza." With a sigh, he turned away. "I'm fully aware of the pitfalls of second- and third-hand information. However, like you, I can feel it in my bones. She is waiting for me to act."

Grace shivered, unsettled by the astute observations. Tobias removed his coat and held it out to her. Seeing her dilemma, he said, "Lean forward, and I'll wrap it about you."

She did as he instructed. His thoughtfulness washed away the last lingering traces of anger. "I hope Eliza will acknowledge the risks and appreciate the effort you are about to undertake in order for the both of you to be reunited."

He stood and ran his hand through his hair, giving him a disheveled appearance. It was the first indication that Tobias might have doubts or concerns about his scheme. "There is not much time remaining, and there is still one critical piece outstanding that needs to be resolved in order for my entire plan to succeed." He walked about in a circle and then came to stand before her. "I need your help."

Tobias had either come to trust her or she was his last resort. Either way, she didn't have much of a choice but to aid him. "How am I to assist you?"

"Harrington is in possession of the crown jewels that Burke believes contain an extraordinary item. A desperate man is a dangerous one, and that is what Burke has become. You need to convince Harrington to hand over the jewels to Lord Hadfield."

Grace tilted her chin to her chest and snuggled deeper into Tobias's coat. How peculiar that Matthew had not informed her that the crown jewels remained in his possession. Matthew had asked her to trust him, yet he didn't trust her. Her anger threatened to reemerge.

Tobias's booted footsteps had Grace looking up. He paced in circles.

She said, "*If* Matthew does have the jewels, he more

than likely already has plans in place. The likelihood of accomplishing what you ask of me is remote at best."

"Then we are doomed."

The man was being overdramatic. "Explain to me why the treasure should be handed over to Hadfield. He isn't an agent of either office. Nor is he a member of the Privy Council."

"I suspect you already know the reasoning, and I'm in no position to expound upon the facts. Don't forget you agreed to trust me."

"My memory is not faulty—but I begin to question my judgment." His pacing was making her dizzy. She lowered her gaze to the floor and said, "Anyway, Matthew resigned. He no longer heeds my orders."

Tobias stilled and turned to face her. "That's not the impression I received when I came upon you."

Her thighs pressed together. Blast the man for reminding her of her intimate encounter with Matthew. She shouldn't have fallen into old habits, but she was done waiting for Matthew to act first. Action—that was what was required. She needed to cease reacting and begin instigating her own scheme. First, she required details. "Suppose I was able to convince Matthew to relinquish the jewels. What next?"

"Now that Hereford is entrenched in the court, you will order him to report back with Burke's activities and task Hereford in gaining the ear and trust of the Prince Regent."

"Were you the one responsible for Hereford's appointment? I know it wasn't Archbroke. He would have chosen one of his own agents."

"It is neither here nor there who was responsible for Hereford's appointment. The man is in place; now you need to issue the orders." Tobias tugged at his left sleeve, nearly yanking it out of its seam. As if he was covering something.

"I shall not agree to assist unless I know all."

"Not possible. Convince Harrington to hand over the jewels. Use whatever means necessary…" Tobias's eyes lowered to where his coat had slipped open. "Harrington did appear rather partial to those lovelies. And don't forget to issue the orders to Hereford." Chuckling, he left the gazebo without another word.

Tobias was a conundrum. She stood and exited her sanctuary, ready to return to her chambers. Flanked by two footmen, Grace returned to the house. As she crossed the threshold into the kitchens, she froze at the sight of her papa seated at the kitchen table.

"Papa, why are you down here alone?"

He drummed his fingers on the wood. "Merely waiting for you to return."

"It's late. I'll assist you back to your rooms." She placed a hand on his shoulder, which was hard and tense.

Clear, all-knowing eyes looked up at her. "Not before you tell me the outcome of your meetings with Harrington and Ellingsworth."

Good lord, she'd have to be more circumspect. If Burke were to hear gossip, it would place everyone in jeopardy. Grace took a seat on the bench opposite her papa and laced her hands on the tabletop. "They both share the same objective, to be rid of Lord Burke…"

"And to see to it that you are compromised." His eyebrows were knitted severely.

"What?"

"Child. Your gown is ripped, and you are wearing Ellingsworth's coat. Which of those two scoundrels shall I be calling out to meet me at dawn?"

"Neither. You said it was your wish for me to marry

Harrington and for me to aid Ellingsworth, and I intend to do both."

"How do you mean to go about that?"

Her half-formulated ideas hardly constitute a scheme that would pass muster with her papa, but it was all she had at the moment. "I have a plan."

Her papa raised both eyebrows and resumed drumming his fingers.

She'd simply have to be brief and to the point. "I'm going to convince Matthew to hand over the crown jewels to Hadfield."

"How?"

"By telling him to do the honorable thing and marry me. But in order to do that, he needs to relinquish the treasure."

"Your scheme has more holes than cheesecloth."

That was not the response she was anticipating. She had basically confessed to having been compromised by Matthew, and all her papa could speak of was cheesecloth. Her head rolled forward. It wasn't a precise strategy, but with a few hours of thought, she'd figure it all out. On a sigh, Grace said, "If you return to your chambers, I will adjourn to the study and work on the finer points of my plan."

He patted her hands. "I assume you will be holed up for hours. I'll have your mama take me for my early-morning walk." The bench scraped against the floor as he rose, and he placed a kiss upon the top of her head. "I have faith in you, Gracie girl. All shall work out."

CHAPTER SIXTEEN

*T*hree damn days.

It wasn't by far the longest span of time he'd spent apart from Grace, yet the past seventy-plus hours had been a living hell for Matthew. He wavered between hope for a future with the woman he would love until his last breath and fear that she would discover he was no longer the man she once loved. She deserved more than the skeleton of a man he had become. It had been a mistake to take Grace into his arms again. Her moans of delight, her soft body rocking against his, reminded him of how it used to be. No, not a mistake. He'd been transported back in time to the period in his life when everything made sense and wasn't filled with dark, terrifying moments.

"I see you've started drinking without me." Blake strolled into the study. "You're not still dwelling over Grace's most recent note, are you?" He grabbed the empty glass from Matthew's hands and walked toward the sidebar, which now housed a half-empty decanter of brandy.

Bending to rest his forearms on his knees, Matthew

clasped his empty hands firmly together. If not, they would no doubt begin to shake. "I fully understand the risks if we were to be caught together, but to have all communications be routed through Theo is rather extreme."

"I disagree. For your scheme to succeed, we must take all the necessary precautions to ensure Burke is blissfully unaware of your intentions."

His sanity remained barely intact. The knowledge that Grace still desired him and was close in proximity but far from accessible these past few days had his mind volleying between the idea of kidnapping her and leaving for Gretna Green to be married or murdering Burke and dashing off to America to start a new life together. If he didn't see Grace soon, he'd inevitably end up in an asylum.

Blake handed him a tumbler that held a finger of brandy in it. Damn. He needed more than a meager finger of brandy this evening, but as it had always been between them, Blake was the levelheaded one.

Settling into the chair next to Matthew, Blake took a sip of his drink before continuing, "I had the jewels inspected by Rutherford."

Matthew sat back and turned to face him. "And?" After waiting for days for Blake to come clean with the information, Matthew was impatient to hear the results.

Blake's features remained neutral. "The jeweler found nothing out of the ordinary."

Damnation. Matthew had believed Baldwin's theory that while the crown jewels were extremely valuable, the king used them to hide the PORF rondure. The coin that crowned its holder as the leader of all PORFs and their supporting network.

Matthew shot to his feet. "Do you believe him? Could he be lying?"

"Of course, I trust the old man. What has Rutherford

to gain by lying? You're searching into matters that have been well left alone by others for generations. My advice is to cease looking into stories told in the nursery and focus on ensuring Burke hangs for his misdeeds."

Matthew slumped back into his chair. Blake didn't understand the importance of the coin. If he'd located the rondure, it would have justified his actions—leaving Grace, causing his peers to have suffered alongside him, and the months of agony spent in the dark.

Glancing at his pocket watch, Blake said, "It's time we set off."

"Where are we going?" Matthew trusted Blake, but it was challenging to extract details from the man.

They both meandered over to the sideboard. Blake left his glass that still contained a half finger of brandy next to Matthew's empty tumbler. Shame to let the liquor go to waste, not that the sentiment had ever occurred to him before his captivity.

Opening the door to leave, Blake answered, "Not far from here."

Matthew brooded in silence as the coach continued to rattle over the cobbled street. He glanced at his best friend, who was capable of capturing every little detail of his surroundings and those around him. Blake always appeared relaxed and sedate, but tonight the crinkle at the edges of his eyes told Matthew he was watching out for danger. The carriage came to a stop, and Blake alighted first.

Women in sparkling gowns, some the latest fashion and others more modest, milled about. They were at Covenant Gardens. A gaggle of ladies followed by their escorts strode by, oblivious to their surroundings. The ladies were easy prey for those who might have nefarious intentions. The dandies were absorbed in themselves and their conversation; it rendered them useless should one of the ladies be snatched for a sum.

Matthew followed Blake as he eased his way into the crowd. A bead of sweat rolled down Matthew's neck. Crowds had never made him uneasy before, but after months of solitude, the stench of body odor, the constant rustling of skirts, and the click-clack of canes hitting the path before them had him longing to retreat to his townhouse. He was still discovering the full effects of having been isolated, starved, and beaten for months.

Blake tugged him into the shadows. "Easy. Take a deep breath."

Matthew did as he was told, staring at a nearby gas lamp that provided limited illumination but a source of light, nonetheless. He'd not been bothered by the darkness the other night as he ventured to visit Grace, but then he was aware that the woman was awaiting him. The scent of lilacs filtered through the garden, settling his nerves. She wasn't here tonight. No doubt Grace was at home, preparing for the annual Fairmont ball. His muscles tensed. She would be attending the event on the arm of her fiancé.

As if he had conjured up the man, Ellingsworth appeared before them. "Evening to you both." Grace's betrothed turned to Blake. "I assume you have what I requested. No time to dawdle. Grace awaits my escort this eve."

Both Matthew and Blake had yet to determine why Ellingsworth had requested sketches of certain foreign diplomats and officials. None of them were known to have had dealings with Burke.

Blake reached into his coat and retrieved the drawings. "I've not seen these men in quite some time. They may have altered their appearance since I last saw them."

"Did you share the list of individuals with your superior?" Ellingsworth eyed the papers but did not reach for them.

"I haven't. Have you?" Blake asked.

Ellingsworth smirked. "I share all pertinent information with Grace. After all, one shouldn't start a life together having secrets. Wouldn't you agree, Devonton?"

Blake shoved the papers into Ellingsworth's chest. "Have a wonderful eve at the Fairmont ball."

Matthew had bristled at Ellingsworth's informal reference to Grace. But it was Blake's reaction that had Matthew clenching his hands by his side. It wouldn't be the first time Matthew threw a punch on behalf of his best friend. Most were naturally intimidated by Blake's size, but the man was extremely slow to anger, and Matthew was a willing defender.

"My thanks." Ellingsworth caught the rolled-up parchment and slipped it into his coat's inner pocket. Shifting his gaze between Matthew and Blake, Ellingsworth asked, "Will you be attending?"

Blake remained stock-still as Matthew narrowed his gaze and shook his head.

With a tip of his hat, Ellingsworth said, "Shame. I'm sure Grace would have preferred to have as many of her loyal *friends* as possible in attendance tonight. Seeing it is our first public appearance together."

If Lucy were in town, she would have made sure Matthew attended. But his sister wasn't here to meddle. Given a choice between spending an evening alone in his study or being subjected to the playacting of the happily betrothed couple, the decision was simple. He would seek solace in a drink or two under his own roof. Playacting or not, Matthew didn't care to see Grace on the arm of another man. *If you hadn't gotten yourself imprisoned, she wouldn't be in this predicament.* A pang of guilt nearly had him changing his mind. No. He'd promised Grace to trust her and to stay away until it was safe for them to be together. The agony of not knowing exactly when that day or time was had Matthew focusing on his scheme to reveal Burke for the conniving, double-crossing devil he was.

Matthew found his voice as Ellingsworth turned to leave. "I believe Grace will have the support of Theo and Mary this eve."

An inch away from Matthew, Ellingsworth stopped and replied, "Ah, yes, the lovely Countess Archbroke and Countess Waterford. Both extremely unique women." He leaned in a tad closer and whispered, "She needs you." Ellingsworth's shoulder bumped Matthew's as he left without another word.

Blake's hand landed squarely on Matthew's shoulder, preventing him from going after Ellingsworth and demanding the obtuse man explain his meaning. What the devil did Grace need him for? *Damn. Damn. Damn.* He couldn't merely ignore the man's statement. But to go to the Fairmont ball and have Grace within sight would be the ultimate test of what remaining willpower he had left.

Having read Matthew's thoughts Blake asked, "Do you need me to accompany you?"

Not surprised at his best friend's offer to endure the extravagant affair, Matthew answered, "No. I shall remain in the shadows this eve."

Images of Grace dressed in an elegant ball gown, hair neatly set in her signature style that was sophisticated and simultaneously fashionable, increased Matthew's anxiety. Without question, she'd be the most beautiful woman present tonight.

Blake patted Matthew solidly on the back. "See that you do. Burke has eyes and ears everywhere."

The reminder that Grace was inherently in danger because of his actions sobered Matthew. His plan for the evening was simple. All he had to do was rein in his desires, shut out fond memories of his time with Grace at the event, and maintain a safe distance. *Keep her safe.* It became his mental mantra as he made his way home to change. It was the very least he could do for the woman who saved his life—both mentally and physically.

CHAPTER SEVENTEEN

*T*obias patted Grace's gloved hand that rested lightly upon his forearm. She should have never agreed to this charade. He'd found her hiding, seated next to her Aunt Emily in the parlor. After seeking permission from Aunt Emily to whisk her away for a dance, Tobias led her through the throng of guests toward the main ballroom. She hadn't been this nervous at a ball in years. Then again, she had not attended one since Matthew's disappearance. Guilt at having declined her dear friend the Duchess of Fairmont's invitation two seasons in a row gnawed at Grace's conscience.

"The duchess seemed genuinely pleased to see you," Tobias said as they stalled behind an older couple.

Staring directly in front of her at the lady's elaborately tied bow in the center of the woman's back, Grace admitted, "I've been rather remiss as a friend."

"The Duchess of Fairmont is lucky. I suspect you don't refer to many as friends."

Grace glanced up at her betrothed. Tobias continued

to surprise her with his observations. She detested surprises. "What led you to that conclusion, my lord?"

"You have many supporters, but you consider very few more than an acquaintance. Those you call friends have known you for many years, with perhaps the exception of Lady Theo. But she is like you in temperament, so it stands to reason the pair of you would come to trust each other relatively fast. Am I wrong?"

The man everyone believed a dullard was absolutely on point. When she was younger, her mama called her shy and reserved. She worked hard to appear sociable, but it required a significant amount of effort, and Grace sorely lacked the necessary energy to continue the farce.

"I'll take your silence as an admission I am correct and that I'm right in stating that you draw strength from those you trust." Tobias glanced about the crowd. "I see Lady Mary and her husband by the terrace. Shall we join them?"

His altruistic behavior was unsettling. It was hard to believe that Tobias was sired by the detestable Lord Burke. While he was right that it would be comforting to have friends close by, she didn't want to appear needy or burden them with her sour mood. "I thought you wanted to dance."

"I do, and we shall." He rubbed a thumb over the top of her hand and bent to whisper, "I apologize for the strain our engagement is causing you. Rest assured, my tender feelings will not be offended if you pretend I'm someone else tonight."

His sincere apology prompted Grace to confess, "I'd prefer to dance rather than stand about tonight. And imagining you to be another will not ease my stress."

"I gathered as much." Tobias continued to edge his way toward the ballroom.

Their progress was slow. Grace continued to scan the crush of guests, eager to catch a glimpse of Theo. She could only hope Theo had a new message for her from Matthew. But with each step Grace took, doubts plagued her thoughts. Her last message to Matthew was to inform him that she still had no specifics as to how or when Tobias intended Burke to meet his maker. Her desperation to be useful and provide the information needed tore at her confidence to succeed. Grace wasn't about to give up. The key was to gain Tobias's trust, but the man was obstinately guarded with her. She flickered a glance up at him as his muscles flexed beneath her hand. She smiled at the gaggle of guests as they passed, none of whom she would believe would give him pause, but his features had taken on an edge that he usually hid with ease. As they continued on, he returned eager smiles. He acknowledged the congratulatory comments of guests with a nod or two, but the muscles beneath her fingers remained taut and strained.

Frustrated, she was unable to interrupt his features. Grace dug her fingers into his arm.

He bent his head toward her and asked, "Is anything the matter?"

"You tell me."

He shrugged and pulled on the cuff of his exquisitely tailored jacket, repeating the agitated movement from the night of their engagement dinner. Tobias was hiding something that resided on the tender side of his wrist. If he was a PORF, as Matthew suspected, was it the mark of a PORF that had him tugging on his coat sleeve?

Grace lifted an eyebrow in question. When he didn't answer, she followed Tobias's lead and curled her lips into a smile and nodded to well-wishers as they entered through the wide double doors through to the grand ballroom. Except her smile faltered as all eyes in the room turned to fall upon them. She squared her shoulders and met the stares of the guests. Scanning the room, Grace searched for a pair of stunning emerald eyes that belonged to Theo. Instead of finding her friend, her gaze locked with the Prince Regent, who now stood glaring at her... Or was Prinny staring at her betrothed?

Grace turned to face Tobias. The constant befuddled frown that graced his brow should have made her cringe. But knowing the man was merely role-playing, Grace's lips curved into a genuine smile.

Tobias looked down at her as if she were the most interesting woman in the crowd. "Prinny wants the jewels returned. Have you convinced Harrington?"

Grace, in turn, gave him the most ludicrous besotted smile. "I've not had an opportunity to speak with him about the matter. Not to worry. I'll see to it."

"Is that so?" Tobias cocked his head to one side.

Fluttering her eyes, Grace answered, "Perhaps I'll find him in attendance tonight."

"I'm saddened to inform you he is not coming." Tobias shifted to shield her from the crowd as patrons jostled about in the cramped space.

It was a good thing she momentarily occupied the space in his shadow, for it took every ounce of self-control for Grace to mask her surprise. "Did Matthew inform you himself?"

"He did."

A stab of jealousy that Matthew had not cared to share this information with her first left Grace standing mute. How could this be? She tried to picture the two of them relaxing and having a drink at one of the clubs. Impossible. None of her reports indicated Tobias ever ventured to Brooks's or White's. On the contrary, his favored haunt was purported to be questionable hells.

Grace stiffened as she recognized the male voice that had Tobias swiveling to his right.

Her betrothed let out a loud, obnoxious chuckle. "Lady Grace, it's my honor to introduce to you my good friend, Wilbert Graystone."

Tobias shifted slightly to his left, revealing the dashing Home Office messenger, Mr. Jones, her stepbrother, whom Grace's parents called Alex.

"Lady Grace, might I say you look divine this evening." Alex unfolded from a graceful bow.

It was a rare occasion that her brother emerged from the shadows. Grace weighed the advantages and disadvantages of confronting Alex in full sight of the ton and then said, "How rude of me to stare. But you share a remarkable resemblance to a man that I know, that goes by the name of Alex. You wouldn't happen to have a brother by that name, would you?"

Both Tobias and Alex stiffened, and then both laughed with a little extra exuberance.

Alex said, "I'm sorry to inform you, Lady Grace, but I'm an only child."

She sneaked a glance at Tobias. Her betrothed momentarily dropped his facade as a dullard. There were ladies of her acquaintance who would certainly consider him dashing when his true colors shone through. Grace smirked and turned her attention back to Alex. "I too was raised as an only child."

Her brother slapped Tobias on the back. "It's a pleasure to meet the woman who managed to ensnare this wily fellow."

Oh, she wasn't about to let the man off the hook that easy. "Mr. Graystone, do you dance?"

Grace waited for her brother to catch on.

Alex frowned but presented his hand at the ready to

escort her to the dance floor. He maneuvered them through the crowd in a similar fashion as Matthew used to, anticipating the ebb and flow, ensuring her toes were safe from the masses.

Grace pulled back as she caught sight of Theo huddled with Mary and Waterford standing by the entrance. Where was Archbroke? Scanning the room, there was no sign of the Home Office secretary. Turning back to the spot where she had left Tobias, Grace inhaled a sharp breath.

Tobias was headed for the doors with Hadfield and Archbroke following close on his heels. It was apparent a meeting of PORFs was to occur. Grace would have to hunt Theo down as soon as she was done dealing with her sibling.

Alex squeezed her hand as he took his position opposite her.

The reel began, and as she circled Alex, she asked, "Why the frown, brother?"

"Who informed you?" Alex's smile was in stark contrast to his sharp tone.

They parted, and Grace's gaze was once more drawn to Mary and Waterford, who had moved to the refreshments table. Where was Theo? How irresponsible of Archbroke to leave his wife without protection. Grace twisted and turned, searching the room for a glimpse of emerald-green silk.

Alex came into focus and asked, "How did you discover my identity?"

"It was by pure happenstance." Grace smiled as they came to stand face-to-face. "Did you not want a sister? Is that why you never…"

Alex stepped around Grace, executing the steps with a fluidity that again reminded Grace of Matthew. Except it wasn't Matthew's whispers of love she heard; it was Alex's dire tone. "I know what I am and my place. I'll forever be grateful for your mama's generosity, but you are not my family."

Grace answered, "We share Papa's blood. How can you deny we are related? I don't understand…"

"Everything is as it should be." Before they parted once more, Alex said, "Thank goodness our papa has no concern for social conventions and has permitted you… to, well… you know."

Grace quickly replied, "Yes, I too am grateful he sees no reason for me not to assist him. However, I'd have loved the opportunity to know my brother. We *are* family."

Alex weaved his way back to her. "You are like your mama, not caring a wit about what others might think should you claim me as family. But I have not changed my stance. It would do more harm than good. Your mama has respected my choice for years. I hope you will do the same."

Unwilling to accept his rejection, Grace managed to ask, "You have no room in your life, in your heart, for a sister?"

Alex adopted a grin that their papa donned whenever he was about to put Grace into checkmate. "While you may not have known about me, I've been fully aware of who you are in relation to me. I've always looked up to my big sister and will continue to do so from afar."

Grace had longed for a sibling. Had begged her mama for years until she understood the toll all the miscarriages were taking on her poor mama's body and soul.

The music ceased, and the reel came to an end. Grace dipped into a curtsy and asked, "Why?"

"Not for the reasons you might think. I choose this life-style. Changing identities. Helping others. Being close enough to keep an eye on those I do care for. But after my time on the Continent… I wish for more freedom."

Grace's hopes perked up as she rose and took Alex's offered hand. "If you work alongside me and not for Archbroke, then…"

"No." Alex looked her in the eyes. "That is not the plan."

"Whose plan?"

Alex escorted her from the dance floor as the strains of a waltz began. "Ellingsworth's, of course. I trust you have convinced Harrington to part with his bounty from the Continent."

How is it her brother was privy to Tobias's plan while she was not?

While Tobias hadn't done anything to lose her trust, Grace had the feeling her betrothed wasn't one hundred percent truthful with her.

Grace sidestepped past another guest and whispered, "Not yet."

Alex paused to let a group of revelers past. "You must not dawdle. Time is of the essence."

She bristled at Alex's tone. "I'm fully aware."

"Are you?" He glanced about. "I was going to inform Ellingsworth that Captain Bane has forecasted a change in the schedule. He now intends to set sail early, well before the date arranged for your ceremony. If you do not succeed soon, Ellingsworth will take matters into his own hands, taking whatever action necessary in order for him to board that ship."

Her mind latched on to Alex's last statement. If matters were not being dictated by Tobias, then who was really orchestrating the entire scheme?

Grace retrieved her fan from her reticle and, with one quick flick of the wrist, spread it open and raised it to partially hide her face. "What do you know about Lord Ellingsworth's Miss Eliza?"

Rolling his eyes, Alex answered, "Not much. Although the man is obsessed with her and will do pretty much anything in order to get to her in time." His words were uttered with a mixture of abhorrence and wonderment as if he didn't believe love should drive a man to desperate measures. It was apparent her brother had yet to experience true love.

She snapped her fan closed. "Do you intend to accompany Lord Ellingsworth?"

"What gave you that idea?"

Grace could read Alex's features as if he were an open book. Suspicion as to how she had guessed his intentions narrowed his gaze and caused a muscle in his jaw to twitch as he clenched it tight. It wasn't clever deduction but common sense that he would seek out a new life after his harrowing experience on the Continent. New beginnings in a land where people are not bound by the same social strictures. A place Alex could reinvent himself and choose who and what he became.

Grace blinked, and Alex came back into focus. "It's what I'd do if I wanted to be free."

Alex's features darkened. "In my experience, men are willing to go to extraordinary lengths for their freedom."

"You are no longer referring to Lord Ellingsworth, are you?"

Shaking his head, Alex said, "You are the sole reason why he survived. Why we were rescued. But if it were not for his actions, I'd not have survived long enough to be rescued."

The distant look in Alex's eyes broke Grace's heart. Blast Archbroke for sending an all-too-young Alex after Matthew.

Head bowed, Alex said, "Harrington claims it was entirely his fault that we all found ourselves at the mercy of Burke's henchmen. Regardless of the events that led up to our captivity, it isn't Harrington who should carry the burden. Harrington is better than a saint if there is such a thing. He launched himself at our captor's time and time again when the brutes landed a hand on Hereford or me and even when they touched the weasel, Addington. He took the brunt of the beatings. Most days, he was half-unconscious, and all he spoke of was you. His guardian angel. His partner for life. His reason for breathing. He promised daily that he'd get us all freed, and once we returned, he'd destroy Burke."

Tears welled in her eyes. Grace's attempts to obtain the gruesome details of the men's captivity had been futile. Hereford's report consisted of a mere ten words. *I pledged an oath not to speak of the events.* She was aware it had not been pleasant and not at all surprised to discover Matthew believed it was all his doing. Burke didn't deserve a trial. No, the devil should be drawn and quartered. Even that was too humane for the likes of him.

A younger version of Burke appeared behind Alex. Tobias announced, "I believe it's time I danced with my delightful fiancé."

Tobias's likeness of his sire had Grace wanting to strangle the smug smile off her betrothed's face. Calmly she placed a hand on Tobias's arm. As she walked past her brother, she said, "You shall not leave without allowing Papa to say goodbye."

Alex acknowledged her order with a curt nod.

"I believe the others are awaiting you by the terrace doors," Tobias said to Alex. He then covered Grace's hand with his own and swung her in the opposite direction, away from Alex and her friends. In an unusually harsh tone,

Tobias said, "Balls are for dancing and frivolity, not discussions that cause grown men nightmares."

A few feet away from the dance floor, Grace turned to look over her shoulder. Her nose twitched. Matthew was somewhere close by.

"I see I've lost your attention." Tobias shortened his stride.

Grace whispered, "He's here."

"Who?"

She waggled her eyebrows at Tobias. A scandalous action if seen by others, but Grace dared not mention Matthew's name.

They both scanned the room. From the corner of his mouth, Tobias asked, "Did you see him?"

"I didn't. I just know." Her pulse became erratic. She could feel Lord Burke's eyes trailing them. "Burke is watching."

"Seems the habit runs in the family." With a smirk, he raised his voice slightly and said, "Well, my dear, you do look a tad overheated. Perhaps a stroll along the terrace."

Grace tugged on his arm to change directions. "I believe I'm merely parched. Please escort me to the refreshments table."

Assuming the befuddled look once more, Tobias outrageously said, "Yes, a drink is exactly what we all need." The man added a wink and a blatant stare at her décolletage. Onlookers gasped at Tobias's statement and actions. But they quickly returned to their own conversations as Grace and Tobias meandered their way through the crush of guests.

CHAPTER EIGHTEEN

*L*ady Mary and Waterford stood in front of Matthew, providing a mediocre barricade from the crush of the crowd. For the second time that night, he broke out in a cold sweat as the guests threatened to descend upon him. Matthew tugged on Theo's elbow and pulled her aside. He peered through the small gap between Lady Mary and Waterford. "She is headed for the refreshments table."

"Why did they not go out to the gardens?" Theo went on her tiptoes to peer over Mary's shoulder.

Matthew placed a hand on Theo's shoulder, urging her to shrink back down. "Just go give her the message."

"No need to get snippy with me." Theo slapped his hand away. "You want me to say *lilacs are my favorite*. Are you certain she will understand my meaning?"

Theo's dubious looks reminded him of happier days when they would play pranks on each other as children which continued well into early adulthood. "Yes, now go." He prayed Grace would remember that he had made the claim moments before their first kiss in an alcove not far from the main ballroom and meet him there.

Leveling her eyes on him, Theo said, "I'm a terrible liar. Everyone knows that!"

It was the truth. Theo was a terrible fibber and always had been. Matthew sighed. "Do your best." He gave Theo a reassuring squeeeze and assisted her up. Rolling his left shoulder, which easily fell out of its socket, Matthew whispered, "Waterford, I'll meet you at the docks at first light."

Waterford's back stiffened and shifted to allow Theo to squeeze through to stand in front. Waterford said, "*We* will be there."

Matthew glanced at Lady Mary. The woman had always been the oddly quiet one, muttering to herself in the shadows. He shifted and whispered, "The docks aren't safe."

"Captain Bane, like all good seaworthy men, has a healthy respect for superstitions and the like. He's more likely to heed Mary's advice than if the recommendation comes from either of us." Waterford's chest expanded forward, like a peacock showing off its pretty feathers, a sign of pride. The man was proud of his lady wife and her purported ability to speak to and hear the dead. Grace had stated upon their first meeting with Lady Mary that the woman possessed an extraordinary gift, but at the time, Matthew didn't believe in spirits. His views changed after spending months in the dark upon the land that had seen bloodshed during the most terrifying years of the Peninsula War.

Twisted at the waist, Theo said, "See to it that Captain Bane ceases all talk of setting sail early."

Matthew stared at Theo's back as she set off to deliver his message. The girl he had grown up alongside who wore pigtails and breeches daily had become the sophisticated, trailblazing woman who parted the crowd naturally as if she were the queen. Matthew frowned and spun on his heel to make his way to meet Grace. He had missed much while being held captive—Theo's transformation, Lucy's wedding, and Edward, his little brother's, first year away at Eton. All for nothing. He had failed in locating the rondure. Was seeing Burke tried and hung for treason enough to atone for his mistakes? It would have to be, for he had no clue of how else to apologize to everyone for his rash decision to leave for the Continent.

As he fell back into the shadows to track Theo's progress. Matthew blinked and blinked again. Lady Mary and Waterford trailed Theo in a distinctly protective manner. As they approached Grace and Ellingsworth, the couple separated to stand on each side of Theo. Ellingsworth's covert nods to each were followed by a deep bow as if Theo were royalty. The voice of Theo's deceased brother, Baldwin, filtered through Matthew's thoughts: *PORFs remain on equal footing unless the rondure is discovered. The holder of the coin wields enormous power.* Did Theo have the treasure he had risked everything for in her possession?

Theo flung her arms about Grace in an exuberant hug, then paused a brief moment as Grace's shoulders stiffened. His message had been delivered.

A tap on his shoulder had Matthew grabbing and twisting a delicate wrist.

"Ow." The Duchess of Fairmont muttered, "I should have known better than to sneak up on an agent."

Matthew released his hostess and said, "My apologizes, Your Grace."

"As I said, it's my own fault." She grabbed him by the chin and turned his face to inspect both sides. "Good to see they didn't mar your fine looks too bad, but it is the scars we can't see that worry Grace the most."

Matthew stood mute. He hadn't known that the duchess and Grace were well acquainted.

"Oh, I know all about your *meetings* in my hothouse. Did you really believe I was unaware of what occurred under this roof? I convinced the duke it was all for the good of the Crown, assisting interdepartmental affairs and all." She released his face and said, "When you left, I invited Grace to visit—often. She spent hours in the hothouse, muttering to herself. Her visits ceased the day you returned, but she surprised me with a visit yesterday. She claimed to have missed me. While her reasoning was probably partially true, it was not the primary motive for her return. I convinced her to stay for tea, and we had a lovely chat."

Good Lord, he had put Grace through the wringer with his departure. He was not deserving of her love or loyalty. Deserving or not, he was going to marry her *if* she would have him.

He glanced behind him, relieved to see Grace was still conversing with Theo. "Your Grace, I do appreciate—"

"We are not done. Don't worry. My eyesight is excellent, and as soon as Grace leaves the group, I'll release you, but until then, I have a mind to..." Her hands were balled at her sides, and he could hear her unspoken words, *knock some sense into you.*

"I can't turn back time. I can assure you that I intend to make things right for all."

The duchess nodded. "One more thing. After a few bottles of brandy, my dear husband succeeded in obtaining confirmation that the rumors were true. Burke has plans in place for Grace to come to an untimely death after his son consummates the marriage." With a swirl of skirts, his hostess disappeared into the throng of guests.

Burke's devious plan for Grace wasn't new information.

It was reassuring to know that Grace had the backing of some of the most powerful men and women in England, even if she wasn't aware of the amount of support she had garnered over the years.

Sliding into the alcove where he was to await Grace, Matthew ensured the curtain and the potted plant sufficiently hid the entrance to the small space. Darkness fell around him, and he found himself struggling for breath. His lungs ceased to spasm as soon as he caught the familiar scent of lilac about him. Closing his eyes, he inhaled deeply. He was safe, standing in the alcove where he and Grace had shared their first kiss.

Running his tongue over his lips, the memory of her soft, warm, buttery mouth against his caused his breath to hitch once more. He pictured Grace, eyes fluttering closed as he brushed his lips over hers until she opened for him. Her tentative responses were quickly replaced with eager openmouthed kisses that had left him feeling like the inexperienced one. His hands had roamed over her back and lowered to cup her pert bottom. Grace's sweet sighs had his breeches uncomfortably tight then—and now.

The strong scent of lilac filled his nose as lush lips pressed against his. This was no dream. There was indeed a warm, inviting woman in his arms kissing him passionately. Matthew slowly opened his eyes. A wave of relief washed over him to find that he had not lost his mind and that Grace was real in his embrace. A countless number of times, he'd lain beaten and bruised on a dirt floor, dreaming of Grace kissing him, riding him, writhing beneath him, fantasies so vivid he'd believed she was actually there. But none of those images compared to what he was experiencing now. The gentle strokes of her tongue against his, her fingertips kneading the back of his neck, the purring moans were all real.

Matthew pulled back. Candlelight peeked through the limbs of the potted plant that now only partially concealed the entrance to the alcove. Glassy-eyed, Grace looked back at him. She didn't have to say the words. He could read them in her face. She was still in love with him, despite everything that had occurred.

She whispered, "I've much to share with you."

"And I with you." He leaned his head back against the wall. "I had the crown jewels inspected."

"Why?"

She hadn't even blinked twice at the revelation the jewels remained in his possession.

Matthew answered, "Theo's brother, Baldwin, had believed our beloved King George hid the PORF rondure among the treasure and had it buried. I suspect Burke discovered this information and…"

Her already dilated eyes widened. "You believe Baldwin was killed. Orchestrated by Burke. You left in search of the coin." She sagged against him and then straightened, pressing clenched fists against his chest. "I don't understand your obsession with these legends. What good can come of finding out their secrets?"

He searched his mind for the words to explain his irrational and all-consuming need to prove the existence of PORFs and their network.

Grace cupped his face and searched his features. "You want to be a part of a legend." Her hand dropped back to his chest. "Don't you understand you are already a major asset to the Crown and its activities? You are already needed, wanted, respected…"

"It's not the same. The network is like a family, bonded by an oath passed down for generations."

Grace smiled, "I understand what it is like to want a family, the desire to belong and contribute to the greater good, but I also recognize what I have already been gifted with." She kissed him and then said, "You must return the crown jewels to Archbroke. They are key to Tobias's scheme."

"I can't do that. They are vital to *my* plans." Grace raised a finger and placed it over his lips.

Ellingsworth's hoarse whisper filled with anger filtered through the curtain from the other side, "She must be here somewhere. Find her."

Grace pushed away and said, "If you wish to marry me, you will return the treasure to Archbroke posthaste." She whirled out of the alcove, out of his reach.

Damnation. He wouldn't be forced to choose between the woman he loved and revenge—he'd have both. He simply had to figure out how.

CHAPTER NINETEEN

*F*ingertips pressed to his temples; Matthew stared at his desk. It was a disaster, with correspondence from Lucy, maps, sketches, and notes in random piles. His life was a mess without Grace.

Nine days had passed since his interlude with Grace at the Fairmont ball. Nine social events he had attended in secret—hiding in the shadows, watching Grace and Ellingsworth fawn over each other, waiting for a signal or a message from the woman he loved. But she had ignored his pleas to meet. Each day he received a missive passed along by Theo that contained the same message. *Return the crown jewels and make me the happiest woman in all London.*

How could she place her trust in Ellingsworth's scheme over Matthew's? Night after night, he wrestled with her decision to continue with the sham engagement and demand he relinquish the jewels. The deep cut of betrayal played havoc with his mind. If Grace hadn't daily sent coded messages stating she still loved him, he would have given up all hope of a happy ending for them both.

His meeting with Captain Bane had been the only

successful event since the damn ball. Thankfully, Waterford had the right of things. Captain Bane had delayed his departure date ten days after hearing Mary's dire warnings of disaster if he was to set sail. Ellingsworth had obtained a common license and announced the official date of the wedding in the papers. It was no coincidence the date corresponded with the Quarter Moon's departure.

Matthew had run out of time—the ship was to set sail tomorrow, and the wedding was set for midday. Burke remained hale and hearty, so either Ellingsworth's scheme had failed, or the man never intended to see the devil dead. Matthew's only option was to enact his plan early.

A dark silhouette fell across his desk. Matthew glanced up to find Blake running his hand through his disheveled hair.

"I received a letter from *your wife* today." Matthew waved the missive in the air. "I can't believe Lucy would suggest we leave it to the others to deal with Burke."

"*Your sister* is a wise woman, and you should seriously consider Lucy's advice." Blake sighed, sinking into the chair opposite Matthew.

Blake's forehead was etched with new worry lines. Each day his friend spent away from Lucy and the twins another line appeared. Two more days, then Blake would leave for Shalford Castle. Matthew would miss his friend's companionship and support. Blake's subtle but frank advice was invaluable to his slow but steady mental recovery. The dizzy spells, the black moments, and the tremors hadn't ceased, but after a week spent in Blake's company, Matthew had come to understand these physical afflictions would ease with time. If he was to fully recover, he needed to cease ignoring his demons. He needed to be the man he once was, both inside and out—strong and confident. Most of all, he wanted to be the man Grace had fallen in love with, not this damaged version who struggled to remain still while his valet tied his cravat.

Matthew shuffled the mounds of papers about until he had a clear view of Blake. "Burke's activities went on unprohibited for years. Why should I place my faith in them to deal with the man now?"

"I suspect the rondure is currently in either Hadfield or Archbroke's possession. My guess is Hadfield's, but I can't be certain. The strong alliance and family bonds they share through Theo will ensure they are in agreement with whatever action will be taken."

Matthew's hands returned to the sides of his head. "Regardless, if family ties exist or not, the bearer of the coin holds ultimate power. If it is Archbroke, his actions will be swift. If perchance it is Hadfield, I'm uncertain he will take action. I can't risk this opportunity. Burke must pay."

"Everything has been arranged as you requested for this evening." Blake placed his left hand on his right shoulder and rolled it back and forth. "I shall accompany you."

"What is wrong with your arm? Are you hurt?"

Blake's broad smile at his sequential questions, made Matthew shift in his seat. While some of his irritating habits from the past might have returned, it was by no means indicative that he had resumed his prior preference for diplomacy over retaliation.

"I'm perfectly well, merely eager to return to Shalford Castle and slumber in my own bed which accommodates a man of my size." Blake rose and headed for the sideboard. A drink was exactly what they both needed.

Matthew clasped his hands behind his head and leaned back in his chair. "If my conversations go to plan this eve, then you should be home within a few days. I'm assuming you will stay for the wedding tomorrow and act as a witness." Letting his eyes close, he pictured Grace in a simple but elegant gown of forest green silk with little embroidered pink roses, walking down the aisle of the chapel with a broad, eager smile.

At the sound of glass hitting wood, Matthew sat up as he searched for his tumbler. Damn Blake and his tiny splashes of the amber liquid. He swirled the brandy around and around. Matthew paused and stared at his glass. When had he ceased the habit of consuming the liquor as soon as it was within his reach?

Blake was standing with an empty glass in hand. Something was setting his best friend on edge—but what?

With his back to Matthew, Blake said, "Do I need to remind you of the conditions Grace set for the happy occasion?" Blake turned. Holding up the decanter and waving it about as he added, "And you are mad if you believe for one moment I'd let you go alone tonight."

Earlier in the week, Matthew had met with his lawyers and arranged for a large settlement from his estate be settled upon Grace should anything dire occur. The sum was large enough to ensure Grace had the freedom to choose to wed or not.

Matthew said, "Promise me, if anything should go awry, you will follow through with the rest of my plan."

Blake returned with a full glass of brandy and placed it upon a stack of papers. He leaned forward and placed both palms flat on the desk. Eye to eye with Matthew, Blake said, "I'll make no such guarantee. Lucy would have my head. I'm going with you, and there is nothing you can do or say to stop me."

Unblinking, Matthew replied, "The instructions were for Burke to arrive alone, and I will do likewise."

"I don't trust him to follow through with his word."

Picking up his drink, Blake settled back into his chair. "I have a terrible feeling about tonight's events, and Lucy is rarely ever wrong. We should heed *my wife's* advice."

No one was going to deny him his revenge. Matthew stood and emptied his glass. He made his way over to the window and pulled back the curtain to peer up at the moon, full and bright. The time for Matthew to act was now. He was fully aware of the dangers. The increased chatter and interest in PORFs and the missing crown jewels had provoked Burke into offering twice his original amount for information. The devil was desperate to get his hands on the treasure.

"I won't say it again. I'm going alone. You are going to attend whatever social engagement Grace will be at this eve."

"There's no need for me to attend any such frivolous activity when you might be in danger. Ellingsworth has proved this past week he is more than capable of protecting and caring for Grace." Blake took another healthy gulp of his drink.

Matthew took a deep, calming breath as a stab of jealousy hit him squarely in the chest. Images of Ellingsworth and Grace flashed in quick succession. He had shadowed the couple as they strolled through the paths of Vauxhall, rode on matching grays in the park, attended the theater, and had even dressed in disguise as a footman to keep watch over Grace as she and Ellingsworth attended various dinner parties as the guests of honor. Matthew's blood boiled, thinking of how Ellingsworth made Grace smile and laugh. There had been absolutely no gossip or suspicion that their engagement was feigned. The pair had excelled at convincing the ton and, more importantly, Burke that they were both eager to say their vows in front of a priest at Saint George's chapel.

Matthew recalled the night they had attended the theater. In the dark, during the second act, he had caught a glimpse of Grace with her head bent as Ellingsworth whispered in her ear. For a brief moment, Matthew saw Grace's facade crack—she had shared a genuine smile with the man. It was enough to plant a seed of doubt in Matthew's mind and to question if Grace was starting to care for her faux betrothed.

Captain Bane confirmed that Ellingsworth had purchased two tickets to the Americas, not one. Who was the extra ticket intended for? Every good agent always had a secondary plan, if not a third. Was whisking Grace away Ellingsworth's scheme if his initial plans went awry?

Blake's glass hit the table. "I'll assume your silence to mean there is no changing your mind." Dispirited his brother-in-law released a deep sigh. "I'm off to change for the evening. I suggest you do the same."

CHAPTER TWENTY

*W*here was her blasted fake fiancé? Grace curved her lips into another bright smile for the guests of the Redburn ball as they glided past. Tobias was late as usual. Punctuality was not a quality that most expected from a dunderhead, so her betrothed exploited the trait to its full advantage. It also meant Grace was the one who bore the brunt of maintaining their pretense.

The tension in her shoulders triggered her headaches, which were getting worse by the day. Pain radiated up her neck, piercing her brain, exacerbated by every blasted nod she gave to all the bloody well-wishers who dared to approach her.

Seated next to Aunt Emily, who appeared content to sit along the wall, Grace snapped her fan open and hid her face behind the decorative object in her hand. For a solid minute, Grace allowed herself to relax her aching facial muscles. A short reprieve from smiling, but it also allowed her disappointment to set in. She had thought Matthew would have no qualms in choosing marriage to her over vengeance. Nine days later, she was no longer confident about the matter and questioned the man's love and touted devotion to her. He hadn't abandoned her like before—she was fully aware that he lurked in the dark everywhere she went. No, he still cared, but he had failed to relinquish the bloody crown jewels.

She peered over the rim of her fan and let out a small gasp. Devonton. The man was dressed in his elegant but conservative evening attire and stood in plain sight. He might be her subordinate, but Blake's loyalty belonged to Matthew. The delicate wood frame snapped in half in her hand. Matthew's best friend, a full head taller than the rest of the guests, easily spotted her. As he made his way over to her, Grace fumbled with her fan and managed to stuff the blasted thing in her petite silk reticle. She synched the drawstring tight as a pair of large black polished dress shoes appeared.

"Wouldn't want to be the poor fellow whom your mind is conjuring right at this moment." Blake presented his hand to her. "Care to join me on the dance floor?"

With her head tilted, Grace leaned back in order to see the man's face. "Your manners are atrocious, but considering your wife is not here, I'll excuse your failure to adhere to social etiquette." Grace placed her gloved hand in his and rose. "Where is Matthew?"

Blake's entire body tensed. His lips were drawn into a tight straight line, and the man lowered his gaze to the floor. It was clear he was not in full support of whatever Matthew was up to tonight.

Grace said, "Take me to him."

"No." Blake turned to lead her about the perimeter of the room, edging closer to the dance floor.

"Devonton, it wasn't a request. It was an order." Grace hated to have to exert her authority as the man's superior. Blake was a loyal, honest man who had served his country throughout the entire battle with Napoleon. He deserved to live out the rest of his life in peace and happiness. Grace nearly tripped as Blake quickly altered their course. Instead of leaving through the main foyer, Blake dragged her through to the gardens and then opened a door concealed behind sprawling ivy.

She glanced about, trying to gain her bearings. Blake released a piercing whistle. Moments later, a hackney rambled toward them and rolled to a stop. Grace hopped into the vehicle as soon as Blake had the door open. She couldn't be seen out here with him.

Grace faced him and asked, "Where are we going?"

The back of the hackney dipped, and Blake moved in front of her as the door swung open. Matthew lunged forward and barreled into his best friend. Righting himself, Matthew glared at Blake and asked, "Where the hell are the two of you going?"

Blake tilted his head in Grace's direction.

Matthew's blue-gray eyes were filled with anger. "Why did you leave the ball?"

"I gave the command." Volleying between wanting to launch herself at the man she loved and desired and strangling him for not seeking her out sooner, Grace stared at Matthew until he shifted uncomfortably. She glanced at both men and crossed her arms over her chest. "Where are we headed?"

Matthew scowled at her. "I'm going to instruct the driver to return to the ball as soon as you answer my question."

"And if I refuse?"

"Damnation, Grace." Matthew mirrored her movements. He crossed his arms and continued, "You are supposed to be dancing and awaiting your betrothed at the ball, not traipsing about town in a hackney with Devonton." He slid a glance at Blake, who sank farther into the corner of the rattling hackney.

Leaning forward, Grace softly said, "Who awaits you and where?"

Matthew brought his face within inches of hers and stared. Blast the man. Her eyes locked on his lips as she silently prayed for their conveyance to jostle about and cause their mouths to accidentally meet.

Blinking, Grace refocused on the matter at hand. "I'll not return to the ball until you share with me what has put Devonton on edge this eve."

"You're not coming with me. Thus it's of no matter who, what, or where I'm off to." Matthew reached for the door latch, presumably to order the driver to return to Redburn's. Her heart crumbled as she leaned back against the hardwood bench. What a fool she had been to believe he truly loved her and still intended to marry her. His decision was clear. He valued revenge over love. The Matthew she loved would have recognized the flaw in allowing hatred to rule one's choices. She could feel his gaze on her, but she clasped her hands in her lap and looked steadfastly at the tips of Devonton's shoes. How awkward for the poor man to be stuck in the same vehicle.

Exhaling a long sigh, Matthew moved to the space next to her and placed a hand over hers. "I plan to meet with Burke. I've arranged for senior court members to remain hidden in the dark. I intend to lead Burke down a merry path until he confesses to his underhanded dealings."

Matthew had lost his marbles. Burke was a silver-tongued devil, and there was no way he'd confess to his nefarious dealings. The hackney was slowing; they must have arrived at their destination.

Grace faced Devonton. "I'll wait here. You accompany him and see to his safety."

"No. You both must return to the ball." He squeezed her hand. "I shall see you tomorrow, and we finalize wedding arrangements."

Wide-eyed, she quickly turned to Matthew. He must have been beaten one too many times to believe she'd still marry him after the choices he had made. *You'd marry him regardless.* Grace shook her head to clear her conscience. "Very well, we will both accompany you." She grabbed her skirts and stood ready to exit. With one last narrowed stare at Matthew, she twisted the latch to release the door and hopped down to the pebbled path.

Where were they? Squinting, Grace could see the field before her was wide and deep. Trees lined the path the hackney was stationed on. Inhaling, beyond the strong scent of grass, Grace detected the faint aroma of mint. They were in Hyde Park. The wheels of the hackney crunched over the gravel path as it disappeared into the darkness.

Matthew gripped her by the elbow and led her into the dark. "You are the most obstinate, dangerous"—he stopped and tenderly cupped her face—"and courageous woman I know. Will you do me the honor of becoming the next Countess of Harrington?"

Of all the times and places, Matthew had to go and catch her totally off guard. His wicked smile proved he knew exactly what he was about. Unable to resist the man, Grace answered, "You better not be late…"

Matthew leaned in and kissed her, stealing her breath away and banishing all rational thoughts from her mind, the thump of her heartbeat loud in her ears. Seeking out Matthew's warmth, Grace wrapped her arms about his waist.

"Praise the saints, it's about bloody time," Blake grumbled from behind her. Clearing his throat, he added, "We must disappear from sight and let Matthew attempt to achieve the impossible."

Matthew leaned back and said, "Thanks for the support, dear friend."

Releasing her hold, Grace stepped back. "Very well. Let's be off, Devonton. Which is the quickest to route back to Redburn's?" Blake was the finest cartographer in all of England. Surely he could figure the best way out of the park.

Her subordinate's gaze flickered to Matthew. After a silent exchange between the two, Blake said, "It's too far to walk all the way back, but I know where we can find a ready vehicle to take us home. Follow me."

They turned to walk toward the path, leaving Matthew behind. Hidden in the shadows, Blake muttered, "I have a bad feeling about his meetings. I fear they will not go to plan."

"I agree." Scanning the area, she tugged on Blake's sleeve. "Let's stay and observe." She moved farther into the brush that was barely tall enough to conceal Blake's towering form. "Merely as a precaution."

CHAPTER TWENTY-ONE

*T*he skin on the back of Matthew's neck chafed against his collar, but it was the tingling sensation that piqued his interest. He tugged the lapels of his coat tighter together as he scanned the trees and the shadows. There was no sign of Grace, yet his body screamed that she was indeed near. It must be the lingering effect of her agreeing to marry him. But even as the rationalization drifted through his mind, Matthew narrowed his gaze and searched his surroundings. He'd have to trust that Blake would see to Grace's safety. Damnation, he needed to focus on the meeting.

Two distinct booted footfalls crunched along the gravel path at least three yards away. There was no indication the men had arrived by horse or carriage. Hereford and Lord Wallace, a well-respected senior member of the court, briefly appeared and then slid back into the shadows. Hereford was considered by many as one of the best agents the Foreign Office had. Trained to remain undetected, Hereford wasn't a concern. It was Lord Wallace's reactions

173

to the events that were about to unfold that gave Matthew pause.

The beat of horse hooves vibrated through the ground. Matthew's peculiar habit of walking barefoot had increased his feet's sensitivity. It brought about a whole new sensory skill he'd not thought possible. Moments later, Burke dismounted from his horse and flung the reins around a sapling. The devil paused and glanced about. He retrieved his timepiece from his coat pocket and flipped it open. Burke shook his head as he angled the face of the watch to capture the dim rays of moonlight. He slid the timepiece back into his coat and turned to face the field. Standing indolently, Burke inspected his right hand, the back, and then the palm and the back again before he stuffed both hands into his gloves. A signal. But to whom and what did it mean?

After months of staring into the dark, Matthew's eyes were well able to see with minimal light. He quickly scanned the perimeter for movement. All that was about were trees and shrubs that cast dark shadows, but nothing that moved.

The crown jewel replicas that Rutherford had created weighed heavily in Matthew's coat pocket. The real treasure was in Theo's safe hands. She had agreed to present them to Archbroke after Redburn's ball. Extracting the pocket watch Grace had gifted him on his birthday three years ago from his coat, Matthew brushed a thumb over the glass face and confirmed it was at the top of the hour.

Emerging from the shadows, Matthew asked, "Did you bring the deed?" The terms of the exchange were simple —the crown jewels for a large parcel of land that boarded Halestone Hall that Burke had swindled away from Matthew's childhood neighbor Lord Taylor.

In the dark, Matthew had expected the man's features

to have a menacing quality to them. Instead, he faced a gentleman whose ruddy complexion and plump cheeks spoke of his overindulgent lifestyle. Burke would hang for his traitorous schemes, a punishment that suddenly seemed too soft.

Burke tipped his hat and said, "A good eve to you, Harrington."

Moonlight fell upon the worn, yellowed parchment that the devil held against his chest. It was a misdeed that had irked Matthew for the past five years, which neither Grace nor he had been able to prevent or rectify.

Matthew reached for the papers, but Burke withdrew them and said, "The jewels first."

"Not until I confirm you have signed the document over to the rightful owners."

Burke unrolled the parchment, and Matthew scanned the deed. Satisfied all was in order, Matthew retrieved the pouch and held out the jewel replicas with an unusually steady hand. He preferred Burke to remain oblivious to the toll months of captivity had upon him. Burke's meaty paw grabbed the bag and reached inside, jingling the jewels about. The man's eyes widened, and then he retracted his hand and tightened the string.

Lifting the treasure in the air, Burke said, "I shall return these to the Palace. The king, along with Prinny, will be most pleased. I had not pegged you for a thief, Harrington. Such a shame for a peer to resort to such behavior. Wouldn't you agree—Lord Wallace, Lord Hereford?"

What!

The devil was accusing him of stealing the crown jewels. A crime he'd hang for if the Prince Regent were to find him guilty. Matthew stiffened as a breeze brushed against his cheek—along with it, the distinct scent of lilacs. *Damnation.* He narrowed his gaze and searched the tree line. Unable to locate Grace, Matthew's attention was drawn to the gentlemen who were to be his witnesses, not Burke's, as they emerged from the dark. He wanted to wipe the smug grin from Burke's face with his fist.

Hereford's monotone voice broke the silence. "Lord Burke, we appreciate you informing us of the situation." He turned to face Matthew. "Present yourself tomorrow. The Prince Regent will expect you an hour before noon."

Tomorrow. An hour before noon. That was when Grace expected him at Saint George's chapel. Damn. Damn. Damn. There was no way he'd make his own wedding in time. The streams of moonlight turned from bright white to a glowing red. Matthew's gaze narrowed on Burke's neck. He could wring the life out of the devil. The idea had its merits, considering he might hang for treason anyway.

"It's a shame I won't be present. I have my progeny's wedding to attend." Burke's smile widened, baring his aged, yellowed teeth. "Gentlemen, there is a ship to set sail tomorrow morn. We wouldn't want anyone to go missing. Perhaps Harrington should be escorted now."

Hereford and Lord Wallace turned their backs to them. Huddled, the pair spoke in hushed whispers. With a nod, Hereford swiveled and addressed Burke directly. "I think not. We shall arrange matters and given you will be preoccupied with your son's wedding, why don't I see to the return of the crown jewels." Hereford held out his hand and waited.

Burke's eyes widened. "As a senior court member… I believe it best if the jewels remained in my position."

Lord Wallace shook his head. "Hand over the jewels. We will attend to the matter of returning them."

Burke's entire body tensed. It appeared Burke's seniority within the court didn't hold much weight with the older, wiser Lord Wallace. Matthew waited for Burke to begin weaving a tale that would see him retain possession of the treasure. Instead, the man simply shoved the pouch into Lord Wallace's chest and said, "Ensure Prinny deals with the traitor."

Burke's actions were totally out of character. But the man had placed his hand in the pouch earlier, and his smirk had held a deviousness to it. With a sleight-of-hand move, Burke could have easily placed a piece up his sleeve, a maneuver often employed by pickpockets. Burke was after the rondure, not the entire set of crown jewels. Matthew spied Burke tugging at his gloves as the devil turned on his heel to leave. He released a pent-up breath, knowing Burke wouldn't find the rondure for it wasn't hidden within, whichever of the finely made replicas Burke had managed to palm.

Lord Wallace stepped forward and placed a hand on Matthew's shoulder. "I'm too old to be involved in all these shenanigans." The man's fingers squeezed Matthew. "Don't be late."

Matthew stood rooted to the spot as Hereford and Lord Wallace disappeared into the night.

A familiar tingling sensation ran down his spine. It wasn't the panicked reaction he'd experienced on the brink of death after a beating from his captors, and it wasn't precisely the same stirring feeling he experienced when Grace was close—but it was alarming.

He took a step in the direction of where his coach was instructed to wait for him. Matthew halted. There was no vehicle waiting for him. He had given Blake leave to commandeer his vehicle to take Grace back to the ball. Matthew's heart seized. Grace. He looked down at his booted feet and fell to his hands and knees. Tears threatened to emerge. He hadn't shed a single one since the death of his papa. Attempting to inhale deeply, his ribs ached, but the pain was minuscule compared to the agony in his heart. How was he to explain to Grace the sequence of events that now prevented him from appearing at the church tomorrow?

A twig snapped to his left. Matthew rolled over onto his butt and jumped up onto his feet. He came face-to-face with Ellingsworth.

With a scowl, Ellingsworth said, "You should have heeded your sister's advice."

Matthew grabbed the man's lapels, pulled him forward, and growled inches from his face. "How do you know the contents of my personal correspondence?"

"Everything can be purchased for a price." Ellingsworth lowered his eyes to Matthew's hands.

"Not everyone is lured by money." Matthew released Ellingsworth and shoved him away.

Ellingsworth smoothed out the wrinkles in his coat. "True. Some are enticed by legends. Why the preoccupation with PORFs?"

He didn't need to explain his motivations to Grace's betrothed. Turning, Matthew walked away, but his steps faltered as Tobias said, "Being one myself, I can assure you there is nothing magical or amazing about the network, and there is certainly nothing special about those who are referred to as PORFs."

Matthew marched back to stand in front of the man. "You are claiming to be a PORF?"

"Yes, but you already suspected it, so I'm not sharing anything you haven't already discovered for yourself. But let me enlighten you with the whole truth. The woman who gave birth to me was not the Countess of Burke. She was a sweet, innocent member of the network whom Burke took a liking to. When the Countess of Burke was found to be barren, my sire ordered my mum to work in the kitchens of his country estate. Desperate for a child, Countess Burke claimed me as her own. I was fortunate to have two loving parents, the woman who gave me life and the Countess who imparted to me the knowledge and skill on how to avoid my sire's attention. For your own good and for Grace and any offspring you may have, cease your investigations. Never share your theories or the information you have accumulated over the years." Raking a hand over his face, Ellingsworth continued, "You've gotten yourself into a fine mess. But now that the crown jewels are finally in the hands of Archbroke, I can assist you. But you have to promise—cease your search and reveal nothing of your findings related to the existence of PORFs and their supporters." Tobias's gaze shifted to the wooded area to their left. "I must be seeing things. I saw Blake escorting Grace to your coach earlier. I'm certain the vehicle adorned your crest."

Matthew peered at the spot that had caught Tobias's attention. "I haven't been able to identify her exact location, but I sense she's close by."

"The crafty woman is probably on the move. She knows you would detect her if she remained in one location too long." Tobias slowly completed a three-hundred-and-sixty-degree turn searching their surroundings. "When will she ever learn to take more care with her own damn safety? I don't understand your rationale for leaving two years past. Grace's willingness to place your safety and welfare before her own is astounding." Tobias glared at Matthew. "I'll admit I am a tad jealous. You have the love of an extraordinary woman. Give me your promise, and I'll help ensure that you are at the church on time."

Matthew wanted to give the man his word, but his instincts told him not to. Being torn apart limb by limb might have been less painful than the agony he was currently experiencing. He was close to fulfilling a lifelong search, but his heart demanded Grace. Ultimately there was no decision to be made—he needed to be at the church. Releasing a sigh, he said, "You have my word. I shall cease investigating and never disclose my findings related to the existence of PORFs or the network."

"Excellent." Tobias slung an arm about Matthew's shoulders and walked toward the path. "Allow me to assist you home. My coach is but a half mile from here."

The lightness in Tobias's step grated on Matthew's nerves. Shrugging off the man's arm, Matthew asked, "How do you intend to deal with Prinny?"

"I don't. Hadfield will. I'll be dealing with Burke." Tobias chuckled. "Don't look so worried. You have my word Burke will be dead by morn, I'll be setting sail on a new adventure, and you will be in front of a priest pledging your life to Grace."

The man was overly confident about what was to occur. Yet Matthew prayed Tobias would deliver on every one of his promises.

CHAPTER TWENTY-TWO

*T*he coach curtains were drawn back, allowing rays of moonlight to illuminate the interior of Matthew's coach. Blake hadn't uttered a word since they left the park. His features were closed off and masked. Grace intently studied her number one agent, waiting for a sign, a wrinkle, the tic of a muscle, something that would give her a clue as to what the man was thinking. Nothing.

"He won't be able to keep his promise, you know." Blake bent and rested his elbows on his knees as he massaged his temples. A habit Matthew had adopted since his return.

"I'm fully aware of Matthew's obsession." She reached out and touched the back of Blake's hand. "Are the headaches from stress or from…" Grace sat back as Blake's eyes opened, and for a flicker, she captured the sight of the depths of anguish her agent had never revealed before. "I'm… I'm sorry for all the years you were assigned to the Continent. I wish I had…"

"The headaches are the result of being separated from Lucy." He closed his eyes and continued to rub the tender spots on the side of his head. "I don't think I ever shared with you… No, I know I've not told you that each time I was captured and held prisoner during the war, not once did I ever doubt that you would send help or have me rescued. I'd wager that similarly; Matthew shared those same thoughts."

"You mean Matthew believed Archbroke was the one responsible for his rescue."

"It was Waterford, a Home Office agent, who ultimately freed the lot of them. But Matthew knows the truth now, not because you told him, but because Theo shared with him the events that had occurred in his absence. Before you marry, he needs to hear from you what all went on." He leaned back and said, "He'll marry you, and then he'll find himself in trouble, for like I said, he won't be able to keep his word and cease his infernal investigations into PORFs and the like."

"Are you suggesting I jilt Matthew?" A strange sound came out of Blake's mouth. Frowning, Grace said, "What was that sound?"

"The noise that I'd be making as Matthew strangled me. If he were to ever hear you utter such a ghastly idea and that it was in some way my idea… I'd be a dead man. Regardless that I'm his brother-in-law and best friend." Blake tugged on his cravat. "No, you need to convince the powers that be that Matthew should be allowed to continue his investigations."

The man was insane. She shook her head and said, "What do you even know of the matter?" Blake did have a vault for a memory, able to recall facts, and he possessed the exceptional ability to illustrate scenes, lands, and people with a precision no one could match.

"More than I'll admit." Blake glanced out the window.

"What makes you believe I have any influence or that my opinions might carry any weight with the PORFs?"

"Because at least two of them care about your welfare. If it were me, I'd seek out Theo's assistance before approaching Ellingsworth. But given there is little time before your betrothed sets sail, perhaps you should seek his assistance first." The coach rolled to a stop in front of her papa's residence, and Blake shifted to open the door.

Grace moved faster, reaching the exit first. "I shall consider your recommendations. No need to escort me to the door, I'll be perfectly safe." She rose and stepped down to leave.

"Then I shall wait here until you have entered."

"Suit yourself." Stubborn man. No one was going to accost her this close to home. With a few quick strides, she was at the entrance of the townhouse.

Silverman swung the door open just as her foot landed on the last step. "His lordship is awaiting you in his study."

Grace must have misheard. Her papa should be abed at this hour. She nodded, slipped off her gloves, and gave them, along with her wrap and reticle, to the butler. "I assume he intends to lecture me on having left Aunt Emily to fend for herself at Redburn's."

"I've not a clue what his lordship intends, but your aunt did pay a visit earlier, my lady." Silverman raised his lit candle and led her down the hall.

She could hear her papa's grumblings from the hallway. He was definitely not in a pleasant mood. Squaring her shoulders, she entered the surprisingly warm room.

Her papa stood by the mantel of the blazing fire. "Ah, there you are, Gracie girl. Come join me by the fire."

The intensity of his gaze and tone made her feel like she was eight years of age again and he had found her reading the paper instead of doing needlepoint. She took her time arranging her skirts that had somehow become twisted like the knots in her stomach.

"Where did you venture off to this eve?" Her papa drummed his fingers on the wood mantel.

What was she to say? That she left because of boredom and had tired of waiting for her faux fiancé to appear? Or because she had an inkling Matthew was in trouble again? Neither seemed a sound enough reason to leave the ball in haste. Grace crossed and uncrossed her legs at the ankles.

The tapping stopped. "Love is confusing. It's illogical, volatile, and painful all the while, it makes one believe they are at the heights of existence, and no matters seem impossible." He moved to sit in the chair next to her. "I've found over time emotions like love can cause one to believe they are acting in the best interest of others but to the detriment of oneself."

Grace was tired, and the constant pounding in her head made it even more challenging for her to follow the direction of the conversation. "Papa, I don't understand your meaning."

"You and Harrington fell in love and from the beginning were in sync with one another."

Grace stared at her papa. His statement couldn't have been further from the truth. Yes, they each claimed to love the other, but they were hardly in agreement from the start. Matthew wanted to marry right away. She wanted to wait. If they had been in accord, he would never have left, or she would have at least understood why he had chosen to venture to the Continent.

Grace said, "I believe his actions prove otherwise."

Her papa shook his head. "Gracie, you are a good girl. Always following the rules, even the ones others often ignore. You care deeply for others and are extremely loyal. Are you sure *you* want to marry Harrington? You're not marrying him because I expressed my wish for it to be so or for other reasons I'd rather not discuss?"

It didn't surprise Grace that her papa was aware and didn't want to discuss the matter of her maidenhood, but what did come as a shock was him questioning her love for Matthew. Of course, she wanted to marry Matthew. She had gone to extreme lengths to ensure his safe return. Yet hadn't she done the same for Blake during the war? Squeezing her eyes tight, she tried to reorganize her muddled thoughts. *Focus on the facts, and the rest will sort itself out.* The motto she had lived by for years. On a shallow breath, Grace said, "Matthew proposed this eve, and I agreed. We are to be wed tomorrow. Assuming Tobias comes through on his promise."

"Why did you say yes?"

"Beg pardon?"

"Why did you agree to marry Harrington? All the recent reports I've received state he has returned a different man."

"Aye. Matthew is not the same, and I'd not expected him to be. After the harrowing events he experienced, how could it not have affected him? Was it not you who told me *life occurrences influence how one makes future choices but do not alter one's soul?* Matthew is fundamentally the same man to me. It may take years or the remainder of our lives for him to be rid of his nightmares and insecurities that were born from his captivity, but I want to be the woman next to him —the one to be there for him."

"Ahh… I understand. You are a replica of your mama." He rose and banked the fire. "It's growing late. We both need rest." He assisted Grace to her feet and escorted her out to the hall where a droopy-eyed Silverman was waiting. As they followed the butler, her papa said, "Have Cook prepare a light affair in the morn and let's partake in an early-morning stroll. I'd like to be of sound mind for your wedding."

He was slightly out of breath as they approached his door. Before he left Grace, he said, "Don't forget."

"I won't, Papa. I'll remember."

At a slower pace, Grace followed Silverman down the corridor to her chamber. Fully aware she was about to break several conventions, she said, "I know you have an opinion on tomorrow's events, and the walls are not so thick you didn't hear of my papa's concerns. Do you think I'm making the wrong decision in marrying Lord Harrington?"

Silverman's gaze shifted from left to right and back again. When she thought he'd not answer, the butler cleared his throat. "I've been in your family's employ since you were but a babe. I agree with his lordship. You tend to think of what matters to others first and especially so when Lord Harrington is involved. Be selfish for once and do as you wish."

"Thank you for sharing your thoughts on the matter."

Grace entered her dark room and leaned back against the door. Her maid was asleep in the chair next to her bed. Remaining quiet, she rolled the back of her head against the solid wood and let her mind roam.

Her papa was a wise man, but her inability to share and display her emotions was the real cause of his concern. It wasn't that she didn't love Matthew; it was that she was reluctant to act upon it in front of others. She used her sham engagement as an excuse not to share her true feelings, even with Matthew. He'd always been able to interrupt her actions and translate them into words that she found difficult to form.

Her shoulders slouched forward as a deep ache formed in the center of her chest. She had assumed Matthew would again simply know how much she cared for him, but how could he? They had rarely spent any time together alone for her to show him the depths of her love, and she certainly hadn't spoken of it when they had a chance to be in each other's company. Eyes closed, she slowly slumped to the ground, and curled her knees to her chest.

A hand brushed over her bent head. Tilman softly said, "My lady, let me help you to bed."

How long had she sat upon the floor? The ache in her chest remained, but she no longer felt tired. "No, I must seek out Lord Ellingsworth. I need his help."

"It's late, and there are but a few more hours before we must start to prepare for the wedding. I'll assist in getting a message to him. What is it that you need?"

The tone Tilman used was one Grace had never heard before. Searching her maid's eyes, there was a clarity to them that told Grace the woman considered the matter serious and would not fail her.

"I need Lord Ellingsworth to know that, while Matthew would never intentionally fail to deliver upon his promise, ceasing his inquiries into PORFs is impossible. No. The message needs to be less wordy."

Tilman let out a laugh and assisted Grace to stand. "Not to worry. All will be as it should be, my lady. The network and Lady Theo have already begun working on setting matters straight."

"Theo? The network?" Grace asked as her maid turned her about by the shoulders and undressed her. After her stays were loosed and removed, she asked, "How do you—"

Tilman pulled her chemise up over her head, cutting off the rest of her question. "You and Lord Harrington have been meddling for years. I was assigned to monitor your progress."

187

"Assigned by whom?"

Slipping a nightgown over Grace's head, her maid started removing hairpins and popped them in her apron.

Grace tried again, "Whose orders do you heed?"

"Yours, my lady." Tilman picked up her evening gown and retreated to the changing chamber where Grace's wardrobe was housed along with a cot that her maid occasionally made use of.

When Tilman failed to reappear, Grace climbed into bed. She would have to trust her friend. Theo would, as Tilman had phrased it, set matters straight.

CHAPTER TWENTY-THREE

hy had he not worn gloves? Matthew withdrew his finger from his mouth and spat out the droplet of blood. Damn climbing rose bush. The overgrown plant significantly slowed his progress. Scratched and pricked by thorns, he heaved himself up the last three inches to latch on to Grace's windowsill.

He rapped on her window. Three quick taps, a pause, two quick taps, a pause, and one last quick tap. It was the code she had insisted he use in order for her to open the damn window.

Moments later, the window opened, and a groggy sounding Grace said, "Matthew?"

He counted to five to give her time to step back, and then he pushed himself headfirst through the window. "I hope I never have to do that again." Matthew straightened and tugged on his coat sleeves. He waited for Grace to enthusiastically wrap her arms about him like she used to. Instead, she stood a good foot away with her hands on her hips.

"What are you doing here?"

"I need to talk to you about our plans for tomorrow." Grace launched herself at him, and he stumbled backward. Arms wound tight about his neck she stared at him with brown eyes filled with worry. "I'm terrible at expressing my feelings. I know you are not the same man as before, but I still love you, and I'll never stop. I'm not the same woman you proposed to either. I'm more cynical and definitely less trusting, but I hope you will still love me and want to marry me." She heaved in a deep breath and rested her forehead against his chest.

Knowing the toll her emotional confessions must have taken, Matthew rubbed her back and squeezed her to him. "I've never stopped loving you, even when I stupidly believed you had accepted a proposal from Ellingsworth. *I'm* going to marry you."

Her breathing evened out, and he guided her back to bed. She crawled up onto the bed, and he was tempted to follow her, but he was in full court attire under his greatcoat. Grace tugged on his hand, inviting him to lie next to her. Her pleading brown eyes were hard to resist. She frowned up at him as he pulled the sheets and the coverlet up over her, but her lips curved into a smile as soon as he shifted to sit on the edge of the bed facing her. Unable to toe-off his boots, he bent to tug them off. Readjusting his coat to sit more comfortably, he sat up to find Grace had scooted down and was mere inches away. Staring at her long, unbound hair, Matthew leaned in and wrapped his hand around the side of her neck, his fingers grazing against her soft locks.

Grace tilted her head and whispered, "Kiss me."

He wanted to give in to her request, but he was uncertain he'd have enough self-control to stop after one kiss. "First, I must tell you…" Matthew paused as the sweet scent of lilacs registered. His fingers tightened about the back of her neck as he gave in to temptation and placed his lips against her soft, inviting mouth. He was right; he couldn't stop at one kiss. Grace opened for him, and his tongue sought out the taste of her. He'd dreamed of making slow love to her, of taking her in every position imaginable and of lying about merely kissing. Hours away from finally making Grace his marchioness, he'd settle for kisses for now.

Lost in their open-mouthed kisses, Matthew froze when Grace slipped her hand under his shirt and ran a finger over his nipple. The minx had somehow managed to breach the many layers that were between them. Her palm skimmed over his puckered and scarred skin. Matthew cringed. His muscles bunched tight as he waited for her to stop and withdraw in revulsion. Instead, her hand drifted down his side and stilled at his waist. Grace pulled back and glanced down between them.

One of his many nightmares was about to play out. Would it be the one where she told him he wasn't half the man he used to be or the one in which she told him she no longer wished to touch him? The latter would be crushing, as physical touch was Grace's way of communicating her love for another. He inhaled and braced himself for what was to come.

Rather than pushing him away or fixing the layers of clothing between them, she said, "You are dressed for court, but you are not due for hours yet."

The swell of relief that she hadn't rejected him was quickly replaced by irritation. Her inadvertent admission to having been at the park throughout the entire ordeal meant Ellingsworth was right. She had no regard for her own safety. With a quick, chaste kiss upon his chin, Grace wiped his irritation away, and his desire roared back. He captured her lips and kissed her until they were both gasping for air.

Matthew sat back and attempted to give her his most serious glare. "So you were there, and I need not have come to see you." He groaned as one side of her mouth kicked up in a grin. Damn, the woman was alluring. After a long period of abstinence and longing for her, he pushed her back to lie upon the bed and loomed over her.

Wrapping her arms about his neck once again, Grace pulled him down to her. "I'm glad you are here. Now, I have the chance to *tell* you how much I'm looking forward to marrying you and working"—she waggled her eyebrows at him and then continued—"with you."

Matthew chuckled as he fondly remembered their time *working* together. Their meetings always began with great intentions of solving the department's problems or planning the newest mission. Images of Grace's head bent over papers and maps and then of her lying naked atop a pile of cushions, rosy-cheeked and satisfied, had Matthew dipping his head and kissing the woman he loved. He'd only ever been with one woman, and she was wiggling beneath him, driving him mad. "Grace, if something… I wanted you to know…"

Grace placed a finger over his lips. "Shh… Have faith in Theo. Try not to be late… but if you are, I will be waiting for you." She replaced her finger with her lips.

Had he heard her correctly? Why was Theo involved? Her kisses were distracting. Rather than focusing on the intricate workings of PORFs, the network, and the Crown, Matthew gave in to the moment and shifted so he could lie next to her.

Lying face-to-face on their sides, Grace asked, "Do you not care for my hands to be upon you anymore? You didn't seem to mind the other night in the gazebo, but tonight…"

He would love to have her hands on his skin, but his body was scarred, and some sections remained numb. Matthew wasn't sure why he had become more self-conscious of his injuries this evening. "I'm sorry, I know how important it is for you to be able to communicate via touch." He rubbed his cheek against her soft palm. "I do love your caresses, but we are to wed tomorrow, and I had the crazy notion that we should wait to be intimate until after the ceremony. I came here tonight to talk, not to take advantage of you."

She closed her eyes for a brief moment, then asked, "Are you worried about your meeting with Prinny?" Grace rubbed her thumb back and forth over his cheekbone with her eyes trained on him.

The answer was absolutely. Matthew had entrusted Ellingsworth, a near stranger, to see to it that Prinny heard his case and did not find him guilty of treason. Matthew simply nodded and closed his eyes.

Grace's soothing strokes stopped, and her hand left his face. She whispered, "Stay with me a while." The rustle of material was all he heard; he dared not open his eyes. Grace lifted his arm and placed it securely about her waist as she snuggled her back against him. "I feel safe with you here, and I admit I'm exhausted."

Her admission was heart-wrenching. He would stay for a bit. It was the least he could do for her. "I'll need to leave before your family awakes."

Matthew wasn't confident she even heard his response. Her breathing was slow and even, as if she had fallen asleep as soon as she settled into his embrace. He didn't seek out sleep immediately. He merely matched his breathing to hers. In the dark with a warm bundle next to him, the silence didn't bring him nightmares. Instead, for the first time in a long time, Matthew allowed himself to picture a future that had them together, happy and surrounded by children. Knowing Grace's opinions on family and how she had longed for a sibling, he hoped he would be able to provide her with a large brood of her own. He promised himself he would start working on it as soon as they were married.

CHAPTER TWENTY-FOUR

*T*he bed linens tangled about her as Grace rolled over. Matthew was gone. Struggling to free herself, Grace mumbled. "Bloody covers."

"Thank heavens, you are awake." Tilman hovered over her and brushed back the wayward strands of hair that covered her face. "Not that it looks like you slept a wink." Her maid's eyebrows scrunched into a fierce scowl.

Glaring at Tilman, Grace sat up and said, "I'll not agree to you placing potatoes over my eyes again."

Tilman winked at Grace before turning to the table next to the bed. "Very well, my lady. Good thing I requested cucumbers from Cook this time." Swiveling back with two slices of the fruit dangling from her fingertips, Tilman ordered, "Lie back, my lady."

Eyes closed Grace reluctantly scooted down to rest her head upon the pillows.

"Let this sit awhile. Promise not to move until I've returned with your wedding dress."

The last thing Grace wanted to do this morn was upset her maid. "I promise."

The door hinge squeaked as the door closed. She would have to see to it they were oiled. Grace's chest contracted. No, she wouldn't. After the wedding, this chamber would no longer belong to her. She wouldn't be returning to her papa's townhouse if all was to go to plan. Grace wasn't due for her monthly cycle for another week, yet her stomach knotted and cramped. She overlapped her hands and placed them on top of her tummy and took deep calming breaths.

The quick tempo of heels striking the wood floors in the hallway could only belong to one person—Lucy. What was her best friend doing back in London? She was supposed to be safely tucked away in the country.

The door creaked open, followed by more swift footsteps. "Grace! Why are you lying about? Are you ill?" A small cool hand touched her forehead.

Lucy's thumb tried to rub the creases from her brow away. "Don't worry. Everything will work out."

Grace repeated, "Don't worry! Ha. All will be well! No one can bloody well know that for certain. If it were Blake who was the one facing charges of treason, I highly doubt you'd be lying here calm and carefree."

The slimy pieces of cucumber were removed from her eyes, and Lucy's gray-blue eyes, similar to Matthew's but not as blue, bore down at Grace. "Well, well. Look who has a temper after all. I need not remind you, but Matthew is my twin. You think it easy for me to sit and wait for the capricious Prince Regent to decide upon my brother's fate."

How selfish of her not to consider Lucy's feelings. "I'm sorry. I shouldn't have lashed out."

Lucy slapped the now lukewarm fruit back over her eyes. "Tilman was right to put those on your eyes. You look dreadful. When was the last time you got a solid night's sleep?" In typical Lucy fashion, Grace's apology was ignored, and the conversation turned around.

"Actually, I managed three hours of solid sleep, just last eve." Grace rolled slightly on to her side as her bed sank. Lucy's hip pressed up against her. She shimmied over to give her best friend more room.

"My hips are wider than a century-old oak." Lucy bemoaned. "Childbirth does strange things to one's body, but Blake doesn't seem to mind."

Of course, her husband wouldn't mind. Grace doubted Blake's infatuation with Lucy would ever die. Grace pictured Lucy's twin boys. Their facial features were the spitting image of their papa, but they both had their mama and uncle's gray-blue eyes.

Lucy patted her arm. "I digress. Never mind about those things now. Three hours of sleep, you say. That's hardly enough for the eve of one's wedding."

Grace raised her hand to remove the fruit eye patches.

Lucy slapped her hand away. "Oh no, you don't. Those stay on until Tilman returns with your freshly pressed gown."

Grace released a sigh as she rested her hands across her chest. "When and what time did you arrive back in town?"

"The roads from Shalford Castle to London are rather well maintained. Fortunately, I was able to arrive before dark. Still, I wasn't able to locate my exhausted husband until well after midnight."

Grace said, "I imagine Blake was delighted to see you no matter the time."

"I won't let you manipulate the conversation back around to me. Explain to me why you decided to place both my brother and husband at risk last night, hiding about in the shadows. If you were caught—"

"But I wasn't."

There was a rap at the door.

Lucy said, "That will be Mary. I believe she and Waterford intend to accompany us to the church."

She didn't need such a large retinue. Was this Theo's doing? Grace called out, "Please come in."

The soft swish of skirts was the only indication that Mary had entered her chambers. The bed shifted as Lucy's feet hit the ground. Grace had a sneaking suspicion Mary was reading Lucy's lips. "Lucille Stanford Gower, you are in my rooms, and you will speak out loud for me to hear."

Lucy grumbled, "Sometimes I wish you didn't know me so well. Where is Waterford?"

"I left my dear husband in Lord Flarinton's company. I believe they were to take a turn in the gardens while they wait." Mary answered.

Frowning, Grace asked, "Should I be worried that Archbroke ordered you and Waterford to accompany me to the church?"

"Beg pardon. No one ordered us to come. I consider you a friend." Mary's voice cracked, but she continued, "I wanted to be here to be of assistance to you."

Lucy interjected, "Don't mind her, Mary. Grace hasn't had much sleep lately."

Argh. Grace removed the cucumber slices from her eyes. She sat up and swung her legs over the edge of the bed to face Mary. "I apologize. Not knowing all the particulars has me on edge."

Tilman rushed into the room with a glorious green silk gown. "My lady, isn't it the most wonderful dress?"

"That's not the gown I ordered." Grace stared at the magnificent dress Tilman was fondling as if it was the most precious thing in the world.

"No, it's the one I had Ms. Lennox design and make for your special day." Lucy smiled. "It's perfect."

"Ms. Lennox?"

It was Mary who grinned and replied, "Aye. Ms. Lennox agreed to outfit us all." She ran a hand down her slender figure wrapped in a ruby-red gown. The color highlighted her mahogany tresses perfectly.

Grace tilted her head to take in Lucy's gown. It was a lovely lavender color. Lucy had worn a similar ensemble the season that Matthew had left. A season Grace wished she could go back and erase.

Mary's concerned eyes captured Grace's attention. "All will be as it is meant to be."

Grace swore she was going to punch the next person who dared to say all would be well.

Leaning in, Mary whispered, "I say that knowing Theo has taken care of matters." Her eyes closed for a moment, and then she added, "But we still need to proceed with caution."

"Why? What do you know?" Grace asked.

Mary shook her head. "I'm sorry, but I can't."

"Can't or won't?"

Before Mary answered, Lucy came to stand beside them. "What are the two of you whispering about?"

Tilman wedged her way closer to her mistress. "My ladies, may I suggest you wait for Lady Grace…"

Lucy relieved her maid of the clean chemise and corset held tightly in her hands. "Tilman, I'm feeling a little parched. Please fetch us some tea. Mary and I will see that Grace is dressed."

Tilman reluctantly let go of the undergarments and bobbed a curtsy. "As you wish, Lady Devonton."

As soon as the door latch fell into place, Lucy said, "I confess I'd had my doubts about Ellingsworth and his intentions, but when Blake woke me this morn to share the news that the royal physician had declared Burke dead, I was relieved, to say the least."

"Burke is dead?" Mary and Grace said in unison.

"Yes." Lucy linked her arm through Mary's and turned, giving Grace privacy to change into her chemise. "Didn't Waterford tell you?"

"No. No one advised me." The annoyance in Mary's tone was clear and mirrored Grace's own thoughts and feelings.

How had Blake and Lucy received confirmation when she had received no news? If her papa had intercepted the information, he might have forgotten to pass it along. Grace shook her head. That couldn't be. The household was well aware she was to be kept abreast of all correspondence.

Grace sucked in a breath as Lucy placed the corset about her ribs. The dastardly contraption was pulled tighter as Grace expelled the last ounce of air left in her lungs.

Mary approached with her dress and said, "I too had concerns over Ellingsworth's ability to see to Burke's demise. But if the royal surgeon is to be believed, it appears his scheme must have worked. Am I the only one concerned for Lord Ellingsworth? His hasty departure after his sire's death will cast a shadow over his inheritance of the title and the duties that come along with it."

"I'm sure Ellingsworth considered the impact of the associated gossip that will ensue," Grace as she punched her arms through the small cap sleeves. "It was his plan."

"Yes, but for him to willingly take on such a burden." Mary absently handed Grace matching silk gloves. "I wonder if the woman he intends to marry will care. That is if such horrid rumors ever reach American shores."

Grace stuffed her hands into the gloves. "If she truly loves Tobias as he says she does, it matters not what the gossips might say."

Lucy said, "We know nothing of this woman nor of her family. We shall just have to hope that Ellingsworth knows what he is about."

Grace ran a hand down her sides, smoothing out the last wrinkles in the gown. She turned to stare at the image in the looking glass. The woman looking back at her appeared calm and reserved, with absolutely no hint of the anxiety that was accumulating within.

Mary appeared behind her in the looking glass. "I'd grown fond of Lord Ellingsworth and Mr. Jones. I shall miss them both."

"Mr. Jones? Per my sources, he didn't possess a ticket." Suspecting her brother might be considering moving abroad, Grace had investigated, but she'd not received confirmation of any plans.

"That is because Mr. Jones hadn't fully committed until they were about to pull the gangplank." Mary smiled and continued to explain, "It is always a tough decision to make when choosing between the life you know and the one that may await in a foreign land."

"I hope they arrive safely."

Mary shrugged. "The trip across the Atlantic is plagued with dangers, but I believe if Mr. Jones sticks with Lord Ellingsworth, he'll be in fine company."

Opening the door, Lucy said, "It's time for us to leave, or we'll be late."

Turning, Mary whispered, "I have full faith in Theo, and so should you."

It wasn't a matter of trust or faith, the shiver that ran down Grace's spine bespoke disaster.

CHAPTER TWENTY-FIVE

*M*uted sunlight shone through the stained-glass window into the cramped quarters where Matthew was ensconced. Head bowed and hands tightly clasped behind his back, he leaned his forehead against the frosty panes of glass. The waiting was killing him.

A Home Office runner had found Matthew descending from Grace's window at first light and passed along a missive written in Archbroke's scrawling handwriting.

Burke is dead.

Ellingsworth and Jones have set sail.

Report to Carlton House immediately.

The news of the loathsome lord's death hadn't allevi-ated the pain and the anger that resided in the middle of Matthew's chest. Ellingsworth had succeeded where he had failed, yet Matthew found it difficult to believe Burke was no longer breathing. His hands clenched. Pushing away from the window, he paced what he guessed was the smallest room in the royal residence.

By rights, Ellingsworth would assume all the duties and

responsibilities that went along with inheriting the Marquess of Burke title, including that of royal advisor. The title alone brought a myriad of obligations. How did the man intend to address them all from across the pond?

As he circled back to face the colorful panes of glass, a shard of green light fell upon his chest right over his heart, and he froze. Damnation. The sight of the sparkling green rays brought Grace to mind. He had no idea exactly how long he'd been detained, but he guessed it must be nearing noon. Matthew let out a frustrated growl. He needed to be on his way to the chapel, not circling about like the animals at the royal menagerie.

It appeared none of his plans since his return were bearing fruit. He had failed to regain his physical strength during the many months of recovery at Halestone Hall. Matthew ran his left hand over this right shoulder, the one that dislodged multiple times and ached incessantly. Over the past week, he had finally gained the courage to speak to Blake regarding his trepidation over revealing his marked skin and damaged body to Grace.

His brother-in-law had listened to his concerns and had empathetically shared, *even if you had returned whole, every man and woman harbor insecurities regarding their form. I guarantee you no one is perfect—nor were you before your imprisonment.* While Matthew acknowledged the fact he was far from perfect, his fears hadn't permeated his every thought and action as they did now.

Booted footsteps from the other side of the door signaled someone was finally approaching.

The door swung open. Instead of a guard entering, Theo preceded Archbroke and then Hadfield into the room. The group formed a semicircle in front of him, with Hadfield in the center, who said, "Tobias doesn't believe you intend to keep your promise to refrain from investigating the matter of PORFs." Hadfield raised a singular brow, and after a brief pause continued, "After many hours of deliberation, we have decided that the best course of action is to provide you with clarity, guidance, and to explain in detail how matters are to be dealt with going forward."

Hadfield's opening words sunk into Matthew's brain. It hadn't been the Prince Regent who had kept him waiting all these hours. It was the trio standing before him.

Theo stepped in front of her cousin and over her shoulder scolded, "You are making this far too complicated."

Matthew was sure Hadfield, an ex-barrister, would make some sort of scathing retort. Instead, the man smiled at his cousin and winked at her. Matthew examined the flow of the conversation and the undercurrent of energy that ebbed and flowed between cousins.

Theo turned back around to face Matthew. "*We* have agreed that it was only fair to grant you the truth. But in return, you will have to swear your fidelity to all current and future PORFs. It will also mean your future wife and your descendants will be bound by your commitment here today."

"Invitations such as this are not granted often." Archbroke came to stand next to Theo.

Matthew shrugged. "If you are truly willing to provide me with answers, I agree."

"I see now why Tobias had his reservations." As Hadfield spoke, Theo and Archbroke stepped back behind the man. Odd. Archbroke typically always took the lead. Hadfield continued, "You are not taking this seriously."

"Au contraire, but I am." Matthew placed his right hand over his heart. "I, Matthew Stanford, Marquess Harrington, pledge my fidelity to the three families who have sworn to protect the royal family. I hereby promise to honor the code of silence."

Hadfield's gaze roamed over his face and down to where his trembling hand rested upon his chest. "Very good. However, I must reiterate you, your wife, and any future children to be born will hereby be sworn to secrecy *and* be pledging their full cooperation and assistance to anyone who bears the mark of a PORF. In return, and as the holder of the coin, it is my responsibility to ensure your safety and the safety of your wife and offspring."

A million items and questions raced through Matthew's mind. His heart pounded with excitement. Years of digging and hypothesizing, all culminating together. Finding his voice, Matthew blurted, "I can't believe it. *You* have the rondure. Have the Hadfields always possessed the coin?"

Archbroke answered, "No. It was missing up until recent months. Without the assistance of Lady Mary, the coin would have fallen into the wrong hands."

"I knew it!" Matthew whirled around and rubbed the back of his neck.

Taking a few steps forward, he muttered more to himself than the others. "Archbrokes have run the Home Office for generations. Hadfields have been known to be great travelers and information seekers. Burkes have held seniority at court for as long as anyone can remember." The rainbow of colors upon the stone floor reminded him of where he needed to be. Walking back to face the trio, Matthew opened his mouth to speak, but Hadfield raised a hand up in the air and lowered it to rest behind his back.

Hadfield said, "As I said, I'm responsible for your welfare. I shall deal with the Prince Regent while you go prepare for your wedding. I have arranged for Hereford to accompany you home and assist with getting you to the church as soon as possible. I suggest you change into a less ostentatious outfit. Prinny might have appreciated your current ensemble, but I highly doubt Lady Grace will."

Was Hereford part of the network? Is that why he was selected for the court appointment?

As if reading his mind, Hadfield answered, "No, Lord Hereford is not my responsibility. His family crest is devoid of the network's emblem. He is, however, a good friend who wants to see that you and Lady Grace are wed. We shall meet, and I'll answer your questions then. But for now, I must meet with Prinny and arrange for the paperwork to be drawn up. Archbroke and Theo will ensure all is ready by the time you arrive at the church." Hadfield leaned down and gave Theo a peck on the cheek. "Come see me after you have escorted Harrington out."

The woman beamed up at her cousin. "As you wish." Theo had adored her deceased brother Baldwin, but it was apparent she worshipped Hadfield. The man smiled and revealed a dimple that Matthew had never known to exist. He expected it was only the first of many new revelations.

Hadfield left the room, followed by Archbroke. Theo hooked her arm through Matthew's and said, "Come along. We are late as it is. I'm sure Hereford is about somewhere."

"What did you have to sacrifice in order to convince your cousin?" Matthew asked.

"Nothing. The man always listens to reason." Theo patted his arm.

The twinkle in her eyes was one Matthew was familiar with. Hadfield may possess the rondure, but Matthew suspected it was Theo who wielded the most power. Matthew looked up to see Hereford quickly descending upon them.

"I got turned about. I've not been granted access to

this section before." Hereford glanced about. "Is this the private wing?"

"It is." Theo nodded.

Matthew whispered, "What is the room I awaited in used for?"

"It was intended for prayer." Theo stepped back and addressed Hereford. "Can you find your way back, or should I accompany you?"

Hereford's brow creased. "I believe I can recall the way back to the private entrance."

"Excellent. We can shorten the distance by going through Saint James's Park. If we hurry, we won't be too late." The mountain of questions he had for Theo and Hadfield would wait. He lengthened his stride and quickened his pace.

Hereford matched him stride for stride. "Regardless, if we are five minutes or two hours late, Lady Grace detests tardiness." They exited Carlton House and jumped into the awaiting coach.

"Do you think she'll forgive me?" Matthew asked.

Hereford shrugged his brawny shoulders. "Hmm. Maybe. Fortunately, you will have a lifetime to make it up to her." The man smiled and revealed a chipped tooth. The damaged pearly white tooth was a reminder Hereford had not escaped totally unscathed.

CHAPTER TWENTY-SIX

*W*hat was keeping Matthew? Where were Lucy and Theo? Good gracious, Grace wasn't even married to the man, and she was already adopting his habits. Sequential questions indeed. Inhaling deeply, she turned and continued to pace along the four walls of the ante-chamber.

Completing her eighty-third circuit of the small room, she was aware the volume of the voices from the other side of the wall was mounting. The chapel was full of guests all expecting her to wed the new Lord Burke. Bloody hell. What would everyone think when it was Matthew up on the dais standing next to her instead of Tobias? Had Matthew even procured a special license? Fustian.

Sidestepping around Mary and Waterford for the eighty-sixth time, Grace narrowed her gaze upon the pair. The smirk on Waterford's face that she had once considered smug was teasing more than anything else. Mary's furrowed brow wasn't so much from scowling but a look of concentration. The woman's gaze tracked Grace as she paced by. Mary's eyes were slightly dilated and gleamed with awareness. What did the woman know that she wasn't sharing? Grace turned around and briskly walked back to confront the couple.

Hands firmly planted on her hips; Grace stared at Mary. "Out with it. Did Theo's plan fail?"

"Lass, what color would describe Lady Grace's exquisite grown?" Waterford pulled his wife a little closer to him.

The protective gesture was unnecessary, and a pang of regret at her aggressive behavior hit Grace squarely in the chest. Yes, she was a little agitated, but she would never harm a friend.

"Emerald green." Mary smiled and then continued, "It's nearly the same shade as Theo's eyes, wouldn't you agree?"

Waterford tilted his head and nodded. "Quite right."

Wide-eyed, Grace stared at the pair. They had totally ignored her question and were being deliberately obtuse. Grace grabbed Mary's hands. "Did the Prince Regent rule against Matthew? Oh, dear Lord…"

Mary squeezed her hands. "Waterford has not yet received an update."

"I'm not talking about Waterford. I'm asking if *you* have received word from *your* sources." Grace searched her friend's face for a clue, any sign that would set her heart at ease that Matthew was well and was merely delayed.

"How long have you known about my…?" Mary asked, lowering her gaze.

"Oh, I've known for years. When we first met, you believed it a curse, but I've always considered it a gift." It was Grace's turn to squeeze Mary's hands. "Please tell me what you know."

Mary bowed her head. "I'm sorry. I can't."

It must be bad news if Mary wouldn't share it with her.

"Very well. I'll go see to the matter myself." She shouldn't have entrusted Theo with the responsibility in the first place. Grace gathered up her skirts to march to the door.

The door burst open, and an out-of-breath Lucy rushed into the room. "Everyone is finally in place. We may proceed."

Grace's hand flew to Lucy's arms to prevent herself from barreling into her best friend. "Matthew's arrived? Where is he?"

Lucy turned to press her back against the door, forcing Grace to release her. Grace's papa stood tall and proud at the threshold. "Gracie girl, you look marvelous. Shall we go?" He was the one who appeared marvelous. He preferred not to have anyone around him with sharp objects should he lapse into confusion and become combative. Yet her papa's hair and beard were trimmed. Grace never doubted her parent's love for her, but it was these minor acts that touched her heart the most.

"What are you doing here?" Out of pure habit, Grace threaded her hand through the crook of her papa's arm. "You were to wait with Mama up front."

"I changed my mind. I shall walk with you to the alter."

Lucy shoved a bouquet of flowers in Grace's hand. "A gift from the Duchess of Fairmont." Grace looked down at the floral arrangement—lilacs, her favorite, were surrounded by white peonies and lavender, all bound together with blue-colored ribbon. Tears welled in her eyes.

Rounding the corner, Theo stood next to the closed doors that barred any more guests from entering the chapel. Her papa paused.

Grace peered up and asked, "What are we waiting for?"

"Your friends want to also walk with you in solidarity."

Lucy and Mary sneaked past them, and the trio formed a line. Lucy, her best friend, in front followed by Theo and then Mary. It was all too much. A tear trickled down her cheek. Her friends were her sisters. Lucy opened the double doors with a whoosh. Heads turned, and a hush came over the crowd.

Grace's gaze immediately sought out Matthew. Unlike Devonton, Archbroke, and Waterford, who were all looking adoringly down the aisle at their wives, Matthew had his back to her. He was in deep discussions with the priest.

As her friends moved to stand next to their husbands, her papa led her all the way up to the altar and said, "Harrington, is there a problem?"

Matthew jumped and spun around. "No issue. No issue at all. I was explaining to Reverend Cottingham that I shall be standing in as groom today."

Grace wanted to stomp her foot. Matthew had yet to acknowledge her presence.

The priest interrupted, "And I was informing Lord Harrington that the banns were read for another gentleman. We simply cannot proceed."

Good gracious, had no one thought to obtain a special license? This was why women should be in charge.

Archbroke coughed and said, "Harrington, I believe these will mitigate the reverend's concerns."

"Why didn't you give this to me earlier?" Matthew snatched the rolled-up parchment from Archbroke's hand and shoved it at the priest.

Reverend Cottingham pulled at the end of the red ribbon and the paper unfurled. The priest's bushy white eyebrows rose. "A decree issued by the Prince Regent."

Grace stepped in front of her papa to better see the order for herself.

Matthew's eyes widened as his gaze finally fell upon her. "You look marvelous."

From behind her, Grace's papa chuckled and said, "Harrington, you will have to be more original than that, she's already received such a compliment from me."

Ignoring the byplay between the men, Grace leaned forward and asked, "May I see the decree?"

Bushy gray eyebrows scowled down at her. "Certainly not." Reverend Cottingham rolled the parchment and held it to his chest.

The Prince Regent was hardly in the habit of issuing such benign orders. Grace asked, "What exactly does the decree state?"

Matthew's body tensed. "Do you no longer wish to marry me?"

"Of course, I want to marry you. I merely think it prudent we both know exactly what the Prince Regent has required of us."

Matthew swiveled to look back behind him. Grace followed and noted the guilty looks upon both Archbroke and Theo's faces.

Grace faced Matthew. "Do you know why a royal decree was issued?" His eyes darted away from hers. He did. The murmurs of the crowd grew. Should she trust Matthew or demand to view the parchment tightly held in the priest's hands?

Reverend Cottingham whispered, "Do you withhold your consent?"

Grace shook her head.

"Then I suggest we start the proceedings." The priest waited and then added, "It is a great honor that the Prince

Regent has bestowed upon your husband-to-be and yourself."

While Grace stared at the priest, who was talking in riddles, Matthew smiled and puffed out his chest as if he had been granted a medal of honor.

Grace made the request. "May I have a word with Lord Harrington before we begin?"

Ignoring her request, Reverend Cottingham opened his prayer book and began the ceremony. None of the men in her life treated her with such little regard. She had taken their liberal ways for granted.

Grace shifted sideways to view her friends. Theo was flanked by Lucy and Mary. Devonton was behind his wife. He towered over Lucy, not in a domineering way but in a loving, protective manner. Waterford stood at attention next to Mary, his eyes sliding over to his wife with admiration and a whisper of longing. Then there was Archbroke, who was slightly in front of Theo but not directly, ensuring that he'd not block his wife's view of the proceedings. It was not so long ago that Archbroke was of a similar mind as the priest, treating women as if they were placed on this earth merely to provide heirs. But it hadn't taken long for him to change his views as soon as he'd met Theo.

Grace inhaled sharply.

Theo.

Mary had stated Theo was the one responsible for seeing things were sorted with Prinny.

Leaning in closer to Matthew, Grace whispered, "Did Theo somehow manage to absolve you of your promise to Tobias not to pursue the matter of PORFs further?"

"She did."

"How?"

Matthew turned his attention back to the proceedings and the priest's prompt to repeat after him. Matthew's unquivering voice rang clear as he vowed to love and to cherish her for the rest of their days. He reached for Grace's hand and placed a ring upon her finger.

It was her turn to promise to honor and obey Matthew. She wasn't concerned about respecting her husband's wishes, and she would have uttered her vows with the same clarity as Matthew if they had shared the content of the decree.

Matthew's eyes were filled with uncertainty as he waited for her to finish repeating the words the priest prompted her to say. She didn't want him to worry about her intentions. But if her suspicion that she was, in fact, vowing to marry Matthew *and* pledging her allegiance and service to the PORFs was correct, shouldn't she be given a moment to consider?

She continued to mechanically parrot words of love and devotion after Reverend Cottingham. Out of the corner of her eye, she could swear she saw a man who looked identical to Burke. But the man was dead, declared so by the royal surgeon. Her eyes must be playing tricks as thoughts of PORFs whirled about in her head. She blinked and narrowed her gaze to the spot where she thought she'd seen a ghost.

Matthew presented his hand to her, and Grace reached for the ring that lay upon Reverend Cottingham's bible.

"What is the matter?" Matthew asked as she slid the ring onto his finger.

"Did you make promises on my behalf without consulting me?"

Matthew gripped her hand. "I'm sorry. I shouldn't have."

The man was infuriating. When would he learn not to act so impulsively?

"If we don't sign the registry, you could seek an annulment."

How could he even suggest an annulment? "You think that is what I want?"

"I hope it's not. But you are clearly disappointed in my decision, and if you prefer not to be bound to serve… well, you know who, then I'll understand." The sadness in his eyes nearly had Grace forgoing the opportunity to prove that in a marriage, one mustn't assume, but it requires healthy communication.

The priest snapped closed the book in his hands and declared to all, "I now pronounce you man and wife."

Following the priest over to the registry, Grace spoke softly for Matthew's ears only. "There was a time when we discussed every matter ad nauseam until we either both agreed, or we decided that there was no reasonable compromise."

For a brief moment, Matthew's pale face flushed pink. "Oh, I remember many a long night debating issues with you."

"There have only been two occasions I'm aware of in which you decided to universally make a choice without discussing the matter with me, and in both cases, the consequences were rather life changing."

Quill poised above the registry, Matthew said, "You want me to promise not to make unilateral decisions that have an impact on both our lives?"

Praise the saints, he finally understood.

"Yes, that is what I wish for."

Matthew dropped the quill to the table, and her heart sank. He wasn't going to sign the registry. She wanted to crumple to the ground, but his strong arms wrapped about her waist, and he rubbed his nose against hers. He waited until she met his gaze and then said, "Marchioness

Harrington, I pledge to thee to rectify my impulsive ways and promise to seek out your counsel, for you are the smartest woman I know."

Rolling onto the balls of her feet, Grace placed her lips upon her husband's and kissed him soundly in front of Reverend Cottingham and all the guests. The priest cleared his throat multiple times before Matthew released her, and then they both promptly scrawled their names and signed the registry.

The ink wasn't even dry upon the parchment when Archbroke and Hadfield whisked them away to an awaiting carriage.

Matthew eyed the pair who occupied the rear-facing seat.

Hadfield said, "Congratulations to you both."

Grace remained silent and shifted her weight slightly closer to Matthew. The intensity of the two men's stares was alarming.

"Our thanks. Where are the two of you escorting us now?" Matthew asked.

"We all shall adjourn to Flarinton's townhouse for a small celebration. Family and close friends only." Archbroke's normally serious features softened and he added, "It will allow Grace to say farewell to her parents before she leaves for her new residence."

As Archbroke finished his speech, Matthew braced himself. Grace never took kindly to men presuming her needs.

"How kind of you both to have arranged everything." The sarcasm in her tone was not lost on any of them.

Both men stiffened. Hadfield's smile faded away. "Lady Grace, as you have probably already deduced, you are now honor-bound to serve the Protectors of the Royal Family."

Grace narrowed her gaze at the unassuming man

opposite her. "For my edification, please confirm for me who those individuals are." She could feel Matthew's eyes on her. If none of them had believed it necessary to talk the matter over with her prior, they were bloody well going to discuss it now.

"There are three titled families—Burke, Archbroke, and Hadfield. You are to assist and protect the current titleholders and their immediate family." Hadfield leaned forward. "I request you personally give me your word that you agree to honor the code of silence and pledge to serve the families as needed."

She wasn't ready to make this easy for any of the men in the coach. "I've already promised to obey my husband in front of everyone. Is that not enough?"

Hadfield's voice deepened. "Lady Grace, it is out of respect that I make this request of you."

"Respect, you say." Grace glanced at Archbroke then back to Hadfield. "Very well. You have my word." Apparently satisfied, Hadfield sat back and lounged as if he had not a care.

In dark contrast, Archbroke's brow furrowed. Excellent, at least her counterpart acknowledged her displeasure at no longer being considered his equal.

The carriage came to a stop.

Hadfield reached for the door handle but pinned Grace with his eyes. "It is an honor to have you join the network."

Grace gathered her skirts and crouched to exit. "I've been told the honor is mine to have been invited." She didn't wait for a response and hopped down onto the path. Matthew alighted from the coach and escorted her up the steps.

From behind them, Hadfield chuckled and said, "Harrington is fortunate she saved his hide."

Her husband leaned in close and said, "I agree. I am an extremely fortunate man, and I promise not to forget it."

Grace replied, "Make sure you don't."

The teasing crinkles about the corner of Matthew's mouth appeared as he gave her a slightly lopsided smile. Her pulse sped up. She had not seen that smile in nearly two years. His lips grazed over hers, and the familiar feeling that nothing could separate them seeped into her bones. She pulled back and took in the sight of her husband. They were finally married, and she, for one, was ready to begin the next phase of her life as Marchioness Harrington.

Becoming members of the network would be a tremendous change. The PORFs and the network were complex entities. Perhaps she should welcome such a change. Grace halted just before they crossed the threshold. A flash of bright light and an image of Burke snickering at the wedding appeared as she blinked. Silverman swung the front door open for them. Matthew moved forward, and she smiled as they walked by the family butler.

The sound of guests filled the hall. If Burke truly wasn't dead, the devil would hunt both Matthew and her down. Trusting her intuition, she squeezed Matthew's hand and then placed it upon the stair rail. "I need to speak to Tilman. I'll join you in a moment."

She raced up the stairs and left her husband behind. She needed to devise a plan to lure Burke out into the open without endangering her friends and family who were now congregating to celebrate her marriage.

CHAPTER TWENTY-SEVEN

*H*is wife was no coward. Grace was lively, engaging, and could manage even the most difficult conversationalists at a social function. But Matthew was fully aware it took an enormous toll on her. Grace needed quiet time to reenergize, and after the day's events, she deserved a few minutes of peace.

As his wife disappeared up the stairs, Matthew squared his shoulders and exhaled. He headed down the hall, ready to greet friends and family he had avoided since his return from the Continent. In the past, the buzz of excitement of those near him fueled Matthew, and he'd seek out the company of the most boisterous groups or forms of entertainment. But crowds no longer held their appeal, and rather than replenishing his energy they now caused vast amounts of anxiety. He was glad the group he was about to encounter would be limited and composed of those who truly cared for Grace and himself.

Clasping his quaking hands behind his back, he walked straight through the large drawing room and out onto the terrace where his father-in-law stood alone. The man might not be the dashing, robust Foreign Secretary he once was, despite Lady Flarinton's continued adoring looks, but Flarinton was still the steadfast gentleman that had counseled Matthew during a time he was left floundering with the mess his papa had left the Harrington estate in. He was the man who had predicted upon their first meeting that Matthew would fall in love with Grace. Flarinton was a brilliant man, even when battling an aging disease. Matthew's views of the man would never change.

Matthew stood next to Flarinton and looked out into the garden. "I apologize for not seeking you out sooner."

"No need to apologize, son." His father-in-law's heavy hand fell upon his shoulder. Without waiting for a reply, Flarinton continued, "Hadfield had the marriage agreements redrawn, said the ones drafted by Burke's men were totally inadequate to protect Grace and her rightful inheritance. I'll have them delivered to you tomorrow." There was a note of confusion in Flarinton's voice, but the man's eyes were bright and clear.

"Certainly. I'll sign and return your copy as soon as they arrive."

Flarinton's hand dropped to his side. "Don't you find it a tad peculiar that Hadfield took it upon himself to intervene?"

A bark of laughter escaped Matthew. "Not at all. The man was a barrister, and his involvement was most likely at Theo's insistence. The woman is rather protective of her friends."

Quick footfalls fell on the stone behind them. Turning, Matthew found himself being descended upon by his sister with Theo and Mary in tow.

Hands on her hips, Lucy stood a scant inch too close and demanded, "Where is Grace?"

While his twin was only six minutes older than him, she

never let him forget she was the elder. "Abovestairs. She went to speak with her maid."

The trio's husbands were not far behind. Waterford was actually smiling as they approached. His jovial manner vanished as soon as he laid eyes upon his wife.

Theo held up a hand, halting the men. "Which of you confirmed Burke's death?"

Archbroke answered his wife's question. "Ellingsworth saw to the details, and the royal physician provided his report to me directly."

Hands planted on her hips, Theo asked, "Are you telling me that none of you actually saw Burke's dead body?"

The hairs on Matthew's arms stood on end. Why had no one physically verified the devil's demise? Matthew's gaze flew to Mary, who was wrapped up in her husband's arms, whispering. He turned to scan the second-floor windows. Grace's room was dark. Panic set in. Running back through the house, Matthew took the stairs two at a time. He ignored the glares he received from the maids scurrying about.

Matthew spotted Tilman at the end of the hall. "Where is your mistress?"

"Out in the gardens. My lady said she needed time to think."

Fear ran down his spine. Surely her footmen were with her, but the woman was a master at evading her well-trained protectors. He should have stayed with Grace; he had sensed she was upset. Rushing through the kitchen doors, Matthew sprinted toward the gazebo. If Burke remained alive, he would have to be crazed to confront Grace with everyone close by. No, the man would lie low, bide his time, and devise some complex strategy and employ others to carry out his wishes. The devil never personally executed any of his horrendous schemes. The bastard was a master manipulator.

Rationalizing that there was no way Burke would attempt an attack on Grace here tonight on her papa's property, Matthew slowed his steps. However, the skin on his forearms still prickled. If she was alone and safe, he'd look like an idiot rushing in like a madman. But if she was in danger, Grace was skilled at self-defense. Matthew shook his head to clear his mind. What was wrong with him? Indecision resulted in the loss of life. He'd always been a man to act first, then modify his actions if necessary. A soft, wheezing sound came from the shadows.

Matthew stilled and called out, "Show yourself."

Out of the shadows, Hadfield appeared, then stopped. He bent at the waist and rested his hands just above his knees. Inhaling appeared to be trying for the man.

Matthew rushed over to the PORF he had sworn to protect and serve. "How can I assist?"

"Burke... He... was sighted... at the church... earlier."

At the church! During the ceremony, Matthew recalled the moment Grace had lost all color, as if she had seen a ghost. Damnation. The woman was attempting to lure Burke out of the shadows.

Matthew broke into a full sprint. A startled cry pierced the night air as he rounded the bend and the gazebo came into sight.

HANDS CLASPED BEHIND HER BACK, Grace paced, and scanned the octagon-shaped floor. Devoid of the rug and cushions that she had carefully arranged against the far side, the gazebo was cold and barren. She needed the area clear of all potential threats. As the seconds ticked by, the temptation to light a candle and dispel the shadows increased. Grace shook her head. The risk of Burke using a small flame to his advantage was too high. Stealing her nerves, Grace froze and inhaled deeply. She should conserve her energy for the battle to come.

Even though she had anticipated Burke's arrival, she still let out a surprised whelp when his large form engulfed the entrance. She couldn't afford to show any signs of weakness. Burke withdrew a shiny steel dagger. There were no nicks or any indication of it ever being removed from its scabbard.

Arms bent at the elbow out in front of her, palms down to protect her chest and face, Grace mirrored Burke's steps to the side. Except she was wiser to know not to cross her legs as they went around and around in circles. Grace waited for Burke to break the silence.

"You turned my son against me!" Burke's dilated but alert eyes followed her every movement. His lips were discolored with a tingle of blue and white spittle pooled at the corner of his mouth. The man was vile.

"It was your own actions that have landed you in this position." Grace angled her head to the left to stretch out the tense muscles in her neck. She readjusted her stance, while her hands remained out in front of her, square to her shoulders. Grace was more than ready and capable of relieving Burke of his knife should he lunge forward. In fact, she wanted him to attempt the foolish move. She should have taken retribution against the man months ago. The devil was overdue in paying for his sins—years of racketeering, having orchestrated the kidnapping of her number one agent, Devonton, coordinating Matthew's imprisonment, and disabusing his power as a PORF. Hatred flowed through her veins.

Grace spied the man's grip on the short blade. *Pfft.* The

fool's thumb lay along the spine. His lack of knife skills would make it all the easier to relieve him of the weapon.

She should be inside, celebrating her union to Matthew, not pacing about with a madman. The notion of abandoning her training and be the one to attack first came and went. No. She needed to be patient. If she could elevate his ire and provoke him to attack, it would allow her the opportunity to knock the blade away.

The moonlight highlighted Burke's crazed eyes as they flickered about. "Poison is the weapon of a lady. I know it was you who attempted to send me off to another world. Did you discover my fateful plans for you?"

Of all the methods to choose to do away with his sire, Tobias had selected poison—typically untraceable, often with the death attributed to natural causes. How fortunate for Burke that the amount administered had been insufficient to kill.

The man was as shifty as they came. She needed to maintain her wits about her and keep him talking. If she was missing long enough, Matthew would arrive to assist. "I heard a variety of scenarios, none of which would have succeeded as they were all poorly designed."

Burke stopped and stepped forward. "You spiteful wench." He swayed as he took another step closer. "Where is Tobias? Why was he not at the church?"

"Tobias is no longer…" She paused, letting her words settle between them. With a shrug, she said, "Your son is gone."

"You bitch! You may have succeeded in taking Tobias, but your attempt to see that I meet my maker failed."

The skin on the back of Grace's neck came alive. Matthew was close by.

Maintaining Burke's attention, she crossed her arms at the wrist to make an X. Then she quickly resumed her defensive position with her hands out front, ready to disarm Burke. She prayed Matthew would heed her command not to attack.

Burke raised his tattered coat sleeve to wipe the excess spittle from his mouth, nearly lopping off his own nose. "Girl, you are no match for me. I'm a bloody PORF, and if the network rumors are correct, you serve me, dammit."

The man's eyes narrowed. He was about to go on the attack.

Grace lowered her stance and shifted to the side. Burke reached out with his free hand, attempting to grab her shoulder, but she was quick, avoiding his meaty hand.

"I'll kill you and your interfering husband when he comes looking for you." Burke raised his arm.

The knife slashed through the air. Without thought, Grace nimbly trapped him at the elbow. She used her body weight to pull his arm and twisted it until Burke growled in agony and released the blade. With the dagger firmly in her hand, Grace pushed the man away from her. But he didn't go down to his knees as she expected. Instead, he rose with his hands stretched out in front of him, reaching for her neck. "You little whore. Get back here."

Burke lunged forward.

She raised the dagger, and a second later it was buried deep into the man's chest—all the way to the hilt. Knocked to the ground, Grace scrambled backward and said, "It is not I who will die this eve." Her gaze never left her attacker.

Burke extracted the weapon, and the stench of blood brought bile up to Grace's throat.

Unsteady, but still on his feet, Burke waved the ruby-red blade. "I'm going to slice that pretty little neck of yours." He staggered forward.

She needed to get back up onto her feet, but her limbs were frozen.

Out from the shadows, Matthew appeared and deftly placed one arm about Burke's reddened neck. Her husband's arm flexed, cutting off Burke's airway until the man went limp. The devil's body slid down the front of Matthew and collapsed to the ground.

Her husband could have killed the bastard with a simple twist of the neck, but he was too damn honorable. It was why his original plan to see Burke tried instead of having a deadly accident had failed.

Grace looked down at her shaking hands. Matthew had the right of it. The death of another by one's hand was a terrible thing to live with.

Matthew crouched down and assisted her to her feet. "I'm so proud of you."

Crushed in his embrace, she placed her hand over her husband's erratic heartbeat. The sight of Burke's blood on her hand made her whole-body shiver. Grace buried her head against his chest and mumbled, "It's over."

A masculine cough came from the gazebo entrance. Grace lifted her head. Hadfield walked over to Burke's unmoving form and, with the toe of his boot, rolled the unconscious man over.

Hadfield ran a hand over his face. "Take your wife inside and send Waterford out here."

Matthew bent, and firmly placing an arm under her knees, he lifted her up and cradled her against him.

Grace asked, "Is he dead?" She needed to hear the words, to know for certain that the devil had finally met his fate and was no longer a threat.

Hadfield squatted and pressed two fingers to Burke's neck. "Yes."

Grace's entire body trembled.

Matthew gathered her closer. "We'll enter through the kitchens. No need to alarm the guests."

Grace nodded, but her thoughts were still upon Burke. For years she'd wished the man dead—and now he was. She had killed Burke. Regardless that she had acted in self-defense, taking a life was a burden she would carry to her grave. Grace peered up at her husband through her lashes. "It's nothing like we practiced."

"I'm glad we did. Otherwise, you would not be standing here." Matthew's voice was gruff, but his eyes were filled with love and concern. He placed a kiss upon the top of her bent head.

Matthew tensed. A man was running along the path toward them—Waterford. He stopped in front of him, not in the least bit winded. "My wife informed me you might require my assistance."

"Hadfield is waiting for you in the gazebo."

Waterford's eyes widened as he saw the blood on her dress. "Are you injured?" He reached out as if he meant to run a hand over her to check for injuries.

Matthew stepped back, placing her out of Waterford's reach. "What do you think you are about?"

"I tended to my men's wounds. I can help."

"It's Burke's blood, not hers." Matthew stepped around a stunned Waterford. "Hadfield is waiting."

Waterford nodded and resumed running down the path.

They made it back to the servants' entrance.

Grace smiled at the footman on guard. "Please inform Lady Oldridge we will not be returning for the evening and have her advise the guests it's time to leave."

Her bodyguard avoided Matthew's gaze, nodded, and quickly left.

"You can put me down now."

Matthew ignored her and carried her up the stairs, despite the fact his breathing was labored. She kept the observation to herself and basked in his warmth. When they reached her chamber door, he bent at the knees. Grace released the door latch and pushed the door open. He gave no indication he intended to let her go.

Matthew walked straight to the bed and sat upon it, settling her upon his lap. Pushing a strand of hair behind her ear, he asked, "Do you want me to arrange to have the coach readied, or would you prefer we remain guests of your parents for the night?"

Leaning her cheek into his palm, Grace smiled. While Matthew's gesture to remain another night under her papa's roof was considerate, the thought of them consummating their marriage while her parents were in their chambers a few doors down the hall was not ideal. Her room was devoid of her personal belongings, and it was time for her to begin as Marchioness Harrington. "Please have the coach readied. I'm ready to go home."

CHAPTER TWENTY-EIGHT

*M*atthew closed his eyes as the coach took the final turn before they reached his townhouse. Home. The word rattled Matthew to his core. Upon his return, England, Halestone Hall, his townhouse, none of them held the same appeal as they had before. With Grace snuggled tightly against his side, he now understood why. She was the key to everything he treasured.

Grace was exhausted. But she didn't appear to be suffering any ill effects from her dreadful encounter with Burke. Keenly aware of the toll her actions would take upon her soul, Matthew reconsidered consummating their marriage. Yes. He'd wait until tomorrow.

Coward. Damn his conscience.

It was out of consideration for Grace. *Liar.*

Why could he not even deceive himself? He swallowed and tried to ignore the mounting anxiety that was building within him. Grace had already seen the scars and the twisted, mangled sections of his chest. But seeing and touching were two entirely different things. She would initially be curious like he had been, but the reality was puckered skin was not at all sensual. It was repulsive, and the associated memories remained painful.

He didn't want her sympathy, and she damn well better not feel any guilt—both of which Matthew was certain Grace would experience, even if she didn't outwardly show it.

Sleepily, she said, "I don't remember your residence being this far."

"We are nearly there, love." Proving his point, the coach slowed to a crawl. Then the coach came to a complete stop, and the door was flung wide open. "Would you like me to carry you up to your chambers?"

"Good gracious, no. I want to greet the staff as I should." Grace looked down at the dark stains on her gown. Green and red were a terrible combination. "Perhaps I should meet them tomorrow."

Matthew stuck his head out and said, "Inform Kirkland her ladyship would prefer to meet the household in the morn." The footman scurried up the path to pass along Grace's wishes. Matthew turned to Grace and asked, "Ready, my love?"

His wife nodded. Matthew rose to exit, but for a moment, his legs remained unmoving, his fear manifesting itself most inconveniently. *Buck up and get on with it.* Throwing himself out of the coach, he surprisingly landed on both feet and straightened.

Grace took his offered hand as she descended from the coach. "Is anything the matter?"

Relaxing every facial muscle possible, he answered, "No."

What was he doing? Why was he attempting to deceive his wife? He'd dreamed of taking her to bed every night for months. The pent-up tension in his groin was unbearable. It had worsened since their interlude in the gazebo.

There was no question he craved her body. It was his damn fear that his damaged body would no longer appeal to Grace that had him behaving like a fool.

Grace arched an eyebrow. "Shall we go in now?"

He winged his arm, but instead of threading her hand through the crook of his elbow, she reached for his hand and interlaced her fingers with his. Walking hand in hand, they entered the townhouse, which was abuzz with activity. Maids and footmen rushed about as if the house was on fire.

Matthew stopped in front of Kirkland. "Is anything amiss?"

"No, my lord. We weren't expecting you for a few more hours. I sent maids up to assist Tilman, and I have the lads getting ready to haul up hot water as soon as it can be boiled."

Grace squeezed his hand. Remembering his manners, Matthew said, "Grace, this is our esteemed butler, Mr. Kirkland."

Color rose to the older man's cheeks. "My lady, it is my pleasure to welcome you."

"My thanks to you and the staff for accommodating our early arrival. I do look forward to meeting everyone on the morrow." Grace bestowed one of her rare bright, heartfelt smiles upon Kirkland.

Matthew led Grace down the hall and up the flight of stairs to the second floor. Each step closer to her chamber, his apprehension grew. He hoped his memory had not failed him. It was nearly three years since he had led her to this room and asked her to describe the perfect bedchamber. She had spun about the room rattling off colors—indigo, cyan, ultramarine, all of which he had thought of as simply blue. But the sparkle in Grace's eyes at the time told him they were more than blue, that the various colors could evoke within the human brain certain emotions. He grinned, recalling her swiveling and declaring she would never care for the color yellow in her bedchamber for she believed it spurred one to anger. While he hadn't any idea if the notion was, in fact, truth, Matthew had ordered the designers to decorate the room in various shades of blue and to avoid any hue of yellow. Pushing the door open, he allowed Grace to enter first.

His wife stopped three steps in and twirled about the room. "Oh, Matthew, it's perfect." She moved to the bed and ran a hand over the silk bed linens. "You remembered everything." Grace stepped out of her slippers and rubbed the sole of her right foot against the plush floor rug and then walked over to the corner where an extraordinary number of cushions of all sizes and fabrics were strewn about. "Where is Tilman?"

Her maid appeared at the entrance of the connecting door that led to a separate chamber he had refurbished for Grace. "Here I am. I have your bath ready, my lady."

"Through there?"

Tilman smiled, "Yes." The maid ducked out of sight.

"I had a chamber refurbished for your use." Pleased at the shocked expression upon Grace's face, Matthew continued, "If Tilman finds you need more cabinets designed and installed, please inform Kirkland, and he will contact the carpenters."

"Cabinets?" Grace raced to the adjoining door that Tilman had occupied moments ago and stuck her head into the room.

The woman gasped, but from across the room, Matthew couldn't decipher if it was in horror or excitement. He used to be able to interpret every single sound and facial expression Grace made. She was probably eager to bathe and be rid of Burke's blood.

Matthew cleared the knot that was forming in his windpipes. "Is there anything else you need from me?"

Whirling around, Grace walked directly up to him. Matthew released a breath as he recognized the emotion in her eyes—joy. She was pleased with what he'd done to the room.

"You transformed an entire chamber for me to bathe and change. I shared my dream with you and…" Grace blinked, she had tears in her eyes. She lifted her gaze and said, "You made it come true."

His heart pattered in his chest. "My hope is that I can make all your dreams come true."

A pink blush appeared at the tops of Grace's cheeks. "All of them?" The minx was up to something. Her voice had dropped an octave.

He nodded, and his wife's lips were upon his. Wrapping her arms about his neck, she leaned up close to his ear. "I've had a few new ones."

"Is that so?"

"Perhaps we could discuss them in the other room?" Her gaze slid to her bathing chamber. "Will you assist me this eve?"

Matthew blinked. His entire body hummed with excitement. One of his favorite reoccurring dreams was seeing Grace soaking in a tub, slick and soapy, and him drying her with soft linens while her fingers massaged the back of his neck. The angels were blessing him with a reprieve of sorts. He could remain fully clothed, while Grace would be naked in the water.

"It would be my pleasure to aid you tonight."

Rewarded with a smile and a kiss, Grace stepped back and headed for the connecting door.

CHAPTER TWENTY-NINE

*G*race crossed the threshold with Matthew in tow. Her husband was behaving strangely. His irises were dilated, and one corner of his lips was curled into a grin. Though his body was responsive, something was preventing him from acting upon his desire.

Tilman rose as they entered. Upon seeing Matthew enter also, her maid quickly bobbed and left, along with the remaining maids and footmen in the room. The sensitive spot on the back of her neck prickled as Matthew placed his hand at the small of her back. Grace clasped her hands tightly in front to prevent from wringing them like a nervous ninny. The notion of Matthew pleasuring her and experiencing the exquisite connection with him once more had her bones turning to pudding.

Needing to be free of her soiled gown and soak in the scented bathwater, she spun around to find Matthew coatless and kneeling next to the bath as steam rose into the air. His lawn shirt sleeves were rolled up to his elbows as he ran his hand through the water.

"What are you doing?"

He stood, and a familiar beguiling smile appeared on her husband's handsome face. "What does it look like? I was checking the temperature to ensure the water doesn't scald you."

He reached out and turned her by the shoulders. His fingers grazed along her spine as he worked the long row of buttons free. The man was taking double the length of time Tilman would require. Grace suspected Matthew's slow progress was intentional. Her breathing became shallow as the green silk gown slid over her hips to the floor.

She giggled at the light tug at her laces. Tonight Matthew was taking extreme care. Grace supposed he did not wish to knot the ribbons, as he had once before.

Matthew chuckled. "I don't have a knife on me tonight, love. You'll have to be patient."

The mention of a blade had her spine stiffening. She had successfully blocked out Burke and her violent actions up until now. The air left her lungs.

"Damnation. I'm sorry. I did not mean to…"

Grace turned and placed a hand over his mouth. Guilt filled his gaze. "Don't apologize. It is not your fault Ellingsworth didn't administer enough poison to ensure Burke's death. It's not your fault. The man was mad and set out to kill us both."

He shook his head, and her hand fell away. "I should never have placed you in danger. I could have intervened sooner."

"Should. Could. Would. I too use these words far too often. They can be extremely dangerous." She cupped his face, ready to confess to the inner turmoil she was experiencing. "I will not lie. My encounter with Burke has my nerves rattled." She raised her trembling hands for him to see. "I feel remorse for being responsible for another's death, but I don't regret my actions. Even knowing the impact on my soul, if I were confronted again by such a danger, I'd take the same actions. There is no reasoning with a madman." A weight from her heart lifted as each word left her mouth. Matthew was the only person she was able to share these innermost thoughts and revelations with without feeling as though she was being judged.

Her corset fell away. Matthew must have been working on the strings all the while. Free and at peace in her husband's arms, she finally breathed easy.

Matthew's soothing strokes along her back ceased, and desire flared in his eyes. She inched her hands down the sides of his neck and then threaded her fingers into his hair. Her husband's lips were upon hers, gentle at first, but when she poked her tongue out, seeking his, Matthew deepened the kiss and devoured her like a starving man.

He pressed her closer, and his hands roamed over her body. Blast the fabric of her chemise. Every inch of her skin tingled and longed for the feel of his palms. When his hand brushed up against her ribs as it moved to cup her breast, her nipples hardened in anticipation. She wanted to feel his fingers against the taut buds. Grace took a step back, and Matthew released his grip on her. Crossing her arms, she gripped the offending material at her hips and drew it over her head. Standing bare before Matthew, Grace finally felt whole once more. Her brazen spirit roared within her. She stepped forward and reached for Matthew's hand. Grace placed his hand upon the center of her chest just below her neck. His thumb and forefinger rested upon her collarbones. His forearm rested along her middle.

Frozen, her husband stared at his hand. It used to be his favored starting position, for she never knew what to expect. She loved the anticipation, and he did too. Would he tease the sensitive skin of her neck? Lower his hand to cup her swollen breasts? Skim it along the center of her to rest at her core? Grace didn't care which he chose.

Matthew's thumb stroked Grace's collarbone back and forth repeatedly. Her breath hitched in anticipation, unfurling throughout her body. In the past, he had been the teacher, guiding Grace to explore. He encouraged her to express which of his touches she preferred. Her preferences tended to closely align with his reactions. If his breathing became erratic or his pulse beat faster, it only heightened her own responses and a desire for more. Matthew's breathing remained slow and steady. Grace stepped back. It was time to see if she could set Matthew on edge as she had long ago.

She raised her leg, exposing her inner thigh, and dipped her pointed toe into the lukewarm water. Easing herself into the bath, she turned back to reach for the washcloth and scented soap, but they were no longer on the stool.

Instead, Matthew knelt behind her, with both items in his hand. "Allow me."

He submerged the cloth in the bath. He squeezed the small square of material, and water rolled down over her shoulder, collarbone, and gently down the slope of her breast. His palm, covered with the soapy cloth, retraced the path the water had made.

Grace leaned her head back and closed her eyes. Matthew's warm breath tickled her ear. His tongue flicked at her earlobe, and then he suckled it. She controlled her breathing, wanting to prolong his attention. If the man detected her already-heightened state of excitement, he would ease up only to build them up once more, over and over, until she was on the edge of bliss without the pleasure of him inside her.

In a steady voice, Matthew said, "I see I'll have to relearn all your preferences."

No. Grace was fairly certain all the spots on her body that were partial to his touch remained the same. She slid her hands under her bottom, preventing them from reaching out for Matthew. Grace refused to be the first to reveal the depths of her true desires. She wanted to hear his voice crack, see him shift with discomfort, or better yet, to listen to his breathing come in fits and spurts. She didn't have to wait long. Matthew drew the cloth over one breast and then the other. He released a moan of pure desire as he lowered the fabric over her slit. Her eyes fluttered open.

Matthew moved to the side of the bath and stared directly at her. "I need you, wife."

Grace needed him too. Her hands twitched, eager to explore his body once more. Her pulse raced as she raked her gaze over her husband. His dark nipples taunted her through his wet lawn shirt. His breeches were strained tight against his enlarged manhood.

Matthew bent over her. For a moment, she pictured pulling him down into the soapy water with her, but that wouldn't allow her to fully explore his form. She wrapped her arms about his neck as he dipped his arm into the water and placed it under her bent knees. With his other arm wrapped securely around her back, he lifted her from the bath. Water sloshed to the floor. Careless of the mess they were making, she kissed and nibbled at his neck. The vibrations of his neck against her lips as he groaned rippled throughout her. Hot flames of desire flared in her belly. Focused on the salty taste of him, Grace was surprised to feel the silk sheets beneath her bottom.

Her smile faded as Matthew stepped back and ran his hand through his hair.

Grace shifted and knelt at the edge of the bed. "Love,

will you share with me what is truly troubling you?" She refrained from reaching out for him; they needed to have this out first.

"I'm not the same man as I once was." Matthew toed off his shoes. "I find I don't like wearing shoes and especially boots that are confining and restricting." He bent and rolled off his stockings next. "My clothing is itchy despite being made from the finest fabrics."

Grace swallowed hard. She was trying to concentrate on Matthew's speech, but in reality, she was silently praying he would remove his soaking lawn shirt next. To her dismay, Matthew stopped disrobing entirely.

"I left England believing there wasn't anything in this world that would stop me from succeeding in my mission. It was a crushing blow to realize that, in fact, I was a pampered, titled gentleman that had seen and been exposed to little."

The distant look in Matthew's eyes told her he was no longer here with her. She needed to bring him back to the present. If she reached out, it might startle him. If she distanced herself, he may assume the worst, that she no longer desired him.

In a voice barely above a whisper, Grace said, "No person is perfect. I loved the man you were before, and I love you now, imperfections and all."

Her husband inhaled deeply and pulled his shirttails out from his breeches. Slowly, as if he was in pain, Matthew lifted the garment over his head and let it fall atop his stockings and shoes. With his chest puffed out, he hadn't released his breath, as if he was awaiting her reaction.

Grace took in the marvelous sight of him. Matthew's skin was no longer silky smooth, and his muscles were not as well defined, but in her opinion, he was perfect. Grace placed her hands on his waist to tug him closer. Instead of exhaling, the man gasped. She quickly pulled her hands away.

"Your hands are like ice blocks." Matthew grabbed her hands and rubbed them between his.

"If you would hurry and undress, we could warm each other." Taking control, Grace deftly unbuttoned his falls and tugged at the waistband of his breeches. Warm hands brushed hers away. She licked her lips in anticipation as Matthew bent, pushing the last remaining garment standing in her way down to the floor.

Pleased to see his full erection, Grace shimmied lower. She wanted him. Grasping him with one hand, she guided the tip of his shaft along the seam of her lips before she opened and took all of him into her mouth.

Matthew's fingers threaded through her hair. "Lord, I've missed you."

His graveled voice had her relaxing her jaw as he gently pushed on the back of her head. She took in every inch of his manhood.

Matthew released a guttural groan. "Love, that feels so damn good."

She tightened her lips about him as she slid her mouth over the length of him over and over until he tugged at her hair and released a deep moan. Moisture pooled between her legs. Pulling back to glance up at Matthew, she stuck out her tongue and circled the tip the way she remembered would drive the man to act. He didn't hesitate. He gyrated his hips forward, and he entered her waiting mouth once more. This time it was Grace who let out a moan as his staff thickened with each stroke. She released him with a pop. "I want you, husband."

Matthew showed no hesitation and sprawled upon the

bed, assuming a relaxed pose with his hands behind his head. "Do as you please, wife."

Grace could barely contain her excitement. She loved riding him—it was her favorite position. His intense gaze brightened as Grace situated herself over him. Matthew let out a groan of relief and satisfaction as she lowered herself inch by inch until she was fully seated upon him. She lifted herself up slightly and then circled her hips as she glided back down. His arms wiggled as if he was about to remove them from their position.

Grace stopped and arched an eyebrow.

"No hands?" Matthew asked.

"Not until I find my release."

He shifted under her as his gaze roamed over her body and back to her face.

"Very well, until your first."

Grace leaned forward and placed her palms flat against his chest, then trailed them down his sides. Matthew wiggled, as he was especially ticklish just below the ribs. They both enjoyed testing each other's limits.

Matthew's movements awakened an urge within her that had lain dormant. She reached one hand behind her and slid his cock between her first two fingers and cupped her bottom. As she rose and fell, his erection pushed against her slick fingers. With her other hand, she cupped her breast and squeezed. Every muscle in her body tightened. Her rhythmic movements became erratic as she came apart. Matthew's hands flew to her hips. He lifted his own hips, entering her over and over with increased speed and force.

Grace commanded, "Don't stop." She was on the verge of climaxing again. Matthew obliged, pumping into her as his hands shifted to her waist and then up and over her breasts. Eyes closed tight; he was on the verge of finding his own release. He tweaked her nipples, sending pure pleasure down to her core.

"Matthew… don't stop until you spill your seed."

If he answered, Grace hadn't heard it over her moans. She rode him hard until he released his bottom lip that was trapped by his teeth, and his thrusts slowed. Circling her hips, she found her second release, and his manhood twitched inside her.

Grace collapsed atop of her husband, who chuckled, "Shall I keep going?"

Pushing herself up, between heated kisses, Grace whispered, "Please."

Her husband again obliged, except this time he rolled her onto her side and took her from behind—her second most preferred way to take him. Grace was determined to find out if he remembered her third, fourth, and fifth most favored positions.

EPILOGUE

HALESTONE HALL 1818...

*F*inally, after two weeks, and a house full of guests, Matthew found himself alone in his study. Without the constant drone of guests' voices, the ringing in his ears was driving him mad. Eyes closed, he rested his elbows upon the desk, placed his palms over his ears, and pressed his fingers against the back of his head. He lifted his right forefinger and began to tap. Fifty would be his goal this morn. Last evening after the last guests had left, it had taken a hundred evenly timed beats to ease the persistent buzzing in his head.

Tap. Tap. Tap... At last, the humming ceased. With a sigh, Matthew opened his eyes.

His beautiful wife was sitting in the chair opposite him with a ready smile. "How many today?"

"Forty-five."

"Ah, you must be pleased." Grace placed four scrolls upon his desk.

Matthew reached for the rolled-up parchments, but his wife pushed them to the side, an inch out of his reach. He asked, "What are those?"

For days, Grace and Blake had huddled together, discussing what he assumed were matters for the Foreign Office. His days were spent sequestered away with Hadfield, Archbroke, and Waterford to go over the training schedule devised for him by the council of network elders. It had been a hellish fortnight, and he was ready to once again spend some alone time with his wife.

Grace retrieved a deck of cards from her pockets. "Care to play a game of brag?"

What was the minx up to? A challenge to a game of brag meant the matter was of some import and had potential impact on their lives.

"What are we playing for?"

Cards interlaced as Grace shuffled. "Winner gets to select one of the four designs Blake created." She pointed over to the scrolls. "Shall we play?"

"I'd like to raise the stakes before agreeing." Matthew paused and grabbed a feather from his desk drawer and placed it upon the desk. "One hour."

His wife's eyes widened at his meaning. An hour of teasing with a feather inevitably had one of them begging for release.

The muscles of Grace's throat worked as she swallowed. "Thirty minutes."

"Very well, I'll compromise. Forty-five and not a second less."

Nimbly squaring the deck with her fingers, Grace nodded and gave him the deck to deal. Not bothering to shuffle the cards, he alternated sliding a card in front of them until they each had two cards face down in front of them. The highest card next dealt would determine the winner of the first phase.

Believing luck was on his side, Matthew arched an eyebrow and asked, "Interested in making a separate wager for this round?"

Grace narrowed her gaze upon him. "What did you have in mind, husband?"

He stuck a finger between his neck and his simply knotted cravat and tugged it loose. Pulling one end away from him, Matthew dangled the silk material in front of Grace. "Winner gets to bind the other." During the first few weeks of their marriage, he couldn't stand to be bound, instantly bringing back nightmares from his captivity and dousing his arousal. But Grace loved the freedom to explore his body without the distraction of his hands upon her. Now, a year later, his mind no longer rebelled against the soft fabric wound around his wrist, but Grace rarely requested the boon that gave her immense pleasure.

His wife's gaze raked over his face. "Very well. I agree to your terms."

He'd not lose either way. If she was to bind him, he'd have the pleasure of her hands and mouth exploring him, and should he be the victor, he'd have her bound and able to take full advantage of his time with the feather, for he was determined to win all the rounds.

Grace frowned at the eight of hearts in front of her. He needed a nine or better. Slowly flipping over his card, Matthew revealed a ten of spades. He'd won.

Graciously his wife conceded the round. "I see luck may be on your side today, husband, but it won't aid you in the next two rounds."

Matthew waited for Grace to peek at the two cards that made up the rest of her hand before he did. The woman was a master at hiding her reactions and feelings, but she still possessed a few tells. Controlled blinking was a sure sign she had a pair. Was it a pair of eights, or had he dealt her a higher?

Lifting the corners of his own two cards, Matthew evened out his breathing and attempted not to reveal any clues as to what his hand might consist of. He glanced down at his cards a second time—a pair of fours. Not strong enough to win, if he had guessed Grace's hand correctly, but if she believed she was beat, she might concede the round. "Wife, I forgot to ask, what does the winner of this round receive?"

Grace drummed her finger over the wood desk. "Might I suggest the winner receives the pleasure of a fruit platter."

An image of brushing a slice of peach along her lips and then kissing the juice from her mouth had Matthew shifting in his seat. "Agreed, and I concede this round." If he revealed his cards, Grace would have been able to calculate the odds of her winning the next and final round, determined by whose total points came closest to thirty-one. "I look forward to feeding you your favorite fruits. I shall speak to Cook to have all arranged for this eve."

"Hmmm. I look forward to it then."

"Care for another card?" If he had read her body language correctly, then she would be wise to pass so as not to go over thirty-one. In contrast, his paltry score of eighteen meant he'd need to at least draw one, if not two cards, to come close to the winning number.

Grace ran the pearl pendant he had gifted her long ago back and forth along its silver chain. His gaze habitually fell to her décolletage, and his eyebrows came together. Grace's breasts were nearly falling out of her dress, or had

Ms. Lennox devised a new design to make them appear that way?

"I don't believe I need another." Grace flipped over her cards early.

A pair of knaves. He would need two cards to beat her score of twenty-eight. Praying luck was indeed on his side, he flipped his two cards over first.

Graced squealed, "I knew it! Now let's see who the winner will be."

With the deck of cards in his hand, he waved to the rolled-up drawings. "What are the designs of?" His guess was they were of the gazebo he had promised to have built for her behind the manor.

Her eyes darted to the feather and then back up to meet his. "First, who is the winner?"

Interesting. Grace wasn't vying for the pleasure of selecting a design; it was the opportunity to torture him with a feather that had her eager to find out who had won. He slid a card off the top of the deck and let it fall to the table face up. Ace of Diamonds. Their scores were tied.

Eyes bright, Grace glanced anxiously at the deck of cards in his hand. "Matthew! Stop dawdling."

"Are they designs of the gazebo?"

"No," Her response was immediate.

Frustrated, Matthew asked, "Then what are they of? Why are we playing for the privilege of picking a design? It makes no sense. I want whichever will make you happy."

He pushed back from the desk as Grace raced around to sit upon his lap.

She reached over the table for the designs and the feather. "Really? You concede?" Grace waved the feather about and then ran it across the top of her chest.

Matthew flipped the top card over to land in front of them—two of hearts. He won with a score of thirty.

"Blast!" Grace expelled the breath she was holding. "You are one lucky man."

Matthew nibbled on her neck, "I am indeed."

He cupped her breast, and Grace swatted his hand away. She leaned forward and unrolled one of the scrolls, placing a paperweight in each corner. Matthew tore his gaze away from her soft skin and blinked at the drawing before him. It was a series of designs, all starting with a replica of his master chamber, which had lain dormant since Grace's rooms were more conducive for the type of bed sport they preferred.

"You're refurbishing my chamber to create two new rooms? Why do we need more rooms?"

Grace turned to face him. "I wish for the children's rooms to be close by—well, at least while they are babes."

While he had suspected that Grace was enceinte, hearing her utter the words had his heart bursting with joy. She wanted a family, a large one, and he meant to provide her with as many children as possible.

THANK YOU for reading CONFESSIONS OF LADY GRACE. I hope you enjoyed the Agents of the Home Office series.

Up Next: The Hadfields
REVEALING A ROGUE available October 2020

THE HADFIELDS

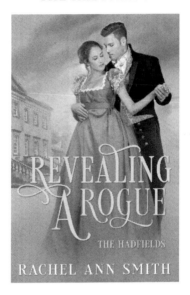

Book 1: Revealing a Rogue

She's sworn an oath to protect him - even from himself.

He's determined to breakdown her walls win her heart.

Will their harried journey to Scotland result in scandal or marriage?

Coming in 2021

Book 2: Tempting a Gentleman

Book 3: Falling for the Dowager

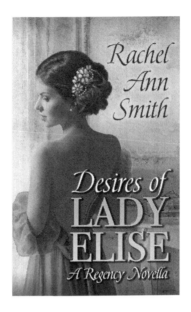

Desires of Lady Elise

He has the reputation of a rogue.

She is too busy with investigations

to bother hunting for a husband.

But when the man who shattered her heart re-enters her world,

will she be able to resist him?

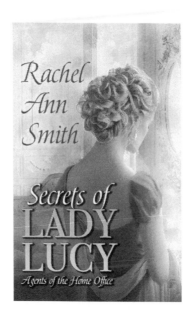

Book 1: Secrets of Lady Lucy

She is determined to foil an attempted kidnapping.

He is set on discovering her secrets.

When the ransom demand comes due—

will it be for Lady Lucy's heart?

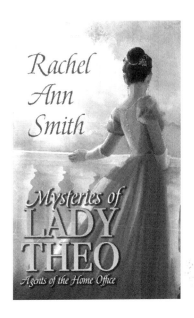

Book 2: Mysteries of Lady Theo

She must fulfill her family's duty to the Crown.

He prioritized his duty to the Crown before all else.

Will the same duty that forced them together be what ultimately drives them apart?

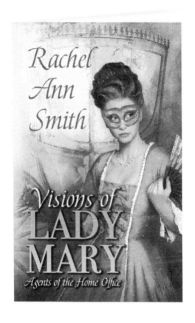

Book3: Visions of Lady Mary

She wants a life of adventure.

He made a promise on the battlefield he's not ready to fulfill.

Can she forgive the man who once called her a witch?

Printed in Great Britain
by Amazon